PERIL

at

SOMNER HOUSE

ALSO BY JOANNA CHALLIS

Murder on the Cliffs

PERIL

at

SOMNER HOUSE

A MYSTERY FEATURING DAPHNE du MAURIER

JOANNA CHALLIS

Minotaur Books 🜲 New York

This is a work of fiction. All of the characters, organizations, and events portrayed in this novel are either products of the author's imagination or are used fictitiously.

PERIL AT SOMNER HOUSE. Copyright © 2010 by Joanna Challis. All rights reserved. Printed in the United States of America. For information, address St. Martin's Press, 175 Fifth Avenue, New York, N.Y. 10010.

www.minotaurbooks.com

Library of Congress Cataloging-in-Publication Data

Challis, Joanna.
    Peril at Somner House : a mystery featuring Daphne du Maurier / Joanna Challis.—
1st ed.
        p. cm.
    ISBN 978-0-312-36716-9
    1. Du Maurier, Daphne, 1907–1989—Fiction.   2. Women authors, English—
20th century—Fiction.   3. Murder—Investigation—Fiction.   4. Aristocracy
(Social class)—England—Fiction.   5. Mansions—England—Fiction.
6. Cornwall (England)—Fiction.   I. Title.
    PR9619.4.C39P47 2010
    823'.92—dc22

                                                                            2010032514

First Edition: November 2010

10   9   8   7   6   5   4   3   2   1

For two very special crows,
Maria Day and Jadan

PERIL

at

SOMNER HOUSE

CHAPTER ONE

"Daphne, hurry up! We'll miss the boat."

Scribbling into my notebook, I pushed back my chair to face an impatient sister. "Angela, you above any ought to understand. I had the most fabulous sentence! A sweeping statement of—"

"That's great. Now you can sweep yourself out the door."

Sighing, I glanced outside. "We still have five minutes. The boat won't leave without us."

"Oh, *yes* it will."

I watched my elder sister storm out of the inn and thought I had better follow without complaint.

Running along to catch up with her brisk, angry walk, I wondered what ailed her. The food? The bad coffee at the inn? Lack of sleep, perhaps? I shook my head. Truly, a fellow writer should know better than to disturb one's sudden inspiration. "Angela! Wait!"

But she did not wait, nor did she answer me as I hastened down to the boat ramp, admiring her poise and skillful attire.

We were going to an island to find inspiration for our art. Why did she have such a glum look about her?

She had been rather irritable of late. But I didn't know the reasons behind her moods. Shrugging my shoulders, I boarded the swaying and weathered old ferryboat, pausing to appreciate the colors swirling in the murky sea below. The sea, so mysterious and changeable, always fascinated me.

"St. Mary's Island." I pointed excitably when we eventually navigated across the rocky waves and land came into view.

Angela snapped the window shut. "It's raining. Can't you see? Really, Daphne, sometimes you just—"

"Live in a world of my own? I know I do. So? What's bothering you? Is it Francis again?"

She sniffed. "Captain Burke can go to hell for all I care."

"Then he won't be joining us at Somner House?"

"He'd better not."

This was news to me, for though she did not share a great deal with me, unlike our younger sister Jeanne, Angela *had* confided that the dashing Captain, hero of the war, had proposed to her last month. Angela had yet to give him an answer; had her delay rattled the Captain's pride enough for him to withdraw his proposal and move to more receptive pastures?

Letting it go, her mulish mood curtailing conversation, I contented myself with watching my fellow passengers: families, lovers, couples, friends, and lone boarders. It was a great mixture of passengers on this mid-morning ferry crossing, always a popular time according to Kate Trevalyan. Or, I should say, *Lady* Kate Trevalyan.

Intrigued to meet this paragon of beauty and sophistication, I had hoped to learn a little more information about her, and about any others we'd be spending the wintry days with at Somner House, but my sister had been resolutely mysteri ous about her friends.

I couldn't wait for our visit. A few weeks dedicated to nothing but the search for inspiration. Though in truth, wherever I went inspiration seemed to find me. During my last vacation, a simple visit to my father's nurse had led to the now famous Victoria Bastion case. "The dead bride on the beach," I whispered to the wind.

"What did you say?"

"Oh, nothing." I smiled, changing the subject. "But I would like to know more about Somner House. It's very selfish of you to keep all the details to yourself."

Despite my rebuke, Angela refused to comply. "I don't know," she'd say, and shrug as I posed question after question. It annoyed me, as I sensed our trip served a particular purpose, a purpose she kept secret. It seemed she needed family support, for why else would she have asked *me,* her troublesome little sister, to accompany her to visit friends at Somner House? She never wanted me to have anything to do with her friends in the past.

"They're sending a car for us," Angela obliged upon arrival at the island, as we waited in line to disembark the ferry. "They say we're to wait at the Three Oaks Inn . . . oh, look, it's over there."

I turned to view the hazy shoreline village. "But what of our luggage?"

"Oh, yes. I suppose we'll need that, won't we?"

Her mind was clearly elsewhere. I wished she would confide in me, even just a little.

Angela's coy smile inspired the boatmen to carry our luggage across the street, leaving us to huddle under my umbrella. At least I had the good sense to bring one.

I'd never been to such a remote island during such a season. Ordinarily our trips included destinations of the obvious choices: Paris, Europe, Italy, and cruising the Mediterranean, where sunny Greek islands differed so greatly from our British ones. Yet I preferred our island to Greece's stark white buildings and still, turquoise sea. There was something wild and ungoverned in the depths of Cornwall, an untamed coastline filled with stories of pirates and legends stretching back to King Arthur's time.

From the grit-smattered Three Oak's window, I first spotted the car lights flashing down the street. A reckless driver sat behind the wheel, consciously ignorant of the common townsfolk attempting to cross the street.

"It's Max Trevalyan!" Gasping, Angela squinted beside me. "Oh dear, he almost ran over that woman! But how kind. I didn't think he'd come to collect us personally."

Yes, how kind indeed, and this is why half the population had paused, even in the rain, to observe the dangerous sleek red sports car with honking horn pull madly to a stop outside the inn.

"We'd best hurry," Angela said, trying to pick up her heavy port. "He looks like he doesn't wish to be kept waiting."

"You'd think the lord of the manor would help us if he were truly a gentleman," I retorted, frowning with worry since we were to be guests of this madman.

We managed to haul our heavy bags a few meters before two

local fellows at the bar, smitten by Angela's damsel in distress routine, relieved us of our burden.

"Lord, dearie, what do ye 'ave in these!" moaned one.

"Books," I replied, smiling. "Well, books for me and shoes for my sister."

Outside, Lord Max Trevalyan dipped his head in mock salute as the two men placed our trunks in the back of the still-running motorcar. The doors were then promptly opened and we were permitted to climb into the cramped space that was left.

Leaving Angela to join Max in the front, I crawled into the back and waved to the fishermen again, seeing that Angela had forgotten her manners in her effervescent greeting to our flagrant host.

Max Trevalyan was nothing like I had pictured him. Ten years younger than his wife, he possessed boyish good looks with his crisp curling chestnut hair, heavy brow, deep-set amber eyes, and slightly Romanic nose.

"What's your sister's name again?" he addressed Angela, speeding down the lane and narrowly missing a young woman about to cross the street. "Blast! You'd think these locals'd know better than to step before a speeding car."

"Are we late for something?" I dared to say, braving Angela's frantic glare.

"Yes!" Rapidly changing gears, Max flicked his car around a sharp right-hand bend. "I'm always late for everything. Kate'll have my neck!"

"But you weren't late," Angela soothed, demonstrating little fear about his driving ability or this incessant, erratic haste. "You were exactly on time."

"Was I?" Cursing his way past a loaded cart going "a hundred miles too slow," Max proceeded with some degree of caution down a narrower country road leading out to the bare fields. "This is the back way," he said to me, whipping his head to have a quick look at me.

"Your sister's pretty," he remarked to Angela with a laugh. "You two'll please the boys. Poor Cousin Bella is much too drab."

"Drab and boring, too?" Angela grinned, and I frowned at her lack of decorum.

"*Intolerably* drab." Max grimaced back, switching to a higher gear.

I glimpsed little of the passing scenery, crammed in the back with the trunks, the light rain blurring the glass, and our reckless driver continuing his mad dash homeward.

"It's not far, Daph. Can I call you Daph?"

"If you wish to, Lord Trevalyan."

"My! She speaks well. I must remember you ladies are the daughters of Gerald du Maurier. How is your father, by the way?"

"Excellent," I answered.

"And happy to be rid of us for a few weeks," Angela put in.

"Then I'm glad of it," Max returned. "And do call me Max, not Lord T. Can't stand it. They called me 'Firefly Max' in the war. That's good enough for me."

He was the strangest fellow I had encountered in some time. Too fast for my liking, and a bit unhinged, yet I could see why Lord Max Trevalyan remained a favorite with the ladies. "Is Trevalyan Castle a ruin now, Max?"

He nodded. "*Ruin?* It's a wretched eyesore. I'd have it blown up but for Rod. Rod has plans to rebuild it." Chuckling at the ridiculous notion, he slowed down to make another turn and to add, "Rod's my older, wiser brother except I'm the elder.

Funny that. In any case, he's the sensible one. He manages the estate for me and all the tenants. Rod has his uses."

Evidently so, as his madcap brother seemed the type to ruin the family's fortunes with his irresponsible ways.

Judging from the way he drove his car, I didn't know what to expect of his home, Somner House.

"We're delightfully apart but close to everything," Max went on, explaining that the house was on the far side of the island as he wound through two sets of forks in the road. "Watch the hills. We're nearly there."

We flew by a village with quaint whitewashed cottages and working farms full of grazing cows gruffly mindful of the noisy racing motorcar disrupting the quiet of the day.

"Trust you brought warm clothes, girls. Can get cold out here, you know. Did get heaters, despite Rod's grumbling about expense, but Katie and I, we're all for *comfort*. Did you ever go to our flat in London, Daph? Sorry, don't remember if you did. Know Angela came once or twice, didn't you, Ange?"

"Yes," Angela was quick to confirm.

Looking up ahead, I waited for a glimpse of the gates leading to Somner House. Whether visiting or touring, exploring old homes was a favorite pastime of mine. Gates always led to interesting places, a thatched hideaway, an abandoned cottage, an old abbey, a ruin by the sea . . . And now, Somner House. Hearing talk of Lady Kate and her connections, I pictured the house old and grand, a colonial-style mansion like one would see in Africa or India during the Empire days. But there were no gates to Somner House, just wide, open fields and a few spare leafless trees. Concealing my disappointment, I waited for some modern monster of a house to loom out of the grim bareness.

"One more corner."

Max Trevalyan revved the gears before making a sharp right-hand turn. Angela gasped, holding on to her hat while I clung to my seat. Thick growth blurred my vision amongst a labyrinth of island trees. To my dismay, and grinning like a schoolboy, Max delighted in weaving his car through the labyrinth of thickly grown trees surrounding the estate.

"Welcome to my paradise," he said at last, reluctantly reducing speed to clamber up the short, smooth drive to the house.

I was surprised to see a landscape bearing lush, exotic wilderness. Parts appeared to be tended—separate gardens, a hidden pergola, and an intriguing maze of beckoning paths curving beyond a manicured French lawn and garden were skillfully married into the existing terrain—but the ruggedness of the island could not be tamed.

"Ten-minute walk to the beach down that path," he indicated.

"And the tower ruins?" I prompted, eager to conduct my own exploration.

"You can only get there via the beach. You'll see."

The house enchanted, too. True, it was not old, and I infinitely preferred something with a decidedly historical feel, but it was charming with its white massive proportions and Tudorish façade lending a degree of the manor house look, further adorned by several individual curved balconies and myriads of French doors and glazed windows. I was eager to learn who designed the house, but Angela sent me a glare to curb my quest for information.

Upon arrival, a slender woman wearing a red dress hastened out of the front door. Snapping open a large umbrella, she skipped down the few stairs in her high heels to greet us.

"Quick!" she laughed. "Before the storm."

Leaving Max to unceremoniously dump our luggage inside the darkened parlor while yelling for "Hugo," Angela and I embraced Lady Kate.

Lady Kate Trevalyan did not look thirty-five, her youthful exuberance of manner and voice masking the tiny telltale lines around her small upturned mouth and vivid blue, almond-shaped eyes. Immediately, I understood her allure. A vivacious, flirtatious beauty rather than a classical kind, she enhanced her image by way of artistry: curling ash-blond hair, painted eyes and lips, and a voluptuous figure, lovely in red chiffon. I shivered. Surely she must get cold in winter wearing such meager clothing?

"Ange, at last! I've been waiting an *age.*"

Grinning profusely, the dimple in her right cheek mesmerizing, Lady Kate took stock of us both. "And this is your sister. Finally. How do you do, Daphne? Enjoy the ride across? I'm *so* pleased you've come for the winter. It gets so deadly dull here."

My mouth dropped open. "The *whole* winter?"

Vastly amused, Kate glanced at Angela. "Naughty Ange. Didn't you tell her?"

"Tell me what? You said only a few weeks "

"Well, you're captive here now," Kate laughed again, "for there's no more boats after tomorrow evening. They can't cross in the bad weather, you see."

I did not see. I was seething inside, and the anger rose in my face.

"Oh dear," Kate laughed, "whatever is the matter?"

"I-I have to be back," I stammered.

"Whatever for? Have you made other arrangements? Your parents expect you? Friends? Commitments?"

"Not exactly but I—"

"Ah, I know what it is. You think us incapable of keeping you entertained. But you needn't worry, for I've arranged a lively bunch. They are coming tomorrow, but if you want to go back on the boat, you can. It's your choice, Daphne."

Tapping her long beautiful fingers across her lips, Lady Kate smiled her beguiling smile, her blue eyes radiantly persuasive. "But you'll stay. You won't be able to resist the island or the allure of Somner House."

The allure of Somner House.

The tempting thought carried me up a curving staircase carpeted in rich burgundy. I followed a hunchback whom Kate affectionately deemed Hugo. Kate and Angela dashed on ahead, chatting and giggling like two long-lost schoolgirls. Taking each step, I savored the landing, the breezy and very dark interior, a contrast to the white-painted veneer outside. Along the corridor, the timber-encased windows were left open, all facing downward toward the sea, and the atmosphere reminded me of a tiny, isolated inn I'd stayed a night in once on the western Cornish coast.

Pity one couldn't see the ocean from here, as one could at Jamieson's Inn, but the fresh salty air with its pungent spirit floated into the house, the windows opened just wide enough to prevent the rain from ruining the red carpet beneath my feet.

I saluted Lady Kate's flair for decorating the house, her wisdom in furnishing it using the old colonial theme. Wicker chairs, open terraces, potted plants, green palms, wooden artifacts, and tribal paintings were featured everywhere. In spite of its newness, the two-story mansion certainly possessed an old-world charm of its own

"Daphne." Kate's crooked finger exhibited itself from one of the large double wooden doors. "We're in here and this is your room to share with Angela. I hope you don't mind sharing? I didn't have time to do up the extra rooms and it'll be a dismal dinner tonight, just Max and I. I invited Roderick but he prefers his tower ruin to Somner."

I asked if Max's brother Rod lived in the tower.

"Yes, he does, more fool him," Kate chuckled, "for it's positively *damp* and very cold, but he loves it."

"Sounds like Daphne will get along very nicely with Roderick." Angela's sly smile widened on inspecting the room's inventory.

"I'll leave you to *play*." Kate grinned. "You'll have to share the bathroom with Cousin Bella but you won't mind, will you?"

She disappeared before we could answer and I sat down on my allotted bed. "Not only have you chosen the best bed but you said nothing about staying here the whole winter!"

Immersed in her unpacking, Angela rolled an indifferent shoulder. "You can go home if you want."

Half turning her head, I caught the haunted look behind her eyes. It vanished as soon as she smiled, offering the best bed to me, but I shook my head. The more time I spent here, even these passing minutes, confirmed the blooming premonition in the back of my mind. Angela needed me. Why, I didn't know. But she needed me.

The bedchamber, a capacious one by any standards, boasted

full-length wooden shutter doors leading out onto our own private little balcony, the shutters being an option for privacy. Two wicker chairs and a table graced the balcony outside, a small bowl of fresh island flowers flapping precariously in the breeze.

Rescuing the flowers before they flew away, I sprinkled the pink, yellow, and white concoction over our beds and un-packed for the night. Hanging two dresses, one for tonight, and one for tomorrow, I took out the essentials and proceeded to find the bathroom.

Across a narrow tiled stretch, the long room consisted of a green bath, with a lion-shaped head as the water spout flanked by two antique golden handles and a modest mirror above a prehistoric washing bowl stand. Little blue and white tiles graced the walls, adding character to the room, and I made swift business of attiring myself, knowing Angela's hourly ritual for adorning herself.

Soon, Kate arrived to collect us for dinner.

"Don't you two look lovely! Pity your efforts are wasted, though Rod may still come. The storm will bring him."

"The storm, Lady Trevalyan?"

Her mouth hardening, Kate slapped me over the wrist. "Just Kate, please. We're on an island and even in London, I abhor all that kind of snobbery. Titles mean nothing."

"To some," Angela reminded, leaning over for Kate to sniff her new perfume.

Back down the same stairs, we turned right to enter the main living quarters of the house. Drawing us into the large open drawing room where a lively fire spluttered and bristled, the chill of the day disappeared and we faded gratefully onto the comfortable velvet reclining divans, each arrayed in a deep purple with long, rounded, cream-colored cushions.

Sets of various African rugs warmed the cool floors beneath, the surrounding walls displaying works of art. "Are they all yours?" I asked Kate.

"Yes," she beamed. "Which is your favorite painting? Choose carefully now. It's my first test for any newcomer to Somner."

Given the pleasant task, I meandered about the room to appreciate each painting while Angela and Kate giggled and whispered together on the far lounge.

"Damnable impudence!"

Sauntering to the fire, Max stoked it. Three aggressive jabs and three unmentionable curses. I recoiled in shock.

"Darling, *please*." Kate blushed. "Don't swear. What has happened now?"

Glaring toward the door, Max's brood intensified. "Ask him. You won't like it."

We all glanced at the tall, dark-haired, caped man paused on the landing.

"Oh, for heaven's sake," Kate sighed, "do come in, Roderick. Whatever this kafuffle is, you *are* staying for dinner. There's no point going back to the tower now with a storm raging, and besides," she teased, gliding across to him to plant a sisterly kiss on his cheek, "you must meet Daphne and Angela, the writer sisters I was telling you about. Here, let me take your cape."

Angela and I rose for the introductions.

Inclining his head to both of us, Roderick Trevalyan looked nothing like his brother. Though a year or two younger, he appeared twenty years older because of his dour expression.

His dark eyes revealed little, a mild passing interest and a weariness, perhaps in regard to his brother. It was a very bleak face, not entirely unhandsome.

"What's the bad news?" Kate prompted, reverting to her usual infectious affability.

"He says we're to sublet the London flat," Max snarled. "For a year. Sorry, Katie. Looks like we're stuck here."

"Oh." A slight frown marred Kate's creamy forehead. "How horrid. But if we must, we must."

"Blast it! I don't want to be trapped here!"

"Let's go to dinner, dear." Kate skipped to the door. "We'll talk about it later. We don't want to ruin the first evening for Daph and Ange do we, my Maxie boy?"

Under her placating look, the aggressiveness slowly dissipated and Max resumed his former attentiveness, leading us into the dining room.

Glaring at his brother across the table, Max whipped out his napkin. "'Spose it's the money again. A year, you say? Why can't we sell off one of the farms?"

"You know very well we cannot sell any of the land," Roderick replied, his voice low and deceptively patient.

"Damned hereditary clauses!" Raising his glass, Max grinned his apology at us ladies. "Ah, well, we'll just have to keep you all here, won't we, Katie?"

He fluttered his eyelashes at Kate, who looked on him with weariness and extended her hand across the table. "Of course, my love. In time, we'll let out the rooms properly and invite fascinating people who pay—"

"Oh, do let us be the first," Angela insisted, looking to me for support. "Our parents will love it."

"Er, yes," I echoed. "You must accept, Mr. Trevalyan?"

After a pithy silence, Roderick said: "I think it's an appalling suggestion to impose upon one's invited *friends,* Miss du Maurier."

"Humph!" Max rolled his eyes. "But Rod, this time I suppose you're right. It's rude, Katie. No, not our friends. The next lot. You do up the rooms and I'll collect the *cash.* Six months and we'll be back in London."

"Provided you don't spend the funds you collect," Roderick dared to caution.

"Let Rod handle the money, darling," Kate implored with an edge to her voice. "He's saved us many times before, *remember?*"

Forced to do so, Max swiftly relented to the wisdom of his younger brother with a perturbed lower lip.

"Dearest Rod, we'd be lost without him." Healing the breach between the brothers, Kate went on to relate how skillfully Roderick handled all of their affairs, farm, estate, and in town.

Listening to her, I thought it remarkable how Kate handled her husband. But I felt sure some hidden tension lurked behind their display of affection.

CHAPTER TWO

A queer sound woke me.

Turning to the window, I opened a bleary eye to see a tiny bird pecking at the glass. The noise hadn't roused Angela yet, and amused by its friendly curiosity, I watched it, afraid to move lest it fly away. Having never before seen a bird of its kind, I mentioned the incident to Kate over breakfast.

She, Angela, and I breakfasted alone in the morning room downstairs. Further along the passage adjacent to the dining room, the enclosed terrace overlooked the open terrace outside where the rain and wind still howled.

"It'll pass," an optimistic Kate said, looking more than a little pale this morning and I wondered whether it was due to the notable absence of her husband. She said nothing of Max and we did not ask.

"There're many exotic birds here," she said, sipping her coffee and tugging the satin-and-fur morning wrap closer about her shoulders. "You'll have to ask Roderick. He knows everything about the island and its species."

"Roderick," Angela mused, the only one of us this morning

who'd taken the time to dress properly for breakfast, even applying color to her cheeks and lips. "Where is he?"

"Oh, he left early. But," Kate teased, "I daresay he'll be back. He's positively enchanted by you two ladies."

"I wasn't asking for that reason," asserted Angela.

"And how *is* your Captain Burke, darling?" the perceptive Kate inquired, and sensing the two friends needed time alone to share their confidences, I took my coffee cup and moved to a quiet corner of my own.

The cane chair nestled off to the side was surprisingly comfortable and, curling my legs up under me, I observed the weather outside. Another hour or so and I could begin my excursion and decide whether or not to stay on the island.

Part of me wanted to stay in order to discover the reason behind Angela's incongruity. Something plagued her and hearing the two whisper together, I felt a little hurt that she chose to confide in Kate and not in me, her sister, the one she'd dragged to this forsaken place.

"Rod gone back?"

The unexpected appearance of a shabbily robed Max sent the remains of my coffee spilling down my shirt.

"Yes." Rushing to her feet, Lady Kate gently corrected his askew hair as I mopped up my coffee spill. "Why don't you get dressed, darling, and offer Daphne a tour of the estate?"

His glum roll of two very shady eyes, remnants of last night's private revelries, led me to rise and insist upon going on my own. I explained this gave me the greatest inspiration and Max swiftly agreed, checking the status of the weather outside. "Best take a raincoat. Got one?"

I assured him I did and, leaving him to the devices of his wife and Angela, whom, I suspected, did not relish his sudden interruption into their private tête-à-tête, I escaped through the sliding terrace door.

The day and its possibilities beckoned. Heading straight for the sea, I smiled at Hugo the hunchback. A person standing with him, the gardener I presumed, a man in his early forties, neatly dressed with a roughened face, clipped whitish beard, and alert eyes, tipped his hat as I passed. I felt intensely sorry for Hugo, having to do a great deal of the work about the place. He served our breakfast, carried our luggage, cooked our meals; did he clean, too? Despite the financial restraint, it seemed there must exist a maid somewhere, even if she worked only a few hours.

Eager to catch sight of the tower where the mysterious Roderick lived, I followed the track down to the beach. The wet sand stuck to the underside of my boots and, shaking them free, I abandoned them for the barefooted approach.

Nothing quite compares to walking along the beach with one's feet bare, the radiance of the morning casting its glow over a sparkling sea.

I located the tower easily, perched high on the cliff. It was a short stretch from Somner House, then a rocky upward climb of a somewhat perilous nature. Obviously, Roderick Trevalyan didn't entertain many visitors at his home.

Evidence of life existed beyond the crows circling above the crumbling jagged proportions. A ginger-haired cat lolling there under the ledge lazily observed my intrusion with its watchful green-yellow eyes. Lifting the wrought-iron handle to the old arched church door, I waited for a response to my call.

There was no response.

I tapped louder.

Suddenly, he came bounding down what sounded like rick-ety stairs to answer the door. Swift annoyance passed his face before a polite, tepid smile emerged.

"Sorry for startling you, Mr. Trevalyan," I apologized. "Lady Trevalyan, oh, I mean, Kate, said you'd left early so I thought you wouldn't mind if I . . ."

I had already stepped inside, forcing him to let me through the door. Roderick Trevalyan guarded his privacy in a fierce fashion and I refused to allow him any chance to think of an excuse to send me away.

"What a fascinating place! I love ruins."

And a ruin it was. Open to the sky, the last vestiges of stone staggered about the place in splendid disarray. The tunnel over the door preceded two meters and extended up the in-stalled wooden stairs where part of the old stone had disinte-grated. The shell of the tower, up the rickety stairs, seemed to enclose one livable space.

I must have looked like a puppy hankering to go upstairs with large, hopeful eyes. "Can I have a quick look, Mr. Trevalyan? Ever since Max mentioned the old castle, I knew I had to see it and I might not have another opportunity."

A mild brow rose.

"I may be returning to the mainland this evening."

I waited for him to ask why and during the flagging quiet-ness, I began to move toward the stairs. Roderick's lumbering feet reluctantly followed. He presented a bizarre image in his casual overalls and rolled-up shirt. He was the worker of the family, the diligent one. I smiled to think of him managing Max's estate and visiting his tenants and farmers in his overalls.

The tower room was as I imagined: small, circular, quaint, and compact; stone walls and floors, a lone square rug of tribal print, reminiscent of Kate's decorating at Somner, one slim-line monkish bed, a tall wardrobe, dressing stand and bedside drawers with lamp, and a chair and bookcase by one of the four windows. Going to a window, the one near the bookcase, I inspected how the glass panes sat inside the iron casing of the old turret windows.

Next, running a gaze across the line of book titles gracing his shelf, I noted the usuals: Shakespeare, Walter Scott, Dickens, no women authors amongst random fiction titles, fishing and books on Cornwall, and . . . "Boatbuilding?" It certainly went with the overalls.

"Yes," confirmed the stark presence looming at the door, preluding my exit.

"Fishing boats? My family has a home in Fowey. Heard of it?"

"No, I rarely leave the island."

Rarely leave the island? Inherently curious, I returned the boatbuilding book back to its place. "Thank you for letting me see your tower, Mr. Trevalyan."

He stared at me as I darted down the stairs and out the door.

"You think he's a boatbuilder?" Angela laughed later in our room, throwing a pillow at me. "Admit it, his austerity has intrigued you. You'll stay."

I didn't like her drawing conclusions about me. "Maybe not. Why *am* I here, Ange? What's troubling you? I'm your sister. You can trust me."

"I know." Nodding, she quickly turned away to view her face in her hand mirror. Frowning at certain parts, her right eye sent me a furtive glance. "You're prettier than Jeanne and I now. I saw how Max looked at you."

"Ha!" I nearly choked though a fiery red stained my cheeks. "He who *rolled* his eyes at the suggestion of doing me a guestly duty? Are you mad?"

"Poor Kate . . ." Sitting on the edge of her bed, Angela continued raiding her little makeup bag. "She suffers so much with his affairs and his drinking, among other things."

I had guessed as much. Max lived life to the extreme. Did those habits and lifestyle grate on Roderick, wishing he were the elder brother, resenting the fact Max held the title and estate when he least deserved it?

"Did you find the tower?"

"Yes. Is it possible Roderick and Max have different mothers, do you think?"

Angela lifted a weary brow. "Oh, please, we're not writing books here!"

"Isn't that why we came?"

"Well, not at this moment, and not using our *hosts* as character studies. Though," she paused on reflection, "I think an austere boatbuilder would feature nicely in your Cornish family saga."

I thought so, too, and skipping luncheon, as everyone seemed to arrange their own midday meals at Somner, I took out pen and paper and stopped by the kitchen to fetch an apple.

A singing maid mopped the floor nearby. Admiring her graceful hips dancing to some tune, I was loath to interrupt her.

"Ayeee!" A few more expletives flew out of her mouth as the mop flew out of her hands. Twirling wildly, she gaped at me in horror. "Oh, sorry, miss! Didn't know it were you."

She had a very strong Cornish accent, her upturned beauty enhanced by straight, short chestnut hair and impish green eyes. "Have you worked here long, er . . . ?"

"Fayella. Just once in a while, miss. When they need me." Her lips curled at some private joke.

Retrieving an apple, I snuggled up in a chair on the outdoor terrace to write. One or two pages later, wishing I'd brought my typewriter, I recalled Fayella and her wanton smile. Arrogance existed on that stout upper lip. Was she a plaything of Max's on the side? *When they need me,* she'd said.

"Ah, so you're a writer!"

Plonking himself down opposite me, Max snatched the notebook from my hands and flicked through the pages, his lips twitching in amusement. "This one's been on the boil for a while? Do I feature in it now?"

Chuckling to himself like an amused child, he scanned the lines before tossing the book back to me. I hoped he failed to notice my slight fluster, and wondered how he'd react if he knew my suspicions.

Smirking, he asked, "Mind if I smoke?"

I shook my head, looking out for Angela and Kate. Something about Max disturbed me. It was more than a wildness, I decided, and continued writing. Using my senses to guide me, to conceal the rapid flutter of my heart, I tried to ignore his presence.

"See the old castle?"

"Yes. Yes, I did."

"And my brother, Rod? What d'you make of him?"

I hesitated. At length, I said, "Odd."

Max laughed, moving his chair closer to mine. "I like you, Daphne. I like you *very* much. Do you have a boyfriend?"

I tensed. Is this how he intended to conduct himself with his wife's guests?

"Ah, your face went red! That means there is *someone*."

"There is someone," I conceded. "But I'd rather not talk about it."

"Why not? I need a diversion." Glaring at dried mud on his boots, he kicked the ground to get rid of it. "Not everyone loves me. Kate . . . she treats me like a child."

I didn't know what to say.

"And Rod's just waiting to get his hands on the estate. He says he should have been the elder. Gosh, he even looks older!"

I nodded my agreement and blushed when I felt his keen gaze upon me.

"Pity you have a boyfriend . . . and pity he's not here to protect you." Chuckling, he left and I breathed an acute sigh of relief. He acted master of the house too well for my liking, taking liberties with everybody, from servants to guests.

His wife, however, failed to show true unease at her husband's imprudence, and despite Angela's manifestation of her continual sufferings, I doubted any real love existed between the couple.

Love replaced by convenience, I jotted down, with a question mark.

I decided to stay.

I couldn't resist a mystery, especially one so beguilingly set on an island.

"So you're swapping the city for the Secrets of Somner House," Angela joked, seeing I'd fully unpacked and my clothes hanging neatly in the closet.

I ignored her caustic, mocking tone and continued to sort out my books.

"But *are* you prepared to uncover all the secrets, whatever they may be?"

Leaning by the wall, her arms crossed, I registered the same smirk I'd seen on Max's face earlier this afternoon.

"Well, I'm glad you're staying," she said finally when I remained silent.

Watching her leave the room confirmed my resolve.

Angela was in possession of a secret . . . and I had to uncover it.

CHAPTER THREE

We dressed in silence that evening.

Angela's thoughts were far away, introspective. She often behaved so before dressing for an important social function.

"Daphne, pass me the violet lipstick, would you?"

Awed by the theatrical aspects of her appearance, and the process involved in which to achieve such a spectacle, I had paid scant attention to mine.

"You're not really going to wear *that*, are you? You look positively a hundred years old!"

Thus chastised, I shrugged, swapping my dismal skirt and blouse for a cream-colored lace gown, one I'd worn to my cousin's wedding last summer.

Using Angela's hand mirror to brush and curl my hair into shape and apply more than the usual scant makeup, I waited for her return from the bathroom.

"They'll be here any moment and we have to make an impression," she said, twittering about the room, searching for her handbag.

I dumped the hunted item into her hands.

"You seem on edge, Daph; are you regretting you stayed? Wished you were on your way to the boat and boring old Fowey?"

"No, you have it wrong."

A vague smile of vacuity passed her lips. "Of course. I always have it wrong."

On our way down to the parlor to await the celebrity guests, I sensed her flurry of nervousness, her excitability, and I hurried on to press her hand. She glanced at me then, a faint smile on her lips, and pressed mine back. No words were needed but she knew I was here, and that I had decided to stay for her.

I was glad I stayed, too, if I was honest. This place intrigued me as much as any old church or mansion, and staying here presented more possibilities than dreary London or Fowey.

"Beautiful!"

Angela's mood considerably brightened for Kate's benefit, who embraced us both, robed in her own sequin ensemble, shining emerald green and silver.

Max stood beside her, suitably sober and dressed in a black evening suit of impeccable quality. Roderick was there, too, seated in the far corner, his face characteristically inscrutable. Acknowledging our presence with a brief incline of the head, he gazed ahead at a painting on the far wall that had somehow escaped my notice.

A large, long canvas hung above the fireplace, shocking in its gruesome intensity. It was a wartime painting of a village under siege, a French village judging from the labyrinth of cobbled streets and quaint rust-colored roofing. Openmouthed mothers screaming for their children, blood-splattered aprons, anguished terrified faces dotting the scene, like unwanted ants on a picnic blanket, and in the far corner, the German tanks steaming onward with their brutal and deadly approach.

"See the children hiding in the wine vats?" Max's hot breath scathed my ear, "half dead with disease, fright, and starvation? I saw them."

I blinked at him. "What did you do in the great war?"

"Pilot," he saluted. "Firefly Max. We crashed in the forest. I was wounded. These villages brought us food. Kept us alive. Hid us from the Germans."

Now I understood his penchant for wild, reckless behavior. Anything to escape the dormant terrors of his mind. "Do the fires still burn, Max?" I whispered softly.

Losing his haunted expression, an open vulnerability suddenly usurped the boyishly handsome face. "Yes . . . they still burn. They burn every day, curse it."

"Oh, darling." Lady Kate glided toward us and I stepped a little apart, a trifle intimidated by her luminous, magnetic presence. I didn't know what it was about her. At various times I suppose we all meet with someone who has the power to startle a room. Even if she were mute, I believed she would possess the quality to silence any room at her entry and commandeer a second look.

The others had arrived, three entering the room. The first, Cousin Arabella Woodford of Devonshire, a girl of my age with upswept dark brown hair and a pale, thin face hiding behind spectacles, wearing a sensible gray woolen suit, stockings, and unfashionable boots.

"May I present Sir Marcus Oxley." Dismissing Bella, Kate betrayed her weakness for nobility. "Sir Marcus has a lovely house just north of London, don't you, Marky?"

A short, stocky man of thirty or so, Sir Marcus Oxley had a

fresh face if not a handsome one, and an adaptability to exude wit, charm, and intelligence all at once. I liked him immensely.

"And Josh."

I noted the way Kate's voice softened at the name. Was he a special friend of hers, a relative, perhaps? Whoever he was, I was placed next to him at dinner.

"Josh Lissot," he obliged as he took his seat and my hand. "Of a modest yard in Ireland."

He was not only young and bright, but quick-witted, too.

"Don't listen to a word he says," Max said rather too loudly from his end of the table. "Josh lies for a living."

"Oh?" Angela lifted an amused brow. I'd seen her acknowledge Bella and Sir Marcus, but she didn't seem to know Josh.

"I'm a poor struggling artist, actually," Josh relayed merrily, quite attractive with his unruly, curling black hair and short, slim stature and kind eyes.

"On the hunt for a new commission," Max further supplied, tipping his wineglass in mock salute. "Katie's always plugging her contacts for Josh's benefit. How's the sculpting business, old chap?"

"Miserably slow." Josh smiled. "But I'm working on something entirely new . . . and hope to finish it while I'm here."

"Are you staying the whole winter, Mr. Lissot?" Angela asked.

"That depends," he said, smiling at us all, "on the inspiration factor, and, I suppose, on the tides! We may all be stranded here at your mercy, my lord." He tipped his glass in polite gesture to Max. "Thank you for having us in your home."

Typical of his mood, Max ignored this gesture. I had seen his brow glower, and also noticed Kate's sudden edginess, a glassy fear sprinkling her eyes.

As it happened, Sir Marcus carried most of the conversation, helped by Kate, Josh, and occasionally, myself. Bella stared at her plate or bowl or whatever came next throughout dinner, and Roderick, in usual fashion, sat there like a boulder.

I was very interested in Josh's sculpture creation and in Kate's new painting, which she insisted upon keeping to herself. "If one talks too much of it, one won't do it," said she, and I heeded the wisdom, extremely reluctant to discuss my current work.

Angela operated differently.

"I can't wait to write," she murmured to me as we labored up the stairs, full with Hugo's delightful, if plain, feast. "What a wealth of secrets lay here."

I squinted at my watch chain while she saw to the lights. One o'clock! I thought it was late but I hadn't anticipated such lateness, especially considering our guests had endured a long, tiresome journey.

"Did you see Arabella Woodford's face? Dull as a dead horse!"

I checked the door, reminding Angela that Bella's room was directly opposite our own and that she may hear us.

"I doubt it. Sound asleep if I know her type."

I had to ask for an explanation.

"Hmmm, frustrated female, no marriage offers, getting older, looking after her sickly mother, desperately in love with Rod."

"Rod?"

"Yes, him. Didn't you see her face light up when he spoke to her or the one smile of the whole evening during their short conversation? What ails these silent types, do you think?"

I didn't know. Intimidation when in the presence of certain

boisterous people or crowds? Afraid to utter a reply should it fail to impress or sound foolish?

Yawning, I began the routine of undressing, locating nightgown and slippers and carting my toiletries to the bathroom.

"Oh, sorry," I said on bursting through the door.

Bella stood there, brushing her teeth.

Her dark eyes flashed at me.

I promptly shut the door to wait, thinking how strange she looked without her glasses. A very odd girl. And perhaps not entirely devoid of secrets of her own.

Morning light burst through the shutters.

Leaving Angela to sleep in, I fetched my umbrella and coat and headed outside.

I should have changed out of my nightgown, but since it was dawn and the house was silent I shrugged off the notion to change. What did it matter if I explored the house in my nightgown? Who would see me?

The weather looked promising. An icy winter's day, gray skies, but clear of rain and wind.

A still quiet reigned downstairs and I wandered through the rooms, absorbing everything from Lady Kate's displayed paintings to how the house appeared after last night's party. The dining table had been cleared, but the drawing room had not been attended to yet. Cushions and chairs remained all over the place, and the odd wineglass graced the mantelpiece by the fire.

Sneaking out through the whiny terrace door, I glimpsed another hallway to the left, the entrance screened off by a carved wooden dividing screen of exquisite fretwork. The darkness of the wood barred the light from entering, hence concealing the hallway from view. Placing my umbrella on a chair, I reentered the house and slid behind the screen. Heart racing, I prayed Hugo would not catch me in the act.

The floorboards creaked. I paused. Holding my breath but drawn to the light, I tiptoed in my great big walking boots. A door emerged at the end of the corridor, left slightly ajar. Passing two other doors that were locked to my profound disappointment, I proceeded to the far door.

Then I heard a noise.

Crying, footsteps, and two voices whispering, a male and a female.

I had come thus far, I would not recant. Going as close to the door as possible, I lingered in the dim light of the passageway.

"He left no note?"

It was Josh Lissot's voice.

"No. Nothing." Kate . . . and Josh Lissot.

"He's often done this sort of thing. You mustn't concern yourself."

Bare feet and a white satin peignoir crossed toward the waiting arms of her lover, and I started to inch my way back.

The door was soon kicked shut and laughter followed.

Sneaking out from behind the screen, startled by the liaison I'd just witnessed, I hunted for my umbrella.

"Looking for this?"

Planted there like a stalwart rock, Hugo's great eyes bored into mine. There was no accusation in his eyes, but certainly an awareness that I had trespassed where I oughtn't. "Oh, y-yes, thank you," I stammered to the hunchback, extracting my umbrella from his hand as I hastened outside.

Fairly certain Kate and Josh hadn't heard me and that Hugo wouldn't report it to his mistress, I kept to the gardens. I didn't want to stray too far from the house lest I miss something important like Max catching his wife and her lover together.

Unfortunately, to my profound disappointment, their very notable absence during breakfast was the only occasion of the morning.

"Where's Kate?"

Glancing several times at the door, Angela asked the others if they knew her location.

Sir Marcus lifted his shoulders and Bella Woodford said nothing, simply stirred her tea in silence.

Suddenly Roderick Trevalyan emerged. Glaring at us under his heavy, solemn brow, he surveyed each of us, a grim line forewarning an impending announcement. "Where's Kate?" he asked.

"We don't know." Angela tried to be helpful. "We haven't seen her *or* Mr. Lissot this morning, have we?"

Bella rose out of her chair, concern marking her features. "And I haven't seen Max, either, Rod. We were supposed to go fishing early this morning but he never showed."

"No, I'm afraid I've bad news. Hugo! Lady Kate must be found, immediately."

"Aye, milord," the hunchback nodded.

"I think I know where she is," I blurted out after he'd gone, slowly rising out of my chair. "I'll go and fetch her."

Slipping behind the screen before anybody could question me, I went to knock on the door where I had eavesdropped. Silence, a noise, then a terrified, bedraggled Kate appeared at the door. Seeing me, and Hugo not far behind, she froze.

Had she expected her husband? "You must come quick," I breathed. "Rod's here. He needs to see you."

Nodding, new worry sharpening her eyes, Kate accepted the large coat hastily thrown to her by Josh.

"Thanks for covering for me," Kate whispered as we sped up to meet the others.

"Kate." Roderick went straight to her, holding both of her shoulders with his steady hands. "Have you seen Max this morning?"

"No . . . he's disappeared again."

"Then prepare yourself. The boatmen found a body on the grounds and it looks like Max."

CHAPTER FOUR

I don't think anybody spoke for a full ten minutes.

Without a word, Kate disappeared with her brother-in-law, leaving us to stare at each other in shock. Bella's face turned pasty white, and she removed to stand limply at the window. Angela and Sir Marcus broke the silence, discussing the hopeful, if improbable, possibility of mistaken identity.

"I'm going out there." Heaving from the window, a frazzled Bella slipped out the terrace door.

I suppressed the desire to follow her. I knew she was going straight to the beach, where I suppose Kate had the grim task of identifying the body. Would a police inspector be there, I wondered, or was it too early for one to have arrived at the scene?

"Daphne found a body on a beach last year," Angela began to say, filling in the silence with my adventure at Padthaway.

I couldn't bear to listen to it. I didn't want to be reminded of Padthaway, or of Lord David. I had thought I had loved him but how did one define true love? Certainly not by the kind Kate Trevalyan shared with Josh Lissot. Their kind of relationship appeared driven by art, lust, and passion.

Copying Bella's route of escape, I retreated to the gardens. Heading straight for the old pergola, I jumped when a hand touched my shoulder.

"Forgive me."

It was Josh Lissot, glancing frantically around and behind me.

"Are you alone? I saw Bella go this way down to the beach."

He swallowed, his face drawn and pinched with anxiety. Laying a kind hand on his arm, I indicated we should go to the pergola to talk. He nodded and together we climbed up the four crackled, painted steps to a dry, leafless seat in the far corner of the hexagon-shaped decaying vista. Wisteria hovered above our heads, dribbling down from a delightful arched roof.

"Thank you," he said under his breath, "for not exposing us. Max knows, but not the others."

"Does he?"

Mr. Lissot nodded. "Kate and he have an arrangement. The blind eye routine. It's been that way for some time."

It appeared I had been correct in my former assumption. The marriage was not one of love.

"Yes . . . poor Kate's had a devil of a time with Max and his addiction."

"Addiction?"

"To drugs. After the war . . ."

"Ah, I see."

I did see, too, having witnessed many returning soldiers, even amongst my own family, suffering the ill effects of such blatant violence. I remembered all too clearly Max's words to me last evening. "You don't really believe Max is the body out there, do you, Mr. Lissot?"

"Please call me Josh." Correcting the buttons on his shirt, he searched through his pockets before getting up to leave. "To be honest, I hope so. Kate's suffered enough."

He left then, and I sat awhile in the fresh morning breeze, loving the way the draping wisteria swayed, oblivious to its owner's possible tragic demise. Closing my eyes, I pictured Kate and Josh, my sudden intrusion, her husband's disappearance, and now . . . a body. Were all of these events connected?

I didn't stay long outside.

The air had suddenly turned too chilly for comfort.

A little before noon, we heard the first news.

Hugo reported it to Sir Marcus, who'd gone in search of a fresh cup of tea.

"No sign of Miss Woodford or Mr. Lissot," he announced upon entering the room bearing a tray of fine English china. "Hugo obliged. Apparently Kate returned to the house terribly shaken. They've put her to bed."

They? The silent question failed to deploy from my lips for Sir Marcus went on to relate the current news.

"Mr. Trevalyan promises to be back within the hour to speak to us all. He wants us assembled for I believe he's bringing the village police."

"The police!" Angela gasped. "So it's true. It *is* Max out there . . . how dreadful."

"We are not sure of the details yet," Sir Marcus advised in his scholarly, upper-class tone.

Despite his attempt, we all knew it must be Max. Why else

put Lady Kate to bed? Yes, shaken to see anybody reposed in death, not to mention one's own husband. I frowned, thinking of Josh Lissot and the still missing Bella.

"I didn't see Miss Woodford. Did any of you?"

Angela and I shook our head.

"And Mr. Lissot? Still curiously absent? Hm, it's very odd. Not how one behaves in this sort of tragic affair."

Sir Marcus's running commentary amused me, though I suppose it was not how one should react in this sort of circumstance. Affable by nature, his wit refined by superior learning, experience, and observation, he was a man after my own heart. I did not say as much, of course, but I may have implied it while we engaged ourselves over the next hour talking of history and various subjects.

I was annoyed that Angela had betrayed my connection with Padthaway and its notoriety, but Sir Marcus kept wisely away from any topic related to fine houses, aristocracy, or scandal.

Appreciating his acute sense of perception, considering the great case at Padthaway and its sequel, I relished our return to the weighty matter looming ominously over this house.

"Pity," Sir Marcus sighed. "I daresay we'll have to all go home now."

"How? There're no boats," Angela pointed out. Getting out of her chair to walk across the room, she tapped her lips in deep thought. "And no. Knowing Kate as I do, as I am a particular friend of hers, I know she'd prefer that we stay. It will help her to grieve and address all the horrible things associated with a death in the family."

I gaped at her, a trifle embarrassed. Her voice sounded

entirely too cold and analytical for my liking. Why? Did she, like Josh, wish Max dead in order to free Kate from her burden?

"Oh, there's Bella and Josh!" Gleaning from the window, putting aside his tepid, distasteful cold tea, Sir Marcus bid them entry.

Had Josh stumbled upon her on his way to the beach? Shivering against him, a white-faced Miss Woodford smiled her thanks. Guided to a seat, Mr. Lissot depriving a chair of its rug to place around Bella's icy shoulders, he explained his absence, mentioning me and the pergola.

"Why didn't you say you'd seen him?" Angela railed at me. Turning to Mr. Lissot, she said, "We were searching for you *everywhere.*"

She was hunting for more information.

Mr. Lissot supplied none.

Shielded in his attentiveness to the frozen-limbed and silent Miss Woodford, he inquired after Kate.

"Put to bed," Sir Marcus said.

"Perhaps I ought to go to her?" Angela mused aloud.

"I think it's best," Mr. Lissot eventually replied, "that we leave her be for now."

Monosyllabic sympathies ensued until Sir Marcus inquired if anybody was hungry.

"Food!" Arabella shrieked, shooting to her feet. "How could you even *think* of food when my cousin is dead!"

Returning, sobbing, to Josh's compassionate arms, we all stared guiltily at each other.

"She saw the body." Mr. Lissot searched his pocket for a handkerchief to give Bella.

"Forgive me," Sir Marcus began.

"Ah, Mr. Trevalyan!" Rushing to the door, Angela relieved

him of his great, droplet-strewn overcoat. "We've been *beside* ourselves with worry."

Reminiscent of a Spanish inquisitor, Roderick Trevalyan grimly gravitated toward the seat nearest to him, which happened to be the head of the table. Had the fact already occurred to him he was now lord of this house? I searched for an obvious sign of joy in his victory, found none, and consigned myself to my own treacherous imagination.

"You will all be shocked to learn we have positively identified the body as my brother, Max."

It was a glacial, remote voice, not dissimilar to Angela's. Or Josh Lissot's, for that matter. Did everyone hate Max so much as to wish him dead? I felt intensely sorry for the departed. Certainly, he wasn't *dearly* departed, was he?

Roderick now lowered his stoic gaze to address each face, all in systematic order. When he came to me, a slight dent crossed the middle of his forehead. "We have no inspector here on the island. The village county police will handle it until the weather changes."

Sir Marcus coughed. "You lead to my next question. In the circumstances, should we seek alternative accommodation on the island? We do not wish to impose upon your sister-in-law or yourself in your grief."

Good grief, thought I, *he delivers a very pretty speech.* Appropriate and poignantly tactful.

"I shall stay." Bella spoke first, dusting her thick glasses. "I am one of the family. You don't mind, Rod, do you?"

I lifted a brow at her pleading, earnest face, how it transformed where Roderick or Max where concerned. She evidently loved her cousins very much and I suspected they'd all grown up together.

"I cannot speak for my sister-in-law," Roderick murmured, "but I see no need for you all to leave. Accommodation is scarce out here—"

"And Kate needs her friends." Braving his brevity, Angela smiled to soften the impact and to make up for her former insensitivity. "Above everything, she *dreads* being alone. And at such a time . . ."

She left off with an unfinished thought. Supremely clever of her, I thought, and, to be truthful, I was grateful. I had no wish to dither around the island, looking for someplace inspirational to stay. Judging from where we'd disembarked, the choices were dismal.

"No, I am quite determined you shall all continue your stay at Somner House . . . in the interim. Now, if you will excuse me, I have matters to attend to before Mr. Fernald arrives."

"How strange," echoed Angela, agitated to have been sent away not once, but twice, from Lady Kate's door. "They've posted Hugo at her door. He's shelling peas."

No lunch, but dinner seemed to have been ordered and I made a mental note to transmit this news to the starving Sir Marcus.

"And Josh Lissot! Who does *he* think he is! Did you see how he cut me down?"

Storming to her bed, Angela fluffed her pillows, very like the aggressive strokes Lord Max had done to the fire on the previous eve.

"Aren't you being a little overprotective, Ange? Kate's a grown woman. She and Mr. Lissot may be great friends—"

"Great friends," she sneered. "More like . . ."

She couldn't seem to stomach the word.

"Lovers," I finished for her. "Can you blame her? Like you said, after what she's suffered with Max and they do share a love of art. It's perfectly natural. It's more than natural. It's *human*."

"Natural! Yes, but not *Josh Lissot*. He's not right for her."

"Who is?"

Silence answered me.

Brooding upon this, Angela swept up the magazine on her bed. I also did the same, but with a book. *The Tenant of Wildfell Hall* by Anne Brontë. It suited my mood, considering the heroine's suffering and her rakish husband's likeness to Max himself.

Max . . . dead? I had difficulty believing it. So sudden and unexpected, an accident, no doubt, or could it have been a suicide propelled by drugs? No, I had since learned from my experiences at Padthaway. What appeared on the surface, the logical speculations, could mask the truth.

I had barely reached halfway through my chapter of *The Tenant* when we were summoned downstairs by Bella. She knocked on the door, the expression in her eyes partially hidden by her thick-rimmed glasses. I noted some color had returned to her face. What distressed her more, her cousin's death, or her obvious love for Roderick and her fear Angela or I would steal him away?

A dreary milieu certainly awaited us in the drawing room.

Sir Marcus paced by the fireplace, where Max and I had shared our private tête-à-tête; Roderick sat austere in the middle of the most upright divan, Arabella swift to take a place beside him; Josh Lissot preferred to pace along the side wall, feigning the odd glance up at Kate's paintings, and the village police chief hovered behind me.

He was a man of average height, slight build, and hairy arms. Younger than I anticipated, and quite good-looking with short, dark blond hair, even features, and a ready smile.

Once Angela and I made use of the last divan left, Kate entered the room.

Cloaked in a gown of black velvet, a dusky pink crocheted shawl gracing her shoulders, she slipped almost unnoticed into the room. Her hair lank, her face drawn and her eyes downcast, she attempted a tiny greeting to everyone, but it was clear she was still shaken by the news.

"And Lady Trevalyan," nodded the police chief, introducing himself as Mr. Fernald. "Ladies and gentleman, I won't keep ye long today though further questionin' will be ongoing here at Somner."

"Perhaps it would be best if we remove to—"

"Oh, no, Sir Marcus," Kate decreed. "I can't bear to face all this alone. Please," she said, glancing around the room, "I don't want any of you to leave."

"Roderick?"

Covering my mouth to conceal my shock, I couldn't believe the policeman addressed Roderick Trevalyan so informally.

"It's fine with me, Fernald," Roderick Trevalyan replied, not showing the slightest offense. "You may use the study or the library to conduct your interviews."

The new master of the house delivered his first decision. I expected once the grieving process ended, Somner House would embark upon a new era. A dramatic change that would affect Kate above everybody else—a childless, penniless widow now dependent upon the goodwill of her brother-in-law. Poor Josh, Kate's lover, lacked the financial freedom to relieve this impending burden.

"I'll need to speak to everyone privately in the next few days," Mr. Fernald said. "I needn't tell ye that none of ye are to leave the island, for it's clear murder."

Arabella's face turned a maggoty white. "I think . . . I think I'm going to be ill . . ."

As she ran out of the room holding her stomach, we all exchanged horrified glances.

"Murder!" Sir Marcus boomed. "How so, dear fellow?"

"I'm afraid there's no delicate way to put it. . . . Lord Max suffer'd blows to the head and face, such as would look after the work of a pickax."

CHAPTER FIVE

The horrible fact cloaked the house.

I now understood Bella's intense pallor and Kate's sunken, haunted eyes. Both had seen the body.

As had Roderick Trevalyan. However, his inherent detachment gave no indication of his true feelings. I wanted to unravel and stir the dormant layers living inside the citadel that was Roderick Trevalyan.

Angela professed shock several times during the afternoon.

"I went to see Kate. We spoke for a little while but she wasn't in the mood for talking."

"Can you blame her?"

She considered. "You're right. We just have to be ready and there for her when she needs us." Her eyes darkened. "I saw her strolling outside with Josh Lissot before . . ."

" 'Jealousy, a curse,' " I quoted aside from my reading of *The Tenant of Wildfell Hall.* Astounded once again by the similarity between the late Max Trevalyan and poor Helen's dissolute, wayward, alcoholic husband Arthur Huntingdon, I said as much to Angela. Her response provided further insight into the world of the troubled couple.

"I've been there when he's been bad and it's not pretty. What do you think drives a person to drink? Excitement? Pleasure? A buzz?"

"No. Escape."

Angela went on to relate what she knew of Max's involvement in the war. "A fighter pilot. He must have looked dashing in his uniform, and I think that's what drew Kate to him. They were all fighting over her, you know. The whole club, even the married men. On their return, Kate used to sing for them at the club and they'd all fight for first place."

Yes, I began to see shades of the portrait emerge with each passing stroke. "Here, listen to this . . . Helen received several warnings before marrying Huntingdon and here Huntingdon speaks of his rakish friend Lowborough:

He kept a private bottle of laudanum, which he was continually soaking at—or rather, holding off and on with, abstaining one day and exceeding the next, just like the spirits.

And this:

One night, during one of our orgies—he glided in, like the ghost in Macbeth, and I saw by his face that he was suffering the effects of an Overdose of his insidious comforter. Then he drew up and exclaimed "Well! It puzzles me what you can find to be so merry about. What YOU see in life I don't know—I see only the blackness of darkness."

"I think Max suffered like this," I murmured. "The eternal darkness, using his empty 'comforter' between periods of extreme merriness and then irrational gloom and bottomless despair. Do you know if Kate was warned before she married him like Helen?"

"Probably," Angela replied. "Not that it would have mattered to her. She married him for the title."

"Besides money and a handsome, if somewhat uncontrollable husband," I added. "His charms were like a drug to her, too—something she could not refuse."

"Well, she certainly had her choices . . . at least five proposals that I know of."

I seized the opportunity to bring up Captain Burke.

"Oh him." Angela's dismissive tone consigned poor Captain Burke to the grave. I knew then she'd not marry him and he'd not renew his addresses to her. She'd given him an icy or vague answer and men loathed both qualities in a woman.

There was little else to do but to ponder upon the catastrophe of Max's violent end.

A violent end. I noted the phrase in my journal. It was a "clear murder" as Mr. Fernald pronounced in his native accent, for one couldn't disfigure one's own face. "Angela, are there any boats at the house?"

"Boats?"

"Yes, rowing boats."

She rolled her eyes. "I expect so. Why don't you go and find out? I could use some time alone without your endless chattering."

My endless chattering. Strange, for I hadn't seen myself in a chatterer's role. Usually, I preferred silence, like Roderick.

I saw him on my way out, on the terrace taking tea with

Bella. Upon my blundering intrusion through the whiny terrace door, they started out of their chairs. I sensed their combined discomfort, perhaps halfway through an intensely private conversation.

"You may sit with us if you wish, Miss du Maurier." Roderick felt it his duty as host to include me.

I smiled, noting Bella's downcast, brooding eyes upon me, hoping I'd refuse. Clearly, *she* did not wish me present. Thanking them for the kind offer, I pressed on to the refuge of the gardens.

Gardens in winter traditionally suffered during the unfavorable season, but the ones here at Somner seemed to thrive. Giant trees planted by early settlers graced the perimeter amongst the swaying native palms, hedges of crimson bottlebrush and dog-rose berries at their feet. Wild rosemary grew between gardens imbedded with yellow freesias, camellias, creamy hydrangeas, and dusty pink orchids. The red lion amaryllis, a particular favorite of mine, towered above clusters of jasmine, blue cornflowers, and winter chrysanthemums. Everywhere I turned, flowers still thrived in the cold, but the rose garden mourned the loss of its colorful companions, the black baccara rose looking lonely beside the odd wintered red rose.

" 'A strange, nervy kind of creature is Arabella Woodford,' " I whispered to the black baccara rose in my best Arthur Huntingdon voice.

"You know talking to oneself implies insanity?"

Sir Marcus grinned, basking on a shady seat hidden amongst the hedges. Staggering to the side, I upbraided him for his sly behavior in not alerting me to his presence and he laughed.

"I am gloriously incognito," he confided. "And positively

delicious for gossip. What else can we do? Clam the mouth and resume a formal detachment?"

We discussed this at length as it was an intriguing subject. How should one fill the days while we remained at this house of death, I began to wonder. Ignore the brutal murder and continue our creative respite?

Sir Marcus proposed we do the opposite.

"I say we head to that window there where I believe our trusty police chief is interviewing Kate . . . what say you, Sherlock? Or do you intend to lose yourself in sad gardens?"

I swallowed. Eavesdropping upon Kate Trevalyan again? It bothered my conscience. Certainly not twice in one week could I commit such folly.

"Oh, come." Sir Marcus nudged me. "I know you caught her out with Lissot."

I stared at him.

"Your face betrays you. You're a keen observer, Daphne. May I call you Daphne? And keen observers sometimes forget to mask their own keen observations. You, for instance, at the breakfast table this morning."

"What of it?"

"You looked like an innocent girl, shocked by the loose morals of your peers. It was there . . . all over your face when you said 'I think I know where she is . . .'"

Brought to my senses by an unfriendly gust of chilly air, I dissected the ramifications of Sir Marcus's elucidation. Was my face so easily readable? Strange, since nobody in my family thought so. "Close shuttered" was the term, I believe. "Happily close shuttered in my own world," I'd often retort. But never ever had I imagined others could see so easily into my fiercely guarded world.

I put it down to disbelief. And acute astonishment. A death . . . and an exposed affair. These events did not occur every day, and if they did, they did not occur together, did they?

"Come." Grabbing my hand, Sir Marcus propelled the two of us toward the house.

I shivered as we drew near. The panes of the window, splattered with salt spray, encompassed the hazy vision of a sobbing Kate and a military pacing police chief. His heavy frown and blazing eyes suggested direct accusation and obviously no delicacy had been employed.

I did not expect Mr. Fernald to possess the nerve to address a lady in such a manner. It was entirely opposite to the assiduous ministrations of Sir Edward at Padthaway, I recalled.

Concealed from their view, Sir Marcus and I leaned closer to the pane.

". . . you and Mr. Lissot! Why did you not mention this before?"

"I tried," Kate sobbed, "but I couldn't find the words."

"Couldn't find the words, eh? How *convenient* for ye both. I'll be havin' a word with ye brother in-law. He won't take kindly—"

"He knows."

Kate's voice, suddenly calm.

Eyes slit, Mr. Fernald jutted our way. Ducking our heads just before he reached the window, Sir Marcus and I exchanged a halting breath. What if we were detected? How *embarrassing,* and how discourteous to poor Kate.

Yes, poor Kate, suffering from that brute Fernald. How could he be so insensitive? She'd only just identified her husband's body. The overwhelming shock must have been unbearable. Or perhaps it was no shock at all but a *planned* death?

I whispered this theory to Sir Marcus as we scurried back the way we'd come.

"Mr. Lissot has no money and from what I know of Max, all goes to his brother. The widow will be left with nothing, apart from a small annuity entirely dependent on the goodwill of Roderick. Lord Roderick . . . funny to think of the old chap as a lord. He's more a man of the land."

Indeed, I agreed in silence, suddenly recalling my promise to Angela to order afternoon tea.

Sir Marcus decided to accompany me to the kitchen.

"Odd household, isn't it? One man does everything. Not a bad cook, either."

"I suspect you have a full staff to service your needs in all of your houses," I joked, hopefully without sounding peevish.

"Ah, a note of envy." The wily Sir Marcus grinned, usurping a pleasurable delight whilst informing me of his various properties.

I had no idea of his extreme wealth.

"Mostly hereditary," he added, "and no wife to warm my days. Alas, I am still on the prowl. Hard to find one without the booty being the lure."

"Not the lure entirely." I smiled upon reaching the kitchen. "You do have other charms to exhibit, you know. Sharp wit, a jovial nature, and too keen an eye—"

"Aha! You resent my sniffing you out."

I shushed him before we were overheard by Hugo, who labored over the kitchen sink. I strolled to the china cabinet and had half opened it when Hugo's great shadow over-reached me.

"I'll do it, miss. Tea, is it?"

Sir Marcus and I exchanged a glance.

"Actually, we wouldn't mind Indian tea . . . there's a good fellow. Need any assistance, old chap? Can't be easy playing all these different roles. You almost need a cap for each one, eh, and I 'spose they don't pay you nearly enough."

Hugo looked blank and not at all amused.

Before inviting Sir Marcus to take tea with Angela and me, I thought I'd better seek the sisterly approval first. After checking our room, mysteriously vacant when she'd asked for time alone, I joined Sir Marcus on the terrace.

"If you're wondering where your sister is," Sir Marcus said as he displayed his unfaltering prowess in the art of serving afternoon tea, "she's the latest victim of Fernald's interrogation."

Grateful to have Sir Marcus here amongst such dire circumstances, particularly as we sat at the very table where Max had snatched my book, we took bets as to who Mr. Fernald planned to torture next.

"How's your tea?"

"Ghastly." He spat out the word. "Tepid and flagitious."

"Flagitious?"

"Deeply criminal, as somebody it here."

To my intense surprise, Mr. Fernald chose me next for questioning. Setting down my teacup, I waited for Angela to take my place beside Sir Marcus and noted her high color. What had Fernald said to upset her?

The gloom of the drawing room beckoned. Walking into the room, I hardly connected it to the one on the first night of our arrival. Welcoming, lively, spirited . . . now dark, depressing, the walls painted with tales of immeasurable misery, once interesting, now distasteful. The wartime death on canvas had stretched its bitter hand over Somner House.

"Miss du Maurier, the younger. What's ye first name then?"

Failing eloquence, Mr. Fernald barked out his words like a trumpet out of tune.

"Daphne."

He nodded, scribbling a note. "Daphne, then. Do sit down, Miss Daphne. I've a few questions for ye."

They were standard questions. Where I had been on the night of Max's disappearance, what did I think of the relationship between husband and wife, did I know anything of significance, of a private nature?

I sat there, mute.

"I know you know something, Missy."

"Mr. Fernald." I promptly drew to my feet. "I object to your calling me Missy. My name is Miss du Maurier, and yes, I did see Mr. Lissot and Kate Trevalyan on the morning they found the body."

"They spent the night together?"

I rolled an elusive shoulder.

"You think they did it, eh? The lovers? Kill the husband? Make it look like an accident or attacking to defend, eh?"

I shrugged again.

Mr. Fernald glared at me. "You're not as talkative as your sister, Miss du Maurier."

"Oh? What did she say?"

"I question, not you. You may go now, I've no further need of ye today."

Dismissed! In all my character readings, I'd never met anybody like Mr. Fernald. This policeman was beyond rude, he was—

"Flagitious!" I seethed to Angela and Sir Marcus.

"Rightly so," Sir Marcus seconded, rubbing his hands together. "This calls for a winter warmer before dinner, don't you say? Shall we repair to the library, ladies?"

Sir Marcus had located the library before me. Lagging behind the two, I paused to peruse the overflowing shelves whilst they helped themselves to the liquor cabinet behind Max's desk.

"Shouldn't we ask for permission first?" I said.

"Already have." Sir Marcus grinned like a schoolboy. "From Rod himself. We are to make ourselves at home, and that, my dear Daphne, entails free access to the liquor cabinet."

"Does Roderick drink, do you think?" I mused while stumbling across a few interesting titles. "I can't imagine it for I daresay it'd crack the dourness of his face."

"Is that so, Miss du Maurier?" Roderick Trevalyan's voice boomed from the doorway.

CHAPTER SIX

Stunned, I gaped out a fumbling apology as books tumbled to the floor.

"Don't trouble yourself," Roderick said, assisting my dismayed efforts to pick up the mess, a hint of amusement flickering in his blue eyes.

"I find it immensely funny." Chuckling, Sir Marcus waved his finger accusingly at me. "Next time you'll check the door before sprouting derogatory comments about your host, won't you, Daphne girl?"

I flushed scarlet and apologized again, but, to my surprise, Roderick just smiled.

"Here." Angela thrust a glass in his hand. "Have a drink."

An uneasy silence pervaded the room. Sir Marcus gravitated to my refuge amongst the books while Roderick and Angela sipped from their glasses, her attempt at conversation barred by his ongoing austerity and one-word replies.

Clearing his throat, Sir Marcus threw me one of his eyebrow lifts. I sensed his silent request to charge the subject. We began to talk about a book I had begun to read, a historical account of a church and other ancient sites on the Isles of Scilly, filling in the next ten minutes until Roderick deigned to join the conversation.

"Weather permitting, there are crossings to the other islands," he obliged. "But to the mainland, not for another month, I'm afraid."

So we were all stranded for a month, trapped on an island with a violent murderer on the rampage. When Sir Marcus posed the possibility of an island trip, I felt ill at ease when Roderick was only too happy to accommodate the request. I kept thinking of Max's words: *Rod's just waiting to get his hands on the estate.* Angela was noncommittal to the idea of an island trip. She wanted to stay by Kate's side, but as I had never been involved in their particular crowd, I felt slightly unwanted and unneeded. Sir Marcus shared my view. He mentioned again to Roderick the possibility of us finding accommodation elsewhere, but Roderick refused to hear a word of it.

"No. You are most welcome to stay. In the circumstances, there is little else we can do."

Commandeering and precise. He applied the same principle to his grooming and appearance, it seemed, absurdly neat and tidy, slicked-back hair, apart from the day in his overalls at the tower where I rudely intruded, and a bleak rudimentary method of approaching life as a duty. He even walked with a purpose.

"Hope that Fernald chap gets to the bottom of this," Sir Marcus said gravely.

Lord Rod inclined his head.

Collecting the books I intended to read, I escaped the halting uneasiness of the room and on my way out collided with Bella.

"Oh," exclaimed she, "I didn't see you." She appeared more angry than upset. "Is Roderick in there?"

I nodded, lingering awhile in the dullness of the hallway. She didn't say "my cousin," but called him "Roderick." It was almost as if she had chosen her words carefully. But, why? Was it to confirm a special understanding between them or was it meant to warn me of her prior claim? Or both?

Relieved to enjoy a reprieve before dinner, I tossed through the books and sketched some notes and scenes relating to my current work in progress, using, I am ashamed to admit, elements of the circumstances around me.

So I set to work on a short story. After the affair at Padthaway, I had written little but an account of my experiences in Windermere Lane. I intended to use those notes in a novel later, but the idea intimidated me. I knew once the seed started, it must grow, regardless of time, family, and friends. I needed complete solitude to write it.

Angela's noisy arrival into the room murdered my half-written story and, sighing, I tore up the papers and hurled them into the wastepaper bin.

"I'm so late; I shan't have time to set my hair. And Daphne, *do* try to make an effort this evening."

"Effort?" Incredulous, I looked at her.

"Yes. For Kate's benefit."

"How does arraying oneself with fine things soothe an anguished spirit?" I stopped short there, for guilty or no, Kate had her future without such finery to think of once the funeral and investigation business was over. "I think Kate might have killed her husband," I blurted out.

"Kate? A suspect?" Angela rejected even the remotest possibility. "There's entirely no motivation," she retorted, while tying the sides to her muted yellow dress. "Max was her whole source of . . ."

"Income? Living? Do those things mean a great deal to her? She might have wanted to be free of him."

Angela did pause to consider this deduction. "She has expensive tastes, I must admit."

"Do you know much about Mr. Lissot's finances?"

"Oh, don't talk to me about *him*," Angela groaned. "I can't abide the man."

I lifted a brow in question.

She squeaked at the time. "Gosh! And I wanted to wash my hands before dinner. I suppose that Bella creature is in the bathroom. What does she *do* in there? It's not as if the time spent shows. She's horribly ugly."

I deemed Angela wrong in this assumption, confiding my private assessment en route to the dining room. A strange, nervy creature, yes, but not an ugly one. Behind those glasses, I gleaned a face of lean proportions, a curved short, straight nose, a well-shaped mouth crying for color, and eyes only requiring the merest enhancement. Out of her schoolmistress outfit and appropriately draped in a feminine gown, she'd certainly turn more than one head. But that certainly was not the vision that greeted me.

Standing at the darkened end of the room quietly talking with her cousin Roderick, she had donned an atrocious blue cardigan over a hospital nurse–style skirt, a white ribbon scraping her hair back from her face where a dull light shimmered across thick-rimmed spectacles.

On the opposing side of the room, Kate was a vision of

mourning glory. The starkest black dress failed to conceal her elegant frame, nor did the disorderly sweeping fashion of her hair detract from her composed, drawn beauty. Speaking in low undertones to Josh Lissot, she fingered the string of black beads around her neck. When Angela and I entered, she smiled faintly and promptly left Mr. Lissot, whose face exuded a furtive wariness as he shifted from side to side, not sure what to do.

The uncertain atmosphere deepened during dinner, with Sir Marcus atoning for the lack of conversation. Angela tried her best, helped a little by myself and, surprisingly, Roderick. Assuming his role as head of the household, he no doubt felt obliged to offer more than the usual perfunctory remark here and there.

"Mr. Fernald," he announced later over coffee under the subdued lighting and at a morbidly quiet moment, "may return to question a few of us. I thought you should all know."

"Murder," Sir Marcus shook his head, appalled by the crime as much as the tepid coffee. "But why? Who would *do* such a thing. Did the man have any enemies on the island? Someone he'd threatened lately?"

Roderick's eyes shifted westward. He wished to avoid the specific inquiry.

"There is Jackson," Kate began hopefully, appealing to Roderick.

Her brother-in-law frowned. "Jackson's a good man. I can't believe it of him."

"But he is prone to violence," Kate persisted, sharing a quick glance with Josh, who, in turn, bowed his head and inspected the contents of his cup.

Sir Marcus asked who Jackson was.

"The gardener," Kate said in a small voice. "The man with the silver beard."

I remembered the gardener from my walk around his domain. He seemed to treat the house and gardens as his own and probably had been working on the estate his whole life. If this Jackson fellow had respected Roderick and Max's father, could his feelings for the reckless son inspire him to murder? No . . . there had to be more motivation for Kate to mention the gardener than mere dislike. I wondered what it was.

"Well, whoever it is," Arabella vowed, "he'll be brought to justice and punished." She dipped her head, the corner of her right eye drifting toward Josh Lissot while I met Angela's gaze across the room. She, too, deciphered the "he" on Bella's sharp tongue and likewise cast a judicious brow in Josh's direction.

Etiquette thus dispensed, Roderick Trevalyan vacated his chair, acknowledged each of us with a curt nod, and left the room.

Kate followed soon afterward, Josh Lissot careful not to shadow her exit.

"Curious fellow," Sir Marcus murmured, hunting for a divan to sprawl out upon. Snapping out a cigar from the inside of his coat, he freed his feet of his restrictive but highly polished shoes. "You don't mind, do you, ladies? I've no wish to go to sleep yet."

Arabella cast one longing glance in the direction of her disappearing cousin before running after him. I remarked upon her hasty departure and Angela and Sir Marcus swooped upon it like two crows on a stone fence.

"Did you *see* her face? Same as when she arrived. She positively hankers after him like a dog," Angela remarked.

"Perhaps you're missing something." Sir Marcus struck his

match with the edge of his boot. "Perhaps it was *Max* she was in love with, and not Rod. Or perhaps she was in love with them both. Girl like her can't have had too many offers about. Lives inside a cottage with an old woman, you know. Not much chance for a social life, is it?"

"No," agreed Angela.

Keeping my ear open to their musings, I went to peruse the paintings. So many scenes, mostly of the wartime. What happened here at home, in the streets of London, the bombings, the nights of terror, what transpired over on the continent, our valiant men and women going off to fight in foreign lands . . .

I paused before the painting above the mantelpiece. A wintry tree opened the window to the canvas, snow-caked leaves mixed with blood trailing the dirty path to two fallen soldiers hiding beneath a hedge in the distance, one cradling the other's head.

I asked Sir Marcus about the painting.

"Know nothing about it. Bit dark, if you ask me. Should be paintings of flowers and animals, to go with the theme. I've told Katie, but you see it was her wartime endeavors that launched her, so to speak. Difficult for an artist to break the mold of what's required of 'em."

Indeed, but perhaps she'd done so having begun to work on a new project. Was it a project inspired by Josh Lissot, by any chance?

Sir Marcus had made the connection, too. "Poor pair. It's going to be tough for the both of them, for Fernald's got his hooks in there."

"Not on Kate, I hope," Angela said. "*She* is innocent, I swear."

"I tend to agree with you." Sir Marcus puffed away on the

divan. "For if she'd wanted Max out, she'd have done it blizzards ago."

"Blizzards, Sir Marcus?" My lips curled in amusement. "You paint words so eloquently, yet you've failed to say why *you're* here at Somner."

"I'm a pure laze-about," he responded merrily. "Flitting from here to there. A passing wind, no more, no less."

Angela made some sordid joke that would have shocked our mother's ears, but Sir Marcus laughed and shared one or two of his own.

I continued to look at the paintings. There had to be a clue hidden amongst each applied stroke, a clue as to why Kate chose to remain with her wastrel husband. Helen out of *Wildfell Hall* had done so out of duty, out of her own religious sense of propriety, but Kate Trevalyan? She was no innocent maid. She'd wed Lord Max knowing exactly who he was and what kind of husband he'd make her.

"I'm surprised both of you aren't wed and pregnant by now," Sir Marcus dared to say.

Somewhat relieved he'd chosen Angela to interrogate first, I kept one ear attentive while studying the war tanks, the children of London running in terror from the bomb blasts . . .

"You ought to accept this Burke, y'know," Sir Marcus advised, assuming the older-brother manner. "Heard of him. Fine fellow. Well set up."

"We are not exactly *poor*, Sir Marcus."

"Oh, indeed. The du Maurier clan. Famous! Spare me the drum. Notoriety and money don't buy happiness."

"And you believe my marrying Burke will? I can't imagine anything more horrid—confined to the country, joining the knitting society and breeding little Burkes—"

"And going to church on Sunday," Sir Marcus added, the terseness of her tone leading him to sit up and strike another cigar. "I must concur with you, I wouldn't want to be breeding little Burkes, either. Ghastly business, all of that."

Angela brought up the necessity of Sir Marcus supplying an heir as well.

"Oh, done already. Sister. Nephew. No need for me to raise the flag."

"But a man like you needs a wife."

"Perhaps," Sir Marcus considered. "I am fond of the shapely kind, like that saucy creature in the kitchen. What was her name, Daphne? You girls remember that sort of thing."

The kitchen maid . . . and Max. "Yes!" I stared at both of them. "Perhaps that's it."

"Queer kind of name, 'Yes!'" drawled Sir Marcus. "No, truly, the saucy wench's name, Daphne?"

But I was already exploring the idea of a connection. "There has to be a connection between the gardener and the maid with whom Max was having an affair."

"Jackson and the saucy kitchen wench? No, no, no, he's old enough to be her grandsire! Truly, Daphne, I can see why you took so long to sniff out the culprit in the Padthaway affair—"

My face reddened and I sent Angela a glare.

"I didn't tell secrets," she promised, "just the facts."

"A fantastic debacle." Sir Marcus's commiserating tone failed to placate me. "And you and this Major fellow didn't do too badly . . . for a pair of amateurs."

I was about to point out that the Major was certainly no amateur, but stopped just in time. I didn't know whether Sir Marcus was teasing me or in earnest, but how dare Angela speak of my private life to strangers! I liked Sir Marcus. In fact, I liked him more than most relatives, but I protested when it came to my personal affairs. I certainly did not go around and dish out the details of Angela's *failed* romances or her *secret* trips to the country.

"I daresay it is time to take this ungainly body upstairs." Yawning, Sir Marcus rolled off the divan to collect his shoes. "See you two birds in the morning where you can explain the gardener and maid theory."

Leaving Angela with another glare, I sauntered after him. Angela could stay there and repent. Is that why she wanted me at Somner? To use me as a spectacle for everyone's dissection? To deflect attention off herself and to conceal her own secrets?

That night, I dreamt of a tower. A lonely eyesore stranded in a barren, rocky land gazing out across a violet sea. Above, a dash of lightning illuminated the darkness, inflaming the landscape with molten hues of orange, plum, and scarlet reds.

I described the strange dream to Sir Marcus at breakfast.

"Violet sea, eh? I knew a Violet once." He inspected his plate of eggs. "Surprising, the Hugo fellow can do a passable egg. What he simply *cannot* do is coffee. I suppose I shall have to train him for I won't consume another cupful of that ghastly muck."

Arabella passed me the pepper and salt dish. Did I imagine the tiniest beginnings of a smile on her face? Assuredly, one could not fail to smile at Sir Marcus, for he was the sort of person everybody liked. He had a contagious charismatic personality and I intended to keep him as friend.

"Has the coffee always been bad at Somner, Miss Wood-ford?" Sir Marcus went blithely on. "Always knew one of my favorite haunts had to have terrible coffee one of these days."

Angela asked how many times he'd been to Somner House.

"Oh, a few, since the couple married. Knew Katie girl before, you see. Met in the art circles."

"You never said what kind of art you do, Sir Marcus," Arabella piped from her corner.

"Patronage," he replied without any degree of modest hesitation. "I like to support talent when I see it."

I lowered my gaze to the table. The logical feasible reason why Sir Marcus came to Somner: as a patron of Kate Trevalyan.

"Not of Kate. She's a clever one. Secured her own patronage whilst singing at the club. Once a few paintings sold, she was in business. She didn't need *moi*."

"And stopped painting once she married Max," Bella added.

"That's not entirely true," Angela begged to differ.

"Apart from the odd piece," Bella conceded, and thus intimidated, scurried away from the table like a frightened mouse.

Sir Marcus noted as much. "I should take you two hunting, I dare say. You'd work better than my hounds."

Angela reared at the insult. "What *else* do you do than busybody with other people's lives? Flit from place to place, *feeding* off them to satisfy an empty craving? I think you ought to get married, Sir Marcus, and raise a castle full of children!"

And with that, she stormed out of the breakfast parlor.

"I think I upset her," Sir Marcus whispered incredulously to me, even though there was no occasion for him to whisper since we were alone.

"Oh, no," I sighed. "She's always like that. Actresses often are. They act to the zenith for maximum impact."

"A very keen observation there, Daphne. You'll make a fine novelist one day."

"Do you think so?" I scarcely believed it. Angela could sit down and write for hours whereas I contended with too many distractions to ever get published. Of course, in order to have a chance at publication, I knew I had to sit down and simply write.

" 'To labor on, the struggle is worth the prize,' " Sir Marcus encouraged. "So what do you make of this gardener, Jackson, and the maid? Grandfather or father? Pretty girl? Max? Yes, I see the picture. As for the girl, I don't think she's a current installment. More a convenience for Maxie boy, if you forgive my brutality."

I told him I'd always forgive his brutality.

"And whoever she was, the liaison probably happened some time ago. We shall have to investigate, Daphne D."

"Won't we get in trouble?" I had to raise the question. "We *are* guests here . . . and the house is in mourning, remember?"

"Well, if we're turned out on our cars," Sir Marcus said, patting my hand, "I promise I'll look after you."

CHAPTER SEVEN

"*You.* Paint?"

Laughing uproariously, Angela ducked her head out of our bedroom door for the fifth time. "She's still in there. Honestly, how long does it take to clean one's teeth?"

I was still piqued by her denouncing my painting before I even started.

"I'm sorry, Daph," she reneged. "Paint if you must but what you should really be doing is working on your novel. You'll never be published otherwise. Books won't write themselves."

She often liked to toss that jeer at me. She, the elder, the learned, the experienced sister.

I read a little of her latest work. She had just composed a scene where two girls traverse through a creepy part of the woods together, guided by an owl. Upon encountering a wolf, the owl screeches a warning before flying off to leave the girls to face the wolf alone. There's no knight to protect them and the odds look grim. "How does it end?" I asked, breathless, enthralled, and more than a little envious.

"They kill the wolf, but I haven't worked out that part yet. This one's a short. Did you finish your short?"

"Not yet." I hurried over to my notebook but she reached it first and began flicking through, spilling open to the page where Max's name was circled with a question mark. "What's this?"

"Random observations," I replied, thrusting out my hand for the book's prompt return.

Ignoring me, she spun around, reading every scrap on the page from every angle. "Sir Marcus is a grown man but you ought to show a little restraint, you know. Yes, the murder concerns us all but there is a time when we must allow the proper authorities to conduct the case and leave it to their judgment. You two are heading into trouble." The motherly scolding didn't sound like Angela at all. "Mr. Fernald, I agree, is an underling, but we have no business poking our noses around. It might upset Kate. Have you or Sir Marcus thought of her amongst your random plans to pillage the place for the murderer?"

No, I was loath to admit we hadn't.

"I know what you're going to say next." Angela waved her little finger. "You're going to tell me Kate was having an affair with Josh Lissot at the time and is glad Max is dead. But that isn't so. She loved Max, in her own bizarre way. It's why she stayed with him all those years."

I shook my head.

"What's *your* assessment, then?" Flicking back to where my short story loomed, half finished, the words scribbled across the pages in splendid disarray, she chuckled. "My, my, you *do* have a penchant for melodramatic overtures, don't you?" Snapping the book shut, she tossed it back to me.

I felt my face grow hot. *It may not be as good as your story, but one day I will write something that even you will admire.* "I haven't reached an assessment yet, but I *do* think Max was murdered by someone close to him."

"Here at Somner? In the house?"

"Or someone close to it, on the grounds."

Angela nodded, yet her face remained blank as if her thoughts strayed elsewhere. She soon disappeared to the bathroom while I went outside to sit on the balcony. I took my notebook with me, still hurt by Angela's comments on my work. What was wrong with a melodramatic story? Was not *Romeo and Juliet* a melodramatic success?

"Ahoy!"

Blinking as a pebble whished past my head to hit the window beside me, I detected a grinning Sir Marcus below.

"Do I do a good Romeo?"

I leaned over the balcony. "You could have hit my head, you know."

He shrugged. "The occupation has its hazards. What do you think of my outfit?"

He twirled around, clad in a full cape and painter's cap.

"Very nice. Where did you get those?" I pointed to the palette hooked under his arm.

"Katie girl. She says we can use a room over there for our painting endeavors. I don't know about you, but I intend to paint a *masterpiece.*"

Chuckling at his absurdity, I joined him downstairs.

"It's this room here," Sir Marcus guided.

Off to the left of the study, this room required a key that Sir Marcus promptly pulled out of his pocket.

"What of the other locked rooms?" I murmured, looking around for a looming Roderick.

Tapping his nose, Sir Marcus spurred me into the room.

"Now Daphne, that's our code for silence—the nose tap. We may be overheard. This place has ears."

I felt it, too. Mentioning Bella's ongoing bathroom antics and Angela's dislike of her, I inspected the array of painter's tools. The room, though small, possessed good light and lay relatively spare but for three easels, brushes, palettes, wiping cloths, little paint tins, two lamps, and a lonely paint-blotted stool.

"You can have the stool," Sir Marcus said, ever the gracious gentleman. "And here's your cape. Sorry, could find no feathery cap for you. You'll just have to imagine one."

I laughed. He truly was a ridiculous man. "Kate said we can use this room exclusively?"

"Yes. Katie girl understands the need for secrecy when we are to embark upon something great. But for us, painting is purely a façade."

He began setting up the canvases while I asked how Kate fared.

"Saw her looking at breakfast. She ate nothing and looks positively dreadful. No sign of Lissot. Or Rod. Perhaps they've all gone fishing?"

Glancing hopefully out of the window, a boyish glumness appeared in the downturn of his lips for if they had gone fishing, they had not invited him.

I seriously doubted a fishing adventure accounted for the absences. "Josh Lissot is maintaining his distance considering he has the strongest motivation for murder; Kate, too, realizes this; she is afraid, afraid of the future and for Josh, and I think she knows something or suspects something. Whether or not she is party to her husband's death remains to be seen. As for Lord Roderick, he is not entirely exempt, since he inherits what is left. He was the preserver of the family fortune before his madcap brother disintegrated the last of it, sending them all to a speedy ruin."

"My, my, a fine hypothesis." Whistling, Sir Marcus waved his white-tipped paintbrush over two canvases. "Undercoat. Once it's dried, you may begin."

"What are you doing and why, may I ask, is our painting a façade?"

Slipping out the frequency radio from his jacket, he switched the top button and adjusted the aerial.

I gasped. "Where did you get that?"

"Dabbled in the toy department during the war. I was useless, needless to say, but my money helped buy a few of these beauties and I got to keep souvenirs."

"So Angela was right. You *do* like to spy on people."

He shrugged, his thickened lips smacking with amusement. "There are worse pastimes. Take our Max chap, for instance. Or Katie girl. Katie and Josh are the subjects for today. They're in the room above."

I didn't want to ask how he'd come by this information, and watching him adjust the dials on his instrument, I shook my head.

"No prudish reprimand from you, Miss Daphne," he warned, "for I've heard all about you and your quest for adventure."

"From whom, may I ask?"

"From a *particular* friend of yours." Winking, Sir Marcus propped the radio on the sill of his easel. "Now we can listen while we paint. Think of it as a . . . radio reading. We've merely tuned into episode three."

After a brief crackle here and there, two voices became increasingly clear.

"Who? The Major? Major Browning?" I pestered Sir Marcus, but he shoved a hand over my mouth, drawing me to the unmistakable nuances of Kate Trevalyan.

". . . we can't be sure they won't find out. Fernald's not clever, but he's not stupid, either."

"But you've removed the evidence, darling. And so what? You slipped a little extra laudanum in his tea that day . . . to calm him, yes?"

I imagined Kate nodding.

"He went out on a wild rampage. How is that your fault?"

"But the drugs! The mix . . . it sent him wild. You know how he gets when he's in that state. He's unstoppable. Perhaps someone else had no choice but to restrain him, and when that failed . . . what kind of weapon would do that to a face?"

"Something long and blunt," Sir Marcus whispered.

"It's terrible . . . I can't live with myself thinking I am in some way responsible. Yes, I wanted him dead but not like this. . . ."

The voices muffled.

"Oh, darn!" Cursing, Sir Marcus tried to rescue the frequency, to no avail.

We spent a good hour or two afterward painting and surmising. Sir Marcus refused to acknowledge or answer my questions about the Major. His aptitude for vexing me led him to deny me any information, promising to "illuminate me" at another time.

Sketching my dream tower scene on canvas, I was amazed to see that Sir Marcus could in fact paint. Dabbing colors here and there, a landscape began to emerge and I recognized the old pergola as the central focus.

We were both immersed in our creations when Kate entered the room. Her warm smile gave no evidence of her secret lover's assignation upstairs or of her fears regarding her husband's death. The whisper of a shadow, however, hovered over a face too uncertain and fraught with worry. Eager to dismiss any attention on herself, she studied each of our works.

"Very good!" she said to Sir Marcus, and listening to them babble on, I understood they shared a great friendship as well as a love of the arts. Wisely, Sir Marcus mentioned nothing about Mr. Fernald or the investigation, but she soon relaxed and confided a little of the matter on her mind.

"I think they'll blame Josh, but he didn't do it!"

"They cannot charge him without evidence," Sir Marcus assured, adopting his best aristocratic demeanor.

A guttural, almost embittered laugh escaped her lips. "Oh, but they've *found* evidence . . . a leg of my painting easel. It has Max's blood on it and Josh's fingerprints."

"*So sayeth Fernald.* I don't mean to be rude, Katie girl, but the man is somewhat lacking in procedural intelligence. I'd truly like to see how he can prove it's Max's blood and Mr. Lissot's fingerprints."

Kate laughed again, this time, a very nervous laugh. "Oh, the fingerprints *will* match b-because . . ."

You and Josh had made love before it . . . the passionate embrace sending the easel and the couple crashing to the floor, where the easel leg rolled to the door.

Later, the unwanted husband strides into the room. He attacks. Seizing the leg, Josh protects Kate and together, they drag the body out to the beach—

"Daphne," Sir Marcus prodded, "give our Kate your reading of the situation."

Entirely lost in my own world, my paintbrush crashed to the floor and rolled to the door. Watching it, I exuded an uneasy swallow to face the grieving, distressed, and perhaps murderous widow.

"What of the gardener? Could he have attacked your husband?"

"Y-yes, I suppose so. He, er"—she stopped short, reluctant to betray the following—"has a daughter, Rachael. She works in the village pub but used to help out here."

"And she and Lord Max had an affair and produced a child," Sir Marcus finished for her.

Lady Kate looked bemused. "Why, yes, but I never told you—"

"I deduced it." A kindly, sympathetic hand brushed her upper arm. "Maybe this gardening fellow sought to ask ol' Max for a few more bucks and our boy responded. Showing steely strength, the gardener picks up the first thing he sees . . ."

"But that's the problem," Kate wailed, "the leg was in the room and Josh *did* use it."

So I had been correct in my painting of the lover's scene. Max had charged in and the two men had fought over Kate, a woman who exuded womanly charm and confidence on every level. Except she didn't look so confident as she started to cry.

"There, there," Sir Marcus, assuming the comforter's role, invited her into his arms. "You're among friends and we're here to help. But now is the time for complete honesty, Katie. If Josh killed Max, we need to know now."

My eyes flew wide open. He hadn't included me in this duplicity, had he? I had offered no such support, concealing a murderer, who, though he may have killed to defend a woman, should still stand trial.

"Josh thought he had," Kate wept profusely, "at first. We dragged the body out to the beach—"

The truth now came tumbling out.

"—but then I heard Max murmur. Josh," she said, lowering her eyes in shame, "offered to finish him off but I said no. We left then, truly we did."

"And what of the weapon?" Sir Marcus delivered a rendition of the epitome of a Scotland Yard detective.

"We left that, too . . . and his face wasn't like *that* when we left him. It wasn't, I swear it wasn't."

"Did Josh stay with you the entire time afterward? Do you have any witnesses?"

"No witnesses." She swallowed, her great eyes turning in an appealing way to me. "Except when Daphne came to the room in the morning."

Sir Marcus and I digested all of this information, each of us forming our own conclusions. Fernald could arrest Josh Lissot. There was enough evidence to convict him and the indisputable transparent motivation spelled his doom.

Still fighting for her lover, Kate lifted her eyes to both of us. "I'll do anything to protect Josh. I even said I did it but Fernald won't listen and Josh is too stubborn." A whisper of a smile eluded her bloodless lips. "He's from Irish stock, and as proud as they come. He won't hide behind any woman's skirts and I don't wish to see him suffer for a crime he didn't commit. Oh, don't you see? There's nothing we can do if Fernald has made up his mind . . . nothing . . . nothing . . ."

"Yes, there is." Opening the door, Angela sashayed into the room. "I'll say I did it. I killed Max."

CHAPTER EIGHT

Angela stood in the doorway.

We all stared at her as she came into the room. "Dearest Kate, you simply must let me say it."

Sir Marcus's loud cough broke my shock.

"Valiant of you, m'dear, but completely unnecessary. Fernald won't hear a word of it, despite how convincingly you can concoct a story."

Angela was enraged. "It's not the time for pessimism, Sir Marcus. Kate's desperate for our help."

"Not pessimism. *Realism.*"

"But if we can get Josh to agree—"

"Afraid you're wasting your time, ladies. From what Katie implies, he's already *half* confessed, which is good enough for a *full* arrest."

Truth . . . and silence. Perched upon the stool, I tried to concentrate on my sketch. Filling in a few more lines on my tower, I adjusted the window sizes and the door. I didn't know what else to do since everybody sat in brooding silence. A few minutes passed before I sensed Lady Kate monitoring each line I drew. I suddenly felt her soft murmur against my ear.

"No, Daphne; that window ought to go like this."

The languid, precise strokes confirmed her familiarity with the tower and her prowess as a great painter. She worked so fast and so quickly, yet everything was captured perfectly, even down to the last, tiny details.

I asked her if she had ever lived in the tower and, pausing, she shook her head and continued. Within moments, my tower rose up from the canvas, alive and ready for color, and she handed the pencil back to me.

"You must paint, as you write, with great detail."

Her words, and her reluctance to talk about the tower, accompanied me as I dressed for dinner that night. Relieved to see no sign of Arabella hovering around the place, I soaked in the bath for half an hour or so, resting my toes on the lion head spout.

It was then that an idea came to me.

Kate . . . and Roderick . . . in the tower. Kate's knowledge, her *intimate* knowledge, of the tower's architecture and her decorative influence with the African theme alluded to more than a passing, sisterly interest in Roderick's home. Or perhaps I read it wrong. Perhaps Roderick had great respect for his sister-in-law, and often heeded her advice. I thought back to when I first arrived, when she insisted he stay for dinner. He hadn't *wanted* to stay, but he had done so at her gentle command.

Kate Trevalyan. She commandeered men better than a ship's captain and without half the effort. Which led me to ponder: Had she, the wily captain, knowingly or unknowingly ordered her husband's death?

I thought I'd question Angela prior to dinner, as we dressed, our sisterly custom since we'd come to this house.

"Why are you offering to protect Kate? Do you and she share some dark secret?"

"No, no, and no" was the swift reply, to which I pointed out that "no" was not a sufficient answer to a question containing "why."

She growled her agitation, shoving her hands up in the air. "Leave me alone."

I did for a little while, until we were about to leave the room. Closing the strap on my shoe, I spied her frustrated attempts to locate her own. "The blue shoes are over there, by the window."

She marched over, swept them up, and then marched to the door.

"Ange," I pleaded on the way out, forcing her to pause, "does Kate hold some power over you? Did you and she ever commit a folly, something that binds you together? Is that what you're afraid of?"

"Afraid?" she scoffed. "I am *not* afraid."

Spinning on her heels, she started down the corridor, leaving me to lock the door. I don't know what possessed me to take this precaution, since we had little valuables inside. However, my notes on Max's murder lay exposed on my bed and I had a vision of Arabella creeping into our room in search of clues, and I dreaded her reaction to my suspicions. She firmly believed her cousin had been murdered, but whom did she suspect? Kate? Josh? Kate's friends? I hesitated . . . Angela?

"She's got a nasty eye, that one," Sir Marcus drawled,

swooping me aside the moment my feet hit the carpet of the last stair. "Wouldn't want to be shackled to her."

I cast a fleeting gaze over Miss Woodford's thin, tall frame. Standing with her arms crossed, forehead creased and scowling openly in Kate and Josh's direction, she looked ready to blurt out an accusation.

Sir Marcus shivered. "She gives me the frosties and she doesn't like our Katie, does she?"

Open hatred bubbled from Bella's ill-humored snarl of discontent. Was such a creature predisposed to a sulky disposition? Or had it been forced upon her in having to live such a dreary existence?

Sir Marcus believed otherwise. "That creature would find the thorn in any garden."

His words proved true over dinner, as another strange evening of stilted conversation commenced. Kate seemed paler than usual, Josh Lissot unusually quiet and pensive, Roderick an inanimate boulder who may as well have been dead, and Arabella's continually suspicious, downcast eyes surveyed us all. When she finally decided to speak—at the time Hugo arrived to clear the dishes—it was to return to the case.

"When is Mr. Fernald due back, Cousin?"

Forced to elicit a reply, Roderick blinked in Kate's direction. "Friday, I believe."

"Friday! That long when it's obvious that *he* . . ."

Her voice trailed off, her insinuation clear.

Sir Marcus lifted a very high brow to me.

"When it's obvious *what*?" Angela spat. "If you never finish your sentences, Miss Woodford, how can we possibly understand you?"

Sir Marcus's mouth dropped open.

So did mine, and looking around the table, I believe I saw the tiniest tinge of color scathe Roderick's face. Kate lowered her eyes, and Josh challenged the accusation, tapping his hands on the table.

"I take it you're referring to *me*, Miss Woodford?" Pushing back his chair, he shrugged off Kate's calming hand. "No. I will not endure this."

Arabella suddenly clammed up. Cornered, she appealed to her cousin who, true to character, simply stared at the wall.

When no apology issued forth from Bella, Josh seized his jacket and stormed out of the room, tossing his coat over his shoulder.

Kate gazed after him, her eyes full of sadness.

She did not, however, run after him. That would have made their affair obvious and, as Arabella had accused, suspect.

"Come," Angela said, rousing Kate out of her chair, "let's go to the drawing room and I'll order tea."

"Tea sounds good," Sir Marcus chimed, "though I'd infinitely prefer a nip of brandy."

Roderick promptly offered the supply available in the study, but refused Sir Marcus's invitation to join him for a nightcap. He said he had an early start the next morning and excused himself from the party.

Sir Marcus looked at me. "It's you and me."

"Is that a bad thing?" I smiled, accepting his arm.

"Fernald will arrest Lissot on Friday," Sir Marcus murmured as we entered the study, his eye immediately detecting the liquor cabinet while I went to the desk.

"Shrewd Daphne rummages through private drawers." I heard his amused chuckle, offering a glass to me.

"No thank you."

He looked disappointed. "No, you're absolutely right. Young, pretty girls like you should only be drinking champagne and pink lemonade. Nor, I do say, should you be drinking anything at all with an old libertine like me."

Relaxing in my lord's armchair, blissfully unaware of anything but enjoying his brandy, he saluted my efforts. "Shouldn't really be looking through those, Daphne girl . . . what if our erstwhile Lord Rod should return for a midnight nip and catch you out?"

"It's not midnight yet." I continued to turn the pages of an ordinary household ledger book. Nothing interesting dawned on the pages; there were various entries on household accounts and expenses, property improvements, kitchen maintenance, et cetera, all meticulously recorded in a neat black hand. I doubted Max kept such neat accounts, so this work must have belonged to Roderick. "My, my, Max and Kate certainly liked to spend large . . . you should see the drawing amounts labeled 'personal K' or 'personal M'!"

"We estate owners are allowed to draw from our estates, you know. It's our hereditary blessing. Whose drawings are larger out of Katie and Max?"

"They are equal but she draws an extra for housekeeping. Hmm, housekeeping, I wonder if that entails purchases of fine art and supporting lovers?"

I continued to scan each page, dismissing any feelings of guilt. Max had been murdered, I kept reminding myself. *Someone* had murdered him for a *reason*.

Closing the book, I hunted through another neat stack of papers. Obviously, Roderick had cleaned up his brother's affairs. I couldn't see Max's desk looking so organized. Tidiness did not fit his character. "Pity we didn't get to this desk just after Max died," I sighed, moving to the second drawer, which held more papers.

Sir Marcus barely raised a brow, quite happily sipping his brandy while I perused the room. "It's very Spartan, isn't it? I wonder if Rod threw out all those graphic nude Nubian post cards I brought Max from Africa last year?"

I blushed in spite of myself.

"No sign of them languishing under all those papers?" Sir Marcus asked hopefully.

"Why? Do you want them back?"

"Well," he said, clearing his throat, " 'twould be a great waste to throw them out. I spent some time choosing those . . . by the way, heard from Major Browning lately?"

I paused. "What is your association with him? You're not another detective, are you, hiding under the shade of your title?"

" 'The shade of my title,' " Sir Marcus echoed. "I like that, and no, can't abide the fellows. Police. Scotland Yard. I'm more interested in the whys and hows and I suspect from your upturned lip that that blaggard Browning never contacted you after the Padthaway affair."

I tried to lift an indifferent brow.

"It might interest you to know he was called away."

I said I didn't care. How hard was it for a man at sea to pick up a pen and write? He couldn't even spare *one* minute when I'd taken the trouble to post *two* letters. "There's a locked drawer here."

"A locked drawer." Rubbing his hands together, Sir Marcus was inspired to get up out of the chair. "The proverbial bottom drawer in every man's study. Why do you think it's always number three? The lower one, the one to be ashamed of, the one to hide risqué postcards?"

While he pondered, I explored. No way in . . . unless . . . "Do you have a key?"

A cynical brow answered me.

"Trust me. It worked *once*."

"At Padthaway?" Intrigued, Sir Marcus handed me one from his pocket. I asked him which one of his many properties did this key belong to and he grimaced. "A modest cottage. Do you believe me?"

I said I did not, too busy trying to jimmy the key in the drawer.

"You'd better not break that," Sir Marcus cautioned. "His lordship might take offense, especially if he's watching his pennies."

I said "hmmm," though I had difficulty imagining Roderick exhibiting any great emotion. Max, on the other hand, yes. "Do you think Max ever hit Kate?"

Sir Marcus chewed on his lower lip. "Saw him squeeze her neck against a wall once . . . he was drunk, of course, and we intervened. He did seem sorry for it later when he sobered up. Poor fellow was a madman."

I shivered and felt sorry for Kate. It must have been dreadful being condemned to live with a man given to violent outbursts, immoderate habits, and uncontrollable alcohol abuse that invariably led to a beastlike nature. I understood why she'd picked Josh Lissot for a lover. He possessed a calm certainty, and he was a man to look up to, not to fear. "Has she had many affairs over the years?"

"I believe the two had an *understanding* in that department."

"Hence the great marriage façade," I echoed, now frustrated with the drawer. "I *could* break the underlay. Even just a little piece might do the trick."

Ignoring Sir Marcus's cautionary glance, I broke a piece off and pulled it out. A small hole emerged, large enough for two fingers to slip through and probe. "More papers," I moaned, "oh, and something round . . . feels like a scroll." Carefully sliding out the beribboned scroll after a few efforts, I chuckled softly and thought of Ewe Sinclaire and how she'd love to embroil herself in this mystery.

"What have you?"

Sir Marcus peered over my shoulder.

"A last will and testament, I hope." Unrolling the purloined item on the desk, I grinned. "And written by Max Trevalyan himself, it seems."

Down at the bottom written in large legible letters were the words: LAST WILL AND TESTAMENT OF MAX TREVALYAN.

"The usual preliminaries . . . then, ah, here it is: *I hereby leave the bulk of my estate to my son born out of wedlock . . . Connor Jackson.*"

"Jackson," Sir Marcus echoed. "Jackson the gardener's grandson. Any mention of the mother?"

"A 'Rachael Eastley,'" I said, triumphant.

"And duly signed and witnessed." Sir Marcus whistled, coming to stand behind me. "Well done, Daphne . . . I suppose we ought to put the thing back now."

"Yes." But on leaning down to see the name of the witness, we both stammered in unison: "Hugo?"

Feeling the importance of such a find and perhaps a little guilty for allowing my forage through a private desk, Sir Marcus decided to confess our sin to Roderick the next morning.

Lowering my gaze at Roderick's calm acceptance of our confession, I nervously awaited the outcome. He did not speak right away, which increased my nervousness and Sir Marcus's prattle.

"Devilish thing, isn't it? I swear we only read a little and put it back where we found it. I daresay you discovered it only recently?"

"Yes," Rod eventually conceded. "I knew my brother always hid certain things in his bottom drawer."

"I'm sure it won't ever stand up, a frantic note written like that," Sir Marcus sympathized. "I know a good lawyer, but the way I see it, you won't have need of one."

"I sincerely hope not," came his reply.

"You can count on our silence," Sir Marcus vowed, steering me to the door. "Can't he, Daphne?"

"Y-yes," I promised. Part of me wanted to share our find with Angela, but her snappy mood that morning quickly overrode the urge. One could only trust a sister so far, and shared secrets with Angela in the past often lacked confidence on her side. She loved to gossip with her girlfriends, and Jeanne and I had learned to be cautious for good reason.

And Somner House was such a reason.

Still refusing to explain her ridiculous attempt to rescue Kate by offering herself as a sacrificial lamb, I observed her frank glumness at breakfast. The shadows beneath her eyes betrayed lack of sleep and she was more restless than usual.

However, a little life sparked to her listless eyes when a strained Kate entered the room, choosing the seat furthermost from Arabella. No love lost there, the two women sat straight-backed like ships poised at battle over the breakfast table. Battling for whom or for what? I mused.

Roderick tried his best to make conversation for the sake of his guests. He mildly suggested a day trip to the Old Town, if anybody was interested, and Sir Marcus swooped upon it, declaring it would be good for all of us to get out in the fresh air for the day. His lively hand then squeezed Kate's across the table, suggesting this was exactly what she needed.

Josh Lissot remained curiously absent and I asked after him.

"Fernald came this morning," Lord Roderick replied in a grim tone.

"Oh?"

"I'm afraid Josh Lissot's been arrested for the murder of my brother."

CHAPTER NINE

Sir Marcus endeavored to do his merry best as our guide of an island that he frankly admitted to knowing nothing about, but Lord Roderick filled in the blanks along the way.

"This entire island was once a part of the Duchy of Cornwall. Essentially, it is and always has been its very own little kingdom."

I liked that expression. Little kingdom. It suited Cornwall perfectly.

"St. Mary's is the bearer of many ancient sites . . . though archaeological sites are dotted all over the Isles."

As there were six of us, we traveled to the sites in two motorcars, Sir Marcus, Angela, and I in one; Bella, Roderick, and Kate in the other. However, at the first stop, some random monument that professed to be a noteworthy ruin, though I saw nothing noteworthy in it, Kate switched into our car.

"I won't stand another minute of that sour-face." She spoke of Arabella Woodford, of course. "She thinks Josh and I murdered Max. She's happy they took him away. She's happy because finally she's triumphed over me."

"How so?" Angela's reassuring voice expressed doubt.

An odd laugh escaped Kate's lips. "I suppose in a curious way she has triumphed over me, for she loves that I am no longer mistress of Somner. She loves the title and the tower, she wants to live here; that's why we're forever enduring her presence, but Max couldn't stand her and Rod, well, I *thought* Rod tolerated her, but now I'm not so sure."

Deciding, for once, upon discretion, Sir Marcus did not question her comment. I did, but in silence. Was she inferring Roderick and Bella, one or both of them, planned to kill Max so they could inherit and preserve what remained of a dying heritage?

I began to whisper to Sir Marcus at the first opportunity, but he pressed a finger to his lips, his right eye rolling in the direction of Bella, who had her sharp ears poised, armed, and waiting to catch any slight blunder of the tongue.

We stopped at the first Iron Age village, a rambling array of stones and partly uncovered walls, wild and old and enhanced by whispers of the past.

"Enchanting," I murmured, thinking myself alone as I explored, my fingernails scraping along the primeval stone, wondering who had lived amidst the ruins long ago.

"Cavemen and Vikings." Sir Marcus's long graceful fingers traced the other side of the wall. "Any stirrings for a novel, Miss Daphne?"

I looked beyond the wasteland to the hills bathed in wayside flowers, a plethora of color, yellows, pinks, oranges, reds, and my favorite, lavender. Inhaling the fresh hint of jasmine in the air, I closed my eyes and daydreamed. In the picture of my mind, I added wild growing rhododendrons and azaleas and a long, winding drive . . . *at the end of the drive, a man waited, my husband. I was a young and inexperienced bride, afraid of my new life, afraid I should not fulfill the requirements befitting a great lady. I was a girl, really. A gauche schoolgirl, a nervous kind of creature. How could I become the mistress of such a vast estate? I shivered, gazing ahead at the long line of servants standing there to welcome me. . . .*

"I am insanely curious," Sir Marcus's face broke my reverie. "What were you thinking just now? I cannot hope that you were dreaming about me, so it must be a story idea?"

I nodded.

"A romance? What kind of romance? Adventure-romance? Mystery-romance?"

I shrugged off his gibe. "Why do all men assume that if women write, they must write romance?"

Smiling, Sir Marcus explained his theories on the "other" sex all the way to the next ruin. I was glad for his company. His personality alone lightened the atmosphere, yet it did not trivialize the peril looming over Somner House.

"I wager that Arabella has something to do with it, with or without our sturdy Roderick's knowledge. Think. They both love Somner House, they want to protect its future. If left in Max's hands, they'd lose the estate, I guarantee it. Look at the ridiculous note he wrote in his will, leaving the whole lot to his illegitimate son!"

"I agree," I whispered back. "And we were right to suspect the gardener. Rachael must be his daughter and Connor, his grandson. Yes, it all seems to fit, doesn't it?"

"Like a glove," Sir Marcus enthused.

"But the violence of the crime? What kind of heartless villain could do *that* to a face?"

"I know," Sir Marcus pondered aloud. "It's a conundrum."

"What's a conundrum?" Stepping out from behind a tombstone, Roderick studied us both. His somber expression sobered me, and I blushed as Sir Marcus prattled on about the mysteries of ancient civilizations.

"He definitely heard *something*," I said to Sir Marcus a few minutes later, after we'd walked some distance away from Roderick, who'd been joined by Bella. "I feel awful. How can we face him again?"

Rolling his eyes, Sir Marcus proffered his arm. "You worry too much. In any case, I am the one with the criminal tongue; you just agreed, which invariably you must do because I am always right."

"Always?" I teased.

We'd reached the museum and stopped to admire a figurehead from a clipper ship when Roderick happened upon us a second time.

"Something appears to be amusing you two."

I exchanged a glance with Sir Marcus. His guilty face, I imagined, mirrored my own.

"I am sorry, my lord," I began. "We did not mean to cause offense under the circumstances—"

"You mistake me, Miss Daphne. I merely wanted to share your amusement."

Sir Marcus and I exchanged another look.

"Oh, er, we were just debating on the works of contemporary female writers."

"The subjects and so forth," put in Sir Marcus.

"Novels, mainly," I added. "Just random ideas. Nothing of any import."

"Plots and motivations," Sir Marcus confirmed.

"I see . . ."

At that precise moment, Kate drifted over to retrieve Sir Marcus, and I gulped, left alone to face Roderick.

"Sir Marcus," Rod remarked, "has the happy manners to enliven any company."

"Yes, he does," I echoed, asking where we intended to lunch. I still couldn't work out if he'd overheard us or not. His expression gave no indication and his eyes remained a trifle skeptical.

"Hugh Town. I believe, Miss Daphne, you will like it."

When he spoke, he seemed to take a great deal of time to do so and I wondered whether he was merely shy. His brother had been born with lively manners. Had such manners placed him further and further in his brother's shadow? Had he resented his brother for it and had such resentment led to anger and, ultimately, murder?

I loved Hugh Town just as Roderick had predicted. The charming seaside port, the old pubs, narrow lanes, and salt-sprayed weathered houses carried years of history. The hint of yesteryear lingered in the air, on the grimy streets, and in the faces of the friendly locals.

"Don't care much for this Hugh Town place." Sir Marcus screwed up his nose. "Ghastly cold, windy place. What say we head over there to that warm-looking pub?"

While Arabella and Roderick continued to tour the local

attractions, Sir Marcus, Angela, Kate, and I headed to the Old Windmill.

"Appropriate title," Sir Marcus commented on the way in, "full of townsfolk and stranded sailors exploiting windy tales."

Despite Sir Marcus's dislike of the town, the charming old inn appealed to me. It was a modified mill, whitewashed, extended to encompass a newer building where most of the locals congregated. One entered the pub via the round mill tower, stepping down a sharp left-hand flight of stairs to descend into the main dining area full of raucous laughter. It was a quarter to noon and yet every stool, table, and chair swarmed with men of all descriptions. Sailors, farmers, and townsfolk filled the place, with the odd woman amongst the entourage serving cider ale and hot food.

Kate couldn't help but smile, her eyes sparkling for the first time since her husband's death. Perhaps the scene reminded her of happier days, during the war, when she had entertained soldiers in the air force. I ached to hear the beautiful singing voice I'd heard so much about. Angela had used the phrase "hauntingly ethereal."

Sir Marcus guided us to a place in the middle of the thoroughfare.

"We'll have to stand at the bar, I'm afraid, unless one of these gents would be so kind as to give the ladies a seat."

He spoke loudly and achieved the desired result, forcing two lonely sailors away from their table. They looked as if they'd consumed too much ale as they staggered out of the pub.

"You ladies fancy a warm brew?"

Kate answered for the three of us, dispatching Sir Marcus to fetch the island's famous cider ale.

"The funeral will be tomorrow," Kate murmured, accepting her mug of warmed cider from Sir Marcus. "Roderick thought a quick, quiet affair would be proper, under the circumstances."

"Yes, under the circumstances," Sir Marcus echoed.

Kate turned her enormous eyes to him. "Oh, Markie, is there any way . . . any way at all . . ."

"To help Josh old boy?" Sir Marcus finished, his watchful gaze monitoring the room. "Sorry, Katie girl. Fernald's dug his toes in and he's the man in charge."

"But what of his superiors? Surely they can look into the case?"

"Possibly, but with the weather and the tides, it looks like Mr. Lissot will have to spend weeks in a dank island cell. They'll move him later, I suspect, where he'll stand trial and—"

"Oh, no! I can't bear it!" Hands cupping her face, she struggled to hold back tears. "It's my fault. He's a good man. I can't let him die when he only sought to protect me and he *didn't* kill him. He *didn't*."

"It's not *your fault*." Angela rubbed Kate's frozen arms. "You mustn't allow fear to ice your days. Hope is what matters."

A wan smile touched Lady Kate's bloodless lips. It was a troublesome time and depressing to see the self-assured, confident, effervescent, and mesmeric Kate Trevalyan reduced to such a withering despondency.

Angela seized the moment to lighten the mood. "Why don't you sing? Sing for the sailors?"

"What, here? Now?"

"Why not? Like Sir Marcus said, they're stranded and could use some cheering up. We *all* could use some cheering up."

Angela thus took charge, Sir Marcus and I unable to stop

her. Leading Kate to the center of the room, she soon got everyone's attention—easy to do for an actress of her caliber—and elicited a welcoming round of applause from the audience.

Drawing from experience, Kate adopted her stage-actress face and began to sing. I wondered what she'd choose, thrown unexpectedly into the arena, and the emerging tune polished every rough soul in the place. The men's faces softened and became wistful, almost dreamy, perhaps recalling better, calmer days before the Great War.

In amongst the crowd I saw him like an illusion. Yet it wasn't an illusion. He was there, in the crowd, smirking from the back wall.

He saw me, too, dipping his head in mock salute. I turned away, my face resuming a lobsterlike quality. Seething, I pulled at my fingers, resisting the urge to bite my nails. I'd not sit here and watch him adoring Kate Trevalyan and her performance, not now, not ever.

"She's extraordinary, isn't she?" Sir Marcus whistled in my ear. "And not as fragile as she looks. I've seen her shoot a lion, you know."

If I hadn't been so consumed with seeing him, I might have asked where this extraordinary event had transpired. But I could not. I could only seethe, dreading his unwanted entry into my life again, and yet powerless to stop it.

The men shouted for an encore and Kate complied as I was forced to hear another love song. This time it was a famous French tune that proved to be torture, *extreme* torture, for it dredged up my days at Padthaway—of David, and of the Major, later neglecting to reply to my letters. How dare he consider *me* a brief flirtation when I deserved better!

"Not up to clapping?"

Prompted by a curious Sir Marcus, I buried my pride and remembered my manners. Soaring to the occasion, I trusted I put in a good enough effort to divert suspicion of jealousy.

Unfortunately, the frustratingly astute Sir Marcus soon located the source of my discomfort and exchanged a jolly handshake with the Major. Obviously, the two knew each other and Sir Marcus, to my dismay, pointed me out rather cheerfully.

Fortunately, an exuberant Angela partially shielded me from the Major's view. "Look at Kate, Daphne. She's positively glowing. This was good for her."

Good for her.

"What's wrong with you?"

One could never fool a sister. "Oh, it's . . ." I whispered the reason for my frustration, and flattered by this sudden confidence, Angela nodded, her wide eyes quick to detect the Major in the crowd. Assuming immediate sisterly control, she squeezed my hand. "Greet him cordially and coolly and don't show him any emotion."

It was difficult thing to do when all I wanted to do was hurl the remainder of my beer at him. How *dare* he ignore my letters after all we'd been through at Padthaway . . .

"Prepare." Angela's hoarse whisper scathed one side of my face. "He's coming over."

His first port of call was Kate, of course. Hearing her squeal of surprise upon seeing him, I realized I should have expected they'd know each other. In fact, the Major seemed to know every person on the planet, which irritated me far beyond his avoidance of my correspondence. Yes, yes, he had contacts in Scotland Yard. Yes, yes, he made it his mission in life to assume and collect information like one collected seashells or works of art.

"Hello, Daphne."

Angela elbowed me.

"Hello." I smiled through my teeth. "What an unexpected pleasure, Major Browning."

"Is it? Your demeanor suggests otherwise."

He deliberately baited me. But I'd since learned to not bite, and merely smiled and asked, in a spirit of politeness, what brought him to the island.

"The far winds." His reply came slow, his eyes searching mine.

I glanced away. I didn't believe him.

"Thank you for your letters, Daphne. I trust you received mine?"

"You never replied," Angela snapped in response.

Raising a brow, the Major waited to be introduced. I did my duty, my voice sounding strangled and forced for I didn't want him intruding upon our party. It was evident that my indisputable coldness caused more than Sir Marcus's face to flush. Sensing Kate's interest in my acquaintance with the Major, I tried a little harder to mask my displeasure. Cordial and cool, Angela had said.

I rolled my shoulders. I could be cool and cordial. "So what brings you to St. Mary's, Major?" I asked again.

"Shipwrecked by weather," Sir Marcus interrupted, his joking presence very much unwanted.

I glared at Sir Marcus and he soon found a swift reason to excuse himself from our conversation.

I repeated my question to the Major as we stepped away from the party. He looked well, a little paler than when I'd last seen him. Perhaps the winter frost had frozen the last vestige of decency in his black, uncaring soul? I wondered.

"You're angry with me, aren't you?"

"Yes," I began with a vengeance.

"I enjoyed your letters and am saddened you did not receive mine." A glimmer twinkled in his eye as he said it.

"I doubt you even *bothered* to reply, Major. Too busy, no doubt, with whatever nefarious and clandestine operation—"

"Nefarious?" He grinned. "I like that word and I like you." His voice dropped to a low, warm whisper. "I've missed you, Daphne."

"Ever hear of the post?"

"I cannot be held to blame for the error of our postal system."

"I suppose not, just as I suppose you only reply to worthy temptations."

"Oh, I assure you. You are a very *worthy* temptation."

Roderick happened upon us at that moment and seeing me with the Major, detached himself from Bella's side and sidled to my own.

A trifle flattered, I wondered if I had stirred a protective instinct inside the dour Roderick Trevalyan. The absurd notion vanished as soon as it entered my mind, for I truly couldn't see Roderick Trevalyan with any woman, least of all me. Far too monkish and isolated, he preferred his own company to anybody else's and seemed intent on remaining so.

After a round of introductions and pleasantries, the offer to call upon us at Somner House was made. "We are a house in mourning," Lord Roderick advised, resuming a solemn air, and the Major gave me a quick glance, "but you, and your senior officers, are welcome."

Thanking him for the invitation, the Major solicited a few

seconds alone with me and, unable to escape, I had no choice but to suffer his interrogation.

"And what brings Miss du Maurier to St. Mary's and Somner House, hmmm? A *murder* in the making? Who died? And did you kill this person for inspiration?"

"Don't talk so loud," I hissed. "Your ideas are as preposterous as they are thoroughly unwelcome."

"But I hope I'm not unwelcome to you," he grimaced, his dark eyes faintly aroused. "We've a new mystery to unravel, have we?"

"*We,* Major, won't be unraveling anything—"

"This time it is *you* who are mistaken, Miss Daphne. Whether or not you welcome my being here, you will have to suffer it. For however long I am here depends entirely upon the weather. Now, tell me about this death, Miss du Maurier."

"I'm sorry, Major. I have to go." And smiling, for once having the upper hand, I waved from the door. "Cheerio."

CHAPTER TEN

I asked Sir Marcus how he knew the Major as we walked away from the mill.

"Met him around the traps, once or twice. Well set up. Good contacts."

"A veritable busybody," I said.

"No more than you or I." Sir Marcus smiled his best doting smile. "Ah, now, here are the others. Let us return to the House of Mourning, shall we?"

"House *in* mourning," I corrected.

Lunch had been a strained affair. A brief stop in a village halfway to Somner, and nobody was in the mood to endure the rainy weather.

"Thank heavens that's over," Kate breathed out loud on the drive home.

Angela tried her best to rouse her spirits. "You sang beautifully, like an angel, and it's good if you try and keep busy by helping others. It'll take your mind off . . ."

"Help others?" Kate echoed. "How can I think of helping others when I don't even know if I have a home anymore?"

Or a living, I thought as I sat in the front seat of the car with Sir Marcus. Since the reading of the will would take place sometime after the funeral at Somner, I sympathized with Kate. Her nerves grew increasingly raw as her future hung in the balance.

Angela had already suspected the worst for Kate.

"That Fernald . . . he's threatened her. She told me. He'll blackmail her, too." Her voice faded into silence and I joined her as she sat brooding on the edge of her bed.

"Oh, *curse* the weather! Fernald shouldn't be in control. He's enjoying the power. Power over poor Kate."

"But you know he can't arrest her while Roderick speaks for her."

"He *can*." Angela's mouth set into a grim line. "He's a little weed and he's after some sport. Sir Marcus agrees with me. Ask him, if you like. You seem to respect his opinion more than mine."

I was too tired to think upon it further and in no mood to humor Angela. The events of the day, compounded by the arrival of the Major waltzing his way into my world again, left me with a nasty headache. I wanted to do nothing but lie in the bath and read a book and hastened to the sanctuary of the next room.

"Oh, I was going in there just now."

Arabella waylaid me, a towel draped over her arm.

"But you can go first, Daphne," she added upon spying the book tucked under my arm.

Without her glasses, I thought her quite attractive, particularly with the tinge of color in her cheeks.

Astonished by her graciousness, I said I'd go second since she only intended to have a shower. She nodded and marched in, shutting the door promptly behind her.

Returning to the bedroom, I discovered Angela furtively shaking out her purse in the corner. She jerked when I entered, nervous, afraid, obviously not expecting my early return.

I noted her preoccupation with the bag.

"Lost my powder pack," she sighed.

"Oh," I said, but did not believe her. For a long time I had suspected Angela dabbled in the occasional use of a drug, opium or cocaine, I didn't know which, and I didn't want to know. No wonder she often spent weekends away, turning her nose up at our home performance nights. The racy crowd appealed to her sensibilities and I decided I should catch her out and report it to our parents for her own good. But not just yet.

The Major and his senior officers attended the funeral.

I was not unduly surprised by this, having prior experience of the Major's aptitude for involving himself in affairs that seemed to be none of his concern. But perhaps they were, after all. I had to acknowledge the Major's importance in the Padthaway case. However, he certainly could not have been sent here by officials when news of the murder had not yet reached the mainland. Or had it?

I dismissed the idea as soon as it came into my head. The news had shocked Kate too much to think of telephoning friends and relatives. Could Roderick have done it for her? As far as I knew, there weren't many relations to be informed of Max's demise. There was a Trevalyan aunt and a few cousins in America, but Lady Kate, as an adopted child, claimed no living relations. No doubt, there were hundreds of friends and acquaintances Kate could have notified, but I suspected she desired little attention.

The priest's gloomy closing words and prayer at the funeral brought a stiffness to an already cold and emotionless atmosphere. Devoid of flowers, candles, and entirely lacking sorrowful adulations of grieving family members, it was the strangest funeral I'd ever attended. It was filled with nothing but silence.

There would be no graveside burial, considering the body's state and nature of death.

Few locals occupied the empty seats, but I noticed one family, that of Jackson the gardener, sitting near Hugo on the last row.

"What d'you make of it?" Sir Marcus's curious whisper tickled my ear. "Father, mother, daughter Rachael, and little grandson Connor."

Our curiosity heightened when directly after the service, Roderick turned to receive and acknowledge the family. Kate's face blanched at the sight of the clan.

"Spark of anger there," Sir Marcus noted.

We watched their slow progression toward Jackson's family. My interest remained on Jackson's daughter and Max's lover, Rachael: slim, wearing a tailored black suit and a pointed little black hat; her dark hair swept high off a strong brow where sloping eyebrows framed long-lashed dark eyes; a short nose and a reddened mouth. Yes, she was beautiful in an unearthly, unusual way.

"My word," Sir Marcus whistled, "a fine-looking filly, if ever I saw one."

Every man in the room noticed her. The Major and his attendants were in the pleasant process of forming her acquaintance when Roderick and Kate approached. Having strangers present probably helped Kate in formally acknowledging her late husband's lover and his child. Entertained by Jackson, Connor, unquestionably Max's son with the same wispy curls and wild good looks, merely stared up at the great lady staring down at him. Oblivious to her interest in him, he wrinkled his nose and clutched his mother's hand.

Rod, Kate, and Jackson shared an exchange while Rachael maintained a dignified silence. She intrigued me, for she didn't seem the kind of flighty girl Max Trevalyan fancied. Maybe having the child had changed her, and I assumed Max had paid handsomely for the mishap.

"Poor Katie girl," Sir Marcus sympathized. "She did so want a baby awhile back . . . went to countless doctors, but nothing ever came of it."

"This child was obviously born during the marriage. That must have been hard for Kate. But no matter how hard I try, I just can't picture someone with such a serene face working as a maid, can you?"

"No," Sir Marcus agreed, "but I have a tantalizing vision of her pulling out weeds . . ."

I rolled my eyes. To my detriment, the Major caught my expression. His brow lifting, he casually left the others to join us.

I hunted round for Angela. Strangely, she seemed deep in conversation with Arabella.

Blessedly, Sir Marcus stepped in to talk to the Major while I stood pale and still. I wished he would go away. I wished he'd not come to embroil himself in Somner House affairs.

"I have just met the charming Mrs. Eastley," he began. "Jackson's daughter."

"Ah." Sir Marcus looked significantly at me. "Do you know her?"

"Yes, she's a widow. Her husband drowned five years ago."

The widow romanced by the dissolute lord of the manor. Annoyed by the Major's obtaining facts quicker than Sir Marcus and I, who were *actually in residence* at Somner, I lifted a haughty brow. "I suppose you know Mr. Fernald, too, and since you are so remarkably clever, why don't you just tell us who killed Max Trevalyan and why?"

Sir Marcus whistled, disbelief clouding his good-natured face. "I, er, shall go and rescue your sister."

He darted off quicker than I could say "I suppose you know Miss Woodford, too, Major."

He continued to smirk. "The venomous tone doesn't suit you, Daphne."

"It is *Miss du Maurier* to you, thank you."

"Miss du Maurier," he obliged. "I have missed you these past months, as you have evidently missed me. Why else would you use the acid tongue on me?"

I stared at him in dismay.

He touched his ear. "What was that? I didn't quite hear you?"

Aware that we were attracting attention, or rather, *I'd* solicited the unwanted attention by raising my voice, I endeavored to resurrect some sense of decorum. It was hard to be friendly and well-mannered when faced with such adversity. Yet it was better for me to retain a cool distance than to exhibit emotion where Major Browning was concerned, for he was a man whose arrogance mistook feeling for infatuation.

Yes, he thought every woman was in love with him.

Yes, that was his problem.

"Sorry," Angela said later as we hung our coats in the parlor of Somner House. "I got stuck talking to Bella Woodford. Thankfully, you had Sir Marcus with you. What's the Major doing here? Don't believe a gibbet about this stranded by bad weather business."

"Oh, it's not unusual at this time of year." Kate had overheard us. "The coastal winds drive many island-bound."

Angela asked how she knew the Major.

"He came to the club once or twice during the war," she replied, a fondness softening her eyes. "He's a kind man."

Kind! My guffaw produced a warning glare from Angela.

"I'm not feeling well," Kate admitted, swaying a little to the left.

"Then go and rest," Angela advised, taking the weight of her coat from her and readjusting it on the hook. "I'll check on you later."

Nodding, Kate left.

"I'm for a lie-down, too," Angela yawned, starting up the stairs.

"All for lie-downs, are we?" Complaining, Sir. Marcus waylaid me. "Daphne, I do hope I can persuade you to accompany me in a dash of arty asylum."

Grinning, we made arrangements for a painting caper. I said I'd go and change first, dashing upstairs ahead of a silent-footed Bella. Feeling uncharitable for not including her, I asked if she wanted to join Sir Marcus and I, but she refused, resuming her usual sullen outlook. "No, thank you," replied she, "my cousin and I have other plans."

Oh, do you? I thought, hunting for my cardigan and catching Angela extracting a small packet out of her handbag. Slipping the item into her skirt pocket, she flopped onto her bed and rolled over to have a nap. Disturbed by the sight, I tried to banish it from my mind.

"My, my, you're a ferocious painter," Sir Marcus commented over my shoulder. "Striking up a literal storm. What represents the clouds today? MB or some unknown womanly complaint?"

"*Not* Major Browning." I determined to be clear on that score. "My sister, actually." I relayed what had happened in the room. "She behaves oddly sometimes. I don't know what to make of it."

"Oh, I do." Sir Marcus smiled.

I asked him to elaborate, but he didn't seem to want to comply, uttering low, moaning sounds as I persisted. "Very well . . . but compose yourself for a shock."

I nodded.

His brow arched. "I'm not *convinced*. In some ways, you are too innocent, Daphne. Charming trait, but not precisely worldly wise. You'll have to wizen up if you're to transcribe life to paper."

My paintbrush wavered.

"All right." Laying down his paintbrush, he faced me with a sigh. "Your sister, Angela, favors the female kind. There. I've said it."

I stared at him, too shocked to speak. "No . . . she's engaged to—"

"She won't marry him. She won't marry any man, if I am a

correct reader of character, and I'd wager my best thorough-bred on *that*."

"But . . ."

My voice faded into a tiny whisper and I found myself on a spiral of memories, each twisting and turning, and blindly, I followed the paths in my mind. "You may be right," I eventually acquiesced, but it didn't lessen the shock, and I wondered how my parents would take the news, if ever they learned of it.

"Oh." I turned from him to hide my scarlet face. Angela . . . and Kate. The two faces in profile blurred before me, Kate's unsure and tentative and Angela's nurturing and devoted. No . . . surely it *couldn't* be . . .

Yet had Sir Marcus stumbled upon something I didn't want to acknowledge? Was it a secret kept so clandestine as to have played a hand in the murder of Max Trevalyan?

CHAPTER ELEVEN

The room was vacant when I returned.

I suspected Angela had gone to check on Kate. I also suspected she'd taken opium or laudanum, as a tonic for Kate.

A modest review of character suggested Kate may have dabbled occasionally in the usage of such dependents, but thinking back to the fear reflected in her eyes whilst enduring the horrors of her husband's addiction, perhaps she rejected *all* forms, indignantly righteous and hating what it'd done to the man she once loved. I still believed she had loved Max when she married him. How soon afterward that changed, who could say?

The shades of love, I scribbled down in my journal, chewing on the edge of my pencil. I felt enormously inspired by the events at Somner and the reappearance of the Major, along with the jealousies he provoked in me.

I penned a short story about friends meeting at a party: suspicion, old feelings, and a romantic resolution. I thought of the general populace and how most readers preferred happy endings. But all endings weren't happy, were they?

"Kate is beside herself." Sweeping into the room, Angela threw herself into a chair. "I don't know what to do. I tried to give her something to calm her, but she flatly refuses."

"The package in your handbag?" I queried. "What is it?"

She looked away. "Oh, don't go preachy on me. It's relatively harmless . . . a friend passed it to me."

"What news of Josh Lissot?"

Angela shook her head. "She's upset over Josh. She wants to see him but Roderick said it wouldn't be wise."

I thought this was interesting, for if Roderick wanted to neatly involve Kate in the murder of her husband, he'd have encouraged, even *taken,* her to see the man suspected of killing her husband.

Angela chattered on about Josh, rolling her eyes at Kate's anguish for the man she dubbed "as good as dead." I dared to reply I believed Kate's attachment to Mr. Lissot greater than the average *affair d'amour,* but my sister talked off this assessment and I had to accept her truth. She *did* care for Kate Trevalyan, passionately. Whether or not Kate returned her affections remained to be seen.

To divert my mind from the possibility of a romance between my sister and Kate, I raised the subject of the funeral. We discussed the attendance and I received sisterly advice once again regarding the Major.

"Oh, but I forgot to tell you about Bella." Wrinkling her nose, a tiny smirk appeared at her lips. "I spoke to her at great length and, well, emotions are always unveiled at funerals and she positively *hates* Kate. Not that she said it, but I saw it in her dark little eyes, watching Rod fix up Kate's shawl and that kind of thing. And she *loathes* that Eastley woman. Not that she said anything particular on that score either, but it appears

Jackson's been blackmailing Max for some time about the child and now that Max is dead, poor Rod's been hampered with the burden."

I thought of Roderick: the good man, keeper of his brother's commitments. Of course, he'd honor any existing arrangement between Jackson and his daughter. "What does Mrs. Eastley do for work?"

"She works at the local tavern, I believe," Angela said in a caustic tone.

I pictured Rachael Eastley catching Max's eye and becoming pregnant, forced to confess the news to Max and her father. Kate, the wife who'd wanted a baby, must have been devastated to learn the truth and the possibility of a scandal, thus leaving the door open to blackmail. It was a story in and of itself.

"Oh," Angela said offhandedly, "I thought you'd want to know. Rod has invited the Major and his officers to dinner tomorrow night. Apparently, Kate wished it."

Despite my resolve, I felt an excitable apprehension upon hearing this news. The Major . . . *here* at Somner. It reminded me of the first time I met him, when he pretended to be a common fisherman for days before appearing at Ewe Sinclaire's door, shining and respectable. Our spirit then were no different from now. In fact, I think they'd worsened. I could not deny my attraction to the charismatic Major, yet I did not admit it at the time. And I never would, I vowed silently.

I knew why Kate had invited him and so did Angela. She wanted to enlist the Major's support in helping her jailed lover. But did the Major carry any influence here, on the remote Isles of Scilly?

I doubted it.

I also doubted the respectableness of Mr. Fernald. He was

too young to be investigating a murder. Did anybody know anything about him? His family? Background? Connections? Friends?

Oh, for an Ewe Sinclaire! I missed her frank aptness for village gossip, always reliable and for the most part, accurate in her colorful reportage. What does one do without essential village gossip?

I posed this sad dilemma to Sir Marcus when next we met.

"We could try the hunchback . . . yes, I'm in for a spot of culinary endeavors. To the kitchen and Hugo we fare."

It was the hour before dinner.

"I don't think Hugo will like us interfering in his domain," I tried to warn, but Sir Marcus marched on ahead.

Everything appeared orderly when we arrived. A simple meal, roasted chicken, lay warm in its oven and we found Hugo crouched over stirring some kind of sauce mixed with tomatoes, potatoes, and carrots.

His daunting, lopsided brow struck up at our noisy interruption. Wiping his hands across his apron, he grunted. "What d'you want? Sir? Miss?"

No pleasantries there. Recognizing his fault, he colored a little and repeated the question with the appropriate softening tones, his watchful eyes intent on Sir Marcus jovially inspecting the kitchen.

Embarrassed, I shrugged my shoulders while Sir Marcus blithely dithered around, proclaiming the excellence of several archaic utensils, saying, "Yes, yes, we can use that."

"Use what, milord?" Abandoning his sauce, the hunchback followed Sir Marcus about the room.

"I am certain Lord Trevalyan would have said we have special guests tomorrow night? Well, Hugo, this is your lucky day. Miss Daphne and I are here to help. We'll provide three of the dishes."

Hugo looked dumbfounded. "Three?"

"Yes, three."

"Did, er, his lordship—"

"Indeed, he has," Sir Marcus affirmed, shepherding me around the kitchen to share his vision for our three dishes.

I lifted an incredulous brow. He *hadn't* asked Roderick at all. It was a complete falsehood that Sir Marcus made up for during dinner later that day.

"You wish to cook for us?" Rod was astounded.

"Why, yes. I like to dally about in the kitchen . . . unless anybody has any objections?"

Nobody dared to object and the plan was set. Unfortunately, the laboriously quiet meal that eve left a bitter taste in my mouth. In truth, I began to look forward to the Major's arrival the next day. A pleasant diversion was needed and I trusted he and his three companions would break the monotonous sobriety of the silent Rod, the withdrawn Kate, and the petulant, tight-lipped Bella.

Due to their recent tête-à-tête at the funeral, Angela managed to implore the latter to talk of her home in Devon where she cared for a tyrannical aunt and what sounded like a jungle of a garden. Listening along, I pitied Arabella and understood why she fancied coming to the island, to Somner. I pictured her in her little cottage, her aunt badgering her, and Bella, hoping, *waiting* for that letter, that invitation to return to Somner House once again. Somner became her salvation.

"His murder was unduly cruel," Bella said the next morning at the breakfast table to Angela and me, since the others had not yet made their appearance.

"I agree with you." Angela nodded, liberally buttering her toast. "But Mr. Lissot will soon be charged."

"But they haven't charged him yet. They still delay, when it is obvious. *Why?*"

Angela gave a nonchalant shrug. "These things take time. How is dear Rod coping? You know your cousin best, Bella. He'll need your help now . . . living all alone on the island."

Bella's face brightened.

"You should marry him," Angela advised with a tinge of sarcasm in her voice, causing the color to deepen on Bella's face. "*Together,* you could rescue Somner out of deep peril and preserve the legacy."

I could see the thought had already occurred to Bella.

After breakfast, I went for a walk. Trudging along the beach path, the path where they'd found the body, I envisaged Max lying there, his head encased by a pool of blood, his face bludgeoned and unrecognizable. I shivered. It was horrible. What manner of person would do such a thing? Jackson? I had observed a shrewdness in the gardener's face. He would push the Trevalyans for benefits, for his daughter and grandson, but the question remained, how far would he, or *had* he, pushed? I could see him hiding in the bushes, waiting for Max, a sickle in his hand.

I glanced up. My feet had carried me along the beach toward the tower. Cursing my lack of thoughtfulness in not bringing a shawl or my woolen fedora, I climbed up the beach path, my teeth chattering in the face of the icy wind.

The lure of the tower beckoned. How sad and lonely it looked, emblazoned against the wintry sky.

"You there!" Suddenly an old man appeared jabbing a pitchfork at me. "Who are ye? Didn't yer read the sign? It says no tresspassin'."

Gasping for my breath, I raised a friendly hand. "Sorry, sir. I'm not trying to break in. I'm a house guest at Somner House. Lord Roderick's guest, in actual fact," I added in all haste.

"Eck?"

The pitchfork lowered a fraction.

"Yes," I confirmed, keeping my voice calm as I related how I'd come to the island and how my sister knew Lady Kate Trevalyan.

"Ah."

Lowering the pitchfork to the ground, he wiped his mouth on his grimy sleeve. "Ye lost then?"

"Not really." I blushed. "I know Lord Roderick is not at home, but I do so love to explore this island. Have you always lived here? Do you work for the Trevalyans?"

The man frowned at me. Too many questions, I realized, and employing Sir Marcus's tactic, I resumed the cheery conversational mode. "I *adore* the ocean and boats. I watch them from my home at Ferryside in Fowey. I love the way they glide across the water. One can never be freer than in a boat, don't you agree, Mr. . . . ?"

My elaborate friendliness worked. Setting aside his pitchfork, the man gestured to the boatshed. "Pencheff's the name, and if ye like boats, Missy . . ."

"Oh, I do," I assured him.

"Then I'll let ye have a look round. I don't think Mr. Rod'll mind, seein' ye his guest and all."

I didn't know what I expected to find or if there existed a logical point to my current endeavor, but I had not lied. I did live in Fowey and I did admire boats. I could sit and watch them all day, tapping my fingers on the windowsill, except, of course, when there were chores to do. My mother did not like idleness and I often received a stern reprimand for my frequent daydreaming.

Having visited a few boatsheds, this one intrigued me with its rusty tin exterior and cobwebs trailing down from the corners of the haphazard workshop, where tools, machines, and nature collided. "This is the newest boat you're building for Lord Trevalyan?" I asked, caressing the side of the simple schooner. "Where does he keep them or do you sell them?"

"We sell 'em."

Nodding, I continued my quiet tour of appreciation, gaining his respect by mentioning one or two things a woman didn't usually know about boats.

"Er, Missy," Mr. Pencheff grimaced, "not many boats for fancy folk. These are small and built for fishin'. Ye like these ones, do ye?"

"Yes. They are more of a challenge."

He wanted to show me the latest rudder, explaining how "Mr. Rod" designed it and how they'd tested the invention out together.

"Everybody likes Lord Roderick," I said. "But they don't seem to have liked his brother."

"O-ei! *Bad* blood, that one. Good he's dead. Would've happened sooner or later."

"They say it's murder," I murmured, wide-eyed. "The wife's lover did it, they also say. What do you think?"

I received no response, but following my inquiry regarding the painting of the sanded-down boat, Mr. Pencheff gave out a whoop of righteous indignation.

"Poor lady. Don't know how she's put up with Mr. Max all these years. Can't blame her. Pity they've got to lock her friend away."

"She's worried they will lock *her* away," I said, and my companion's eyes rounded, an unknown seafaring curse escaping his lips.

"Mr. Rod won't have it. She should've married him after all."

I agreed, treading upon the subject with a modest degree of caution. "Did Lady Kate ever come to the tower?"

The boat builder neither confirmed nor denied it.

"It would be a nice end if she married Lord Roderick," I said, "but this man in jail was special to her and then there's the cousin—"

Mr. Pencheff spluttered his disgust. "Oh, heard *she's* here again. Funny girl, that one."

"Yes," I said, waiting for him to give me a history of Bella's association with the island and its folk. When none came and the quaint inference hung about unfulfilled, I pressed him on the subject.

"It ain't me ye should be talkin' to but me Mrs."

"Mrs. Pencheff?"

He nodded and I asked for directions to see Mrs. Pencheff.

"It's the first cottage on the hill."

He pointed up to the ridge and I thanked him, walking briskly in case he should change his mind. Salt air assailed my face as I climbed the winding little beach track, only a few yards from the tower.

The stone and slate cottage was easy to find. It was the first cottage on the left, and I noticed the closed shutters; the tended, yet suffering garden; and the weathered roof. I love seaside cottages and this one was undeniably charming.

Taking a deep breath, I knocked on the door.

"Who is it? Ivy? Is that you, Ivy?"

"It's not Ivy," I said through the wooden grooves. "I'm a stranger. You don't know me but I just spoke with your husband."

"Eh?" Pounding footsteps and then the door sprang open to reveal a wiry-haired woman. Her keen eye quickly examined me. "Ye lost then? We don't get any fancy folk knockin' on our doors."

Realizing this woman may be my closest find to a village gossip, I explained my purpose.

Heavy-lidded eyes narrowing, she crossed her arms and I wondered if she intended to keep me standing out in the cold wind. "Please," I implored as the door began to close.

Shrugging, instead of shutting it, she opened the door wider and bid me entry. Without saying a word, I was led inside the tiny cottage, to the warm kitchen out the back. I tried not to look at the stacks of dirty dishes waiting to be washed or the faded curtains at the windows bearing more than a few years of dust.

She faced me from behind the kitchen, clicking her tongue. "I tell me man to keep quiet on the subject, I do. But does he listen to me? What's he say, then, about Arabella Woodford?"

"Not much. He said I should ask you."

She clicked her tongue again. "Why do ye want to know about her?"

"She may be," I cleared my voice, "we *all* may be suspects in the murder of Max Trevalyan."

She smiled. "Always knew it'd happen. Those house parties, bringin' all sorts to the island . . . I said so to Ivy. Ivy's a great friend of mine and we've watched the goings on of Somner House for many a year."

I ached to learn more but she remained closemouthed. She was the kind of gossip, I feared, who collected information to share only for her benefit or among her inner circle. I did not belong to her inner circle and I had nothing to pay her with except news from Somner, news about the murder inquiry, news that might be priceless to a woman like Mrs. Pencheff.

"Did you go to the funeral?" Mrs. Pencheff asked archly.

"Yes, of course. My sister and I had only recently arrived before it happened. We were shocked, naturally."

"And who is your sister and who are you?"

She wanted to know every pertinent detail so I humored her, giving a brief summary of my upbringing, my connections, and how I'd arrived at Somner house.

"Du Maurier," she mused aloud. "I ain't heard the name but that's nothin'. I've been here me whole life, I have, and never ventured off it."

"The island? You've never left the island?"

"No. Why should I? Me parents were same before me and me grandparents before that. All fishermen and boatbuilders, we are."

"And your family has witnessed many things during that time, has it not?"

Mrs. Pencheff huffed. "Maybe we have or maybe we haven't."

I lowered my eyes, trying a new tactic. "It's all very shocking to us, my sister and myself. We don't know what to make of it." And I went on to volunteer information regarding Kate's fears regarding the reading of the will the next day.

This interested Mrs. Pencheff. "The readin's tomorrow, is it?"

"Yes. We all believe Lord Roderick will inherit, which is only fit."

"It *should* be only fit. He's the only good blood in the family."

"What of Max's son?"

"Eh? That little bastard? He's nothing, though ye can't tell Jackson that, can ye? He has grandiose ideas for the boy but he won't be cheatin' Rod out of his rightful inheritance. That boy's a bastard and he's the wild eyes of his father, I can tell ye that."

"I confess I never knew Max Trevalyan very well," I ventured slowly, "but I thought him very wild, very wild indeed."

"Pfff! *Wild* is not the least of it. He was very bad. *Evil,* even. I says so to Ivy and Mr. Pencheff many a time. But do they listen to me? No! Only *now* they listen."

"Lord Max had few friends, it seemed," I went on as Mrs. Pencheff bustled away to boil the kettle. I allowed myself a little smile as I hoped she'd accepted me into her inner circle.

Bringing back a tray of fresh tea, Mrs. Pencheff shook her head. "There's none blamin' Lady Kate over it, poor lass. Who's to blame her goin' off with her gentleman fellow for puttin' up with such a husband as him! I'm surprised Mr. Fernald's locked up the lover. Not fair, if he were protectin' her."

"I agree completely," I murmured, drawing up to glance out the window while she poured the tea. "You have a very fine view here, Mrs. Pencheff."

She shivered. "Not with them winds up. The only place on the island to get warm is down at the pub." Flicking a hand toward the other room, she gestured to the cottage's dismal spurting fire. "So, ye want to know 'bout Miss Woodford, eh? What d'ye make of 'er?"

"She's quiet and reserved, however, there has been an occasional emotional outburst. She loves her cousins, which is natural—"

"Hark!"

A tirade of curses sprang forth in a language unknown to me.

"No *natural* thing there. To the cave, they'd go, first with Max, Max and she, barely off the apron strings and once it were Mr. Rod. Well, I only saw *him* go there once, but that Max"—her mouth took a grim line—"he's a rogue to do *that* with his own cousin!"

Concealing my surprise, for I never suspected Arabella would interest a man like Max Trevalyan, I mentioned his affair with Rachael Eastley.

Mrs. Pencheff raised her eyes to the ceiling. "There's likely half a dozen bastards of 'em around. You've seen Mrs. Eastley, have ye?"

"Yes. She's very attractive."

"Psh! *Attractively* landing her son on Max. Tho' . . . the boy has the look of him and he's the only bastard he's claimed."

"Claimed," I echoed. "So Max accepted the boy?"

"Well," Mrs. Pencheff pressed my hand. "Ye never heard it from me, but Ivy and I, we've seen him visit her and the boy, bringin' the boy presents. If that's not acceptance, I don't know what is. Heard a few other girls over the years tryin' the same sort of thing, but he'd have none of it."

"Mrs. Eastley was different. Perhaps he loved her?"

"Who knows? The person I feel sorry for is that Lady Kate. It ain't right what Fernald's doin'. Who'd blame her or her fancy fellow for protectin' themselves. That's not murder, I say. "

"They will view it as manslaughter."

"Manslaughter my foot! How can it be when ye protectin'

yourself? It don't make no sense to me and that half-baked brain of Fernald, he ain't real clever. Ye watch him now, won't ye, over at the big house?" She looked at me then, archly. "And ye'll come back and visit me with the news, won't ye?"

I promised I would. "Good-bye, Mrs. Pencheff."

She stood at the door watching me, despite the cold, and I wondered what she was thinking as she watched me go.

CHAPTER TWELVE

"Sir Marcus is looking for you."

Languidly sprawled on her bed, Angela directed a lazy eye at me. "He seemed very put out you weren't around. Said something about the kitchen and dinner?"

Oh dear! I'd forgotten completely. Whipping off my coat and gloves, I headed down to find him juggling two steaming saucepans.

"Quick!" he ordered. "Take this."

Muttering under his breath, Hugo stood cross-armed while I hurried over to rescue Sir Marcus, emptying the charred remains of the saucepan down the sink.

"You were supposed to be here at ten," Sir Marcus growled. "Now my minestrone casserole is ruined. Where were you? You'd better have a good excuse."

After tying on my apron, I smiled mysteriously. "I do have a good excuse but first, what can I do to help? We've still time to make another dish."

Giving me one last glare, he fired a series of curt instructions and I followed them to the best of my ability. I seldom ventured into the kitchen, except to extract an apple or a picnic basket, and it never occurred to me the amount of preparation involved in preparing a dish. Sir Marcus's extravagant plan bemused me. "I should call you 'Lord Kitchener,'" I joked while peeling and cutting vegetables and fetching various herbs and spices.

Within the hour, we'd finished. A watchful Hugo still haunted a corner of the kitchen, but Sir Marcus continued blithely on, whistling away. I wished I had his sort of temperament. I couldn't relax in an atmosphere where I knew we weren't wanted. Hugo objected to noisy guests blundering about his domain and making a mess in the process.

Locating a space on the kitchen bench to sit and observe his new creation bubbling away, Sir Marcus struck up a conversation with the unwilling Hugo. "We met Mrs. Eastley at the funeral, old chap."

Hugo's slanted eyes remained uncommunicative.

"Max's son is a nice-looking boy," Sir Marcus continued. "Wonder he didn't leave the estate to him. Oh, but, how silly of me. He's not legitimate, is he? Does it matter with these Trevalyans? I know my own estate can only pass on the well-oiled line, but others are more accepting of children out of wedlock. What say you, Hugo, old boy?"

The hunchback floundered like a fish caught on pavement. "Er . . ."

"Er. Er—yes," Sir Marcus pretended to understand. "All will come out in the official reading of the will. Tomorrow, isn't it? Shall you be there?"

"What, *me*? His lordship said nothin' to me. What's it got to do with me?"

His eyes betrayed the smallest hint of fear.

"But you're always the man about the house," Sir Marcus pacified in his best engaging manner. "You *see* things. You caught Miss Daphne here creeping into a forbidden room, so what else have you seen? What else have you witnessed?"

Hugo became indignant. "I told the police everythin' I know and seen."

"And heard?" I blurted out. "It's funny how one often forgets hearing things in the middle of the night. You must have heard *something,* dear Mr. Hugo," I pleaded in a sweet tone.

The hunchback paused to brood and I gently laid my hand on his arm. "Please, it may be important. I know you wish to protect the Trevalyans and I promise no harm will come to them."

Not sure whether to trust me or not, or whether to speak or not, he groaned.

"There were a squeak," he said eventually.

"A squeak?" Sir Marcus echoed.

"The terrace door. It makes a noise, even tho' I've tried to oil it. Three times, I hear it that night."

"And you told Mr. Fernald this?" Swooping upon the clue, Sir Marcus's eyes glimmered like a cat.

"He weren't too interested in it." Hugo shrugged. "The first two times it were quietlike, as a thief would do, and then the last time it was loud. I left me bed and went down there, but nobody was there." Crossing his arms, he frowned at us. "I told Fernald all this anyway . . . why's it so important?"

"Because little things are important," I said, following his gaze to see Kate hurrying into the room, her mind clearly elsewhere.

"Oh, Hugo," she began, stopping short when she saw Sir

Marcus and me. She smiled a little uncertainly before delivering her instructions to set another place for dinner.

"Max's friend," she explained to us. "They were in the war together and when he received the news, he braved the seas to get here."

She seemed relieved this friend had arrived.

"You'll meet him at dinner. Forgive me." Her voice faltered. "It's been a long day."

"It's all right, Katie girl." Sir Marcus enveloped her in his great bearlike embrace. "All will turn out well. You'll see."

"Somehow," she said, and paused, raising deep, haunted eyes to me. "Somehow . . . I don't think it will this time."

She left Sir Marcus and me, and we used the opportunity to press the issue of alerting us to any little abnormality out of the usual order of things. What Hugo truly thought of his previous master came out in his next words.

"Poor lady. She don't deserve no bad. No bad after what she went through with him."

"You're her best witness," Sir Marcus incited. "If you want to help her and help Mr. Lissott, you must tell Fernald what you saw. Oh, I *know* you must have seen or heard *something*. The lord catching the lady in her lover's embrace? The fight that followed? Wrestling in the hall perhaps? Then dragging a body out through the squeaky terrace door?"

Hugo looked conflicted. "But I told him everthin' I seen and heard."

"But what of all the other times when you witnessed Lady Kate suffering at the hands of her husband?" I implored. "Is there a reason by which she had to defend herself? Is there, Hugo? You must know."

"Mr. Josh will get off and you'll make Lady Kate a very

happy woman," Sir Marcus added. "*And* you'll earn the gratitude of Lord Roderick."

Considering the enviable prospect of keeping his job and pleasing his new employer, Hugo stared down at the floor. "I'll think on it." He nodded and returned to his kitchen duties.

I went to dress for dinner. Wearily climbing up the stairs, I wished I could take my meal in my room, for the day had proved too eventful for me. I just wanted to curl up and go to sleep.

Yawning, I was glad to greet an empty room. When tired, the last thing I wanted to do was to humor Angela, whose strange behavior quite frankly disturbed me. Was she party to a crime? Or worse, was she party to a murder? She seemed pleased for Kate regarding Max's passing and pleased that Mr. Lissot remained incarcerated in the local prison.

"That *stupid* girl's in the bathroom again!"

Storming into the room, Angela kicked off her shoes and threw down her handbag. Commencing to peel off her stockings, she further denounced Bella.

"She's not all prim and proper, either. Caught her *smoking* this afternoon, oh yes, I did. Footed the stub when she saw me but it was too late. She's definitely hiding something," Angela added, her hands diving into her toiletry bag. "Can't quite fix it, though. Is it Lord Rod she's after? The house? Or something else?"

A knock sounded at the door.

Angela smiled in return. "Oh, it's Kate. She's come to dress you."

"Dress *me*?"

I had no time to compose myself before Kate came in, her arms laden with dresses.

"Yes." Angela clapped her hands. "We're going to make you up and parade you before all the gentlemen visitors. *No*, don't deny us the pleasure, and it'll be a good diversion for Kate. Look, she's picked all these beauties from her own collection."

There was a significant pause. Should I show gratitude, being the prized cow of Angela and Kate? I ground my teeth. The notion of being paraded about appalled me. And I hated to be anybody's *hobby*, even for a short period of time.

And knowing Major Browning, he'd assume I had purposely spent hours adorning myself for his benefit. *Coiffuring curls in front of the mirror and pinching my cheeks.* Oh! It was too . . . humiliating. Unfortunately, Angela dismissed the downward turn of my mouth as Kate began to dress me. After examining my hair and skin color, she set about her work, ordering me in and out of gowns too numerous to count.

At last they proudly shepherded me to the bathroom to see the result. I kept my eyes downcast, hoping, *praying* Bella's mocking sneer remained in her room. I still found it difficult to believe Mrs. Pencheff, which I planned to keep to myself. Bella Woodford . . . and her cousin?

Descending the massive staircase, the young bride glowed with nervous pride. She knew, for this one night, she looked beautiful. Tiptoeing in her high-heeled satin shoes, she allowed herself only one backward gaze, waving a shaky hand to the maids lined up to watch her triumph.

She couldn't wait to surprise her husband . . .

"Daphne! My *word*."

Dismayed to see, not my expectant, proud husband, the slender and tall one, his brooding brow vanishing at my glorious arrival, but a bustling, red nosed Sir Marcus, I paused, my hand resting on the balustrade.

Beaming, Sir Marcus let his cultured eye study me from head to foot. "Ah, but wait until Browning sees you."

I stopped short, a sudden fear overcoming me. I didn't want to face the crowd. I didn't want to see Major Browning. I didn't want him examining me.

"You dressed for *yourself,* not for him, I know," Sir Marcus said, tapping my wrist. "You're a sly one, aren't you? What were you dreamin' about just now if you don't mind me asking?"

"A scene for a book," I answered.

"Hmm. Well, I trust it has a bitter, dark twist then, this story of yours. Too boring otherwise."

"I can't go down." I halted again, flushed of face.

"Why ever not? You look better than I've ever seen you before. Look in the mirror, Daphne girl. See for yourself."

Drawn to the hall mirror, I stared at the picture of a girl I didn't recognize. Young, slender, curling honey-colored hair swept up and curled on the sides of her face. Swathed in a gown of ivory silk, strips of pearl-encrusted and silver embroidery framing a delicate neckline, she resembled a bride. Skin of peaches and cream, deep-set wondering eyes, innocent lips, and a face too young for the diamond earrings on her lobes or the diamond-pearl necklace at her throat. My fingers drew up, ready to rip the necklace away . . .

"Come on." Sir Marcus drew me downstairs. "I'm here to protect you."

"I am not frightened," I clarified on the way. "I merely have no wish to be ogled at."

"I thought all girls like to be ogled at. Isn't that how they catch husbands?"

We made our grand entrance, all eyes assessing me. Perhaps it was bemusement. The customarily plainly dressed Daphne was exhibiting herself in the magnetic apparel of a skilled femme fatale. Male hushes ensued and Kate, to my eternal detriment, expressed pride in her creation.

Sensing the Major's proximity, and eager to avoid his mocking eye, I found myself a quiet corner of refuge by one of the paintings.

"Hello," said a voice. "I don't believe we've been introduced?"

A nondescript man leaned gracefully against the wall, his hands shoved in the pockets of his trousers. He was in his midtwenties, with brown hair brushed back, clothing neat and uncomplicated, and a demeanor modest and unobtrusive. He was the kind of person one felt very safe with at social gatherings such as this, the undemanding person lagging in the background.

He introduced himself as Peter Davis, Max's friend from the war. Standing in front of a painting called *The Two Soldiers,* I expressed my condolences and he began to speak of his friend.

"Yes, the townsfolk kept us alive." Mr. Davis nodded, his light brown hair gracing his forehead. "Max and I," he said, pausing to smile, "we were inseparable, you see. We went to college together, then the club, and the war . . . we've been friends forever. Where others would've left him for dead, I dragged him through the forest. I couldn't accept his death, though the severity of his wounds suggested I should have."

"That was good of you," I murmured, noting the grief wash over his face.

He shrugged dismissively. "It doesn't signify now, does it? He's dead. I wish I'd been here." His gaze slowly went around the room. "It's ridiculous to go on normally when something like this happens, yet I suppose we must." Mr. Davis remained bound to his grief. "I just don't know how I'll manage, Miss Daphne, without him. Max and I shared so much together. A lifetime."

"Then you must busy yourself." I laid a kind hand on his arm. "Since his marriage, you can't have been with him all the time. What have you been doing since the war?"

A frank smile passed his lips. "I work at the museum, and I suppose I've given the wild days up to become a bit of a hermit. I keep to myself and my piano mostly."

"Oh, you play the piano? How glorious!"

We launched into a lively discussion, which progressed to the dining room, where Lady Kate shrewdly placed me beside the Major.

"Perfect," the Major breathed, sliding out my chair for me.

I sat down and pretended not to notice his mocking swagger as he drew his chair closer to mine.

"Dare I assume you've dressed for me? After our long parting, I hoped it would be so."

"Your opinion of yourself is grossly overdeveloped," I said, smiling through my teeth, reinstating the former distance between our chairs, "and is unwanted here."

"Unwanted by whom?"

His casual gaze strayed in the direction of our hostess, who, despite her intention to dress deadly dull, had turned out a picture in blue and white. Dispensing with the black widow's weeds, she also made a concession by adding a tiny feather headpiece to her curled hair. I wished, rather enviously, that I could master her becoming smile, so charming and perfect and contagious.

"Our Lady Trevalyan captivates all, does she not?" The Major's observation cast itself to my ear. "Yet, I'm sure you haven't delayed in making conquests of your own." He tilted his glass toward Lord Roderick. "A man of title and in keeping with the mode. Well done."

"Mode?" I hissed at the insinuation lurking in his smile.

"Lord David. Or have you forgotten him so soon? Admit it, you were in love with him."

"I was *not* in love with him."

"No," the Major agreed, "you were infatuated with him."

I seethed in my chair. No matter what I said, it pleased him to say the opposite. "Why are you here, anyway?"

He affected his most charming smile. "I was invited."

"I don't mean *here* at the house, but the island."

"I told you. Rough seas have landed me in your quarter. Aren't you happy to see an old friend? After we've shared so much together . . ."

Devil take him. He had the ability to charm anyone, even Bella. I caught her glancing over once or twice, curious as to our relationship.

"Note Fernald declined the dinner invitation," the Major attempted a conspiratorial familiarity. "Watch. He'll make a dramatic *after dinner* interruption."

"You are misinformed, Mr. Browning. He's coming in the morning."

He grinned. "Shall we make a wager on it?"

His seductive gaze traveled to my lips. I flushed scarlet, wishing I could remain wan-faced like other girls of my acquaintance. But no, whenever embarrassed or enraged, emotion flooded to my cheeks and no amount of powder could conceal it. "You are wrong about Fernald."

"I beg to differ, dear Daphne. He doesn't wish to be seen playing Fido with the enemy."

CHAPTER THIRTEEN

"Playing Fido with the enemy? Truly, Mr. Browning, you have the most preposterous expressions. I suspect you found that one belowdeck."

He grimaced.

"And don't, pray, act as if we are friends, for friends, sir, we most certainly are not. And I am not 'dear Daphne' to you, either. Those dear to you don't ignore letters."

Feigning a look of indignant hurt, he sighed. "We're not going over that again, are we? Acquit me. I'm innocent. It was a misfortune of events, and, for the record, I do consider you a special friend . . . dare I hope we're something dearer to each other, much dearer than friends?"

His twinkling eyes went on to make their own silent appraisal of my outfit and hair.

This time he had gone too far. Sliding out of my chair, more to hide the too-quick beat of my heart, I fled to find a moment's peace and quiet. Finding a darkened corner, I paused to catch my breath. How dare he seek to eye me in that way, almost like a lover! I flushed again, pacing down the hall. I was not one of his playthings existing simply to amuse him—

"Oh, Daphne . . ."

I spun around to face Arabella.

"I saw you leave the room," she began, her dark eyes concerned. "Did the Major upset you?"

"No, the Major *did not* upset me," I expressed with conviction. "It is merely his chafing, *erroneous* audacity I cannot abide—"

"Is that so, Miss du Maurier?"

Strolling to us, the Major bowed. "I am grieved my behavior offended you."

It was only a half apology and he wasn't grieved about a thing. "It's not your behavior but your *manners,* sir, which are in error."

Arabella glanced from me to him, wondering how we knew each other and the depth of our relationship.

Leaving them both in the hallway, I headed back into the dining room. By now, everyone had abandoned their seats and were ensconced around the blazing fire in the drawing room.

I went to the fire to thaw out my hands. The warm flames soothed my temper and I began to regret my childishness. What mature, reasonably intelligent woman took offense to such a minor grievance as the return or neglect of a letter? I had made a scene, which my mother detested, and I should have waited for a better moment, for my dramatics had not gone unnoticed.

Gently tugging my hand, Lady Kate coerced me to the seat she shared with Angela facing the fire. "Ange told me about the Major," she whispered with a flick of a smile across her lips. "He was quick to get up after you. I hope he apologized?"

"If one can call it an apology," I retorted, grimly surveying his reentry and congenial conversation with Arabella.

"Major Browning does have a certain reputation," Kate murmured.

Angela nodded, confirming her intention to divulge the news later. Kate soon shuffled away to assist her brother-in-law, who was having difficulty conversing with the Major's lieutenants. One look at Roderick's heavy brow signaled his distaste at having to play host when he'd prefer the silence and solitude of his tower.

Feeling akin to this feeling myself and tired of Angela's raucous jokes encouraged by too much champagne, I joined Kate. I asked Rod a series of boring questions about island species and the lieutenants soon lost interest, despite my wondrous gown and shining appearance. They gravitated back to Kate, Angela, and Bella, and I secured Roderick for myself.

"You're very close to your cousin, are you not, my lord?"

"Close? Close to Bella?" He sounded surprised. "Not particularly."

"I have a confession to make, my lord."

"Please don't call me that," he began to say as I told him of my jaunt up the tower and meeting the Pencheffs. As I'd hoped, the mention of the name "Pencheff" cast a wary glow across his glacial cheeks.

"You spoke to Mrs. Pencheff?"

"Yes." I followed his gaze to Arabella. "She said you three cousins used to play down in the caves. That must have been great fun."

I was being deliberately cruel, since I knew very well what kind of fun that entailed, but I justified that it was all within investigative boundaries.

"I, er—"

He was saved an answer by the very abrupt interruption of Mr. Fernald and a fat bearded fellow bearing the largest brief-case I'd ever seen stumbling behind him.

"Forgive my intrusion," Mr. Fernald began with an attempt at manners. His very presence, of course, conceded the Major his victory. How did he know Fernald would call tonight instead of tomorrow? A lucky guess? Or did he have prior knowledge? I slanted my gaze toward the Major's face, which showed nothing but the merest surprise. Why was he here?

I watched him greet Fernald, perhaps in order to lessen the anxiety on the deathly white face of Kate, who had gladly accepted his supportive arm.

"Couldn't this have waited until tomorrow, Fernald?" Roderick spoke beside me.

"No, sir, it couldn't 'ave. It's a nice peaceful island we 'ave here and I'm keen to 'ave things all wrapped up."

Too keen, I thought. He was desperate to settle the matter before his superiors arrived from the mainland. Perhaps he fancied himself the highest authority on the island and intended to prove it.

"I've brought Mrs. Eastley and her father with me, too. They're waitin' outside with your family attorney."

Roderick showed no emotion at this statement, nor did he attempt to dissuade Fernald from carrying on his business. I imagined Max Trevalyan would have reacted very differently, raging at the man and ordering him to leave. Was it weak of Rod to give in to Fernald's demands? Or did he do so because one could not stop the inevitable?

Fernald, obviously, had wished to use the element of surprise. The party ended and the guests dispersed as Roderick apologized and promptly guided Fernald and Kate to the study. Bella started to follow but Fernald blocked her efforts.

"No, Miss Woodford, Ye're not required."

Bella's face darkened. She could do nothing but accept the prohibition, but I saw the same question occur to her as it did to me, Sir Marcus, and the Major. *Where could we go to listen?* The library was next to the study and I laid silent wagers as to who left first and on what false pretense.

To my infinite shock, Angela shot to her feet, scurrying upstairs, her heels clanking on the floorboards, and I followed her lead.

"Ingenious of you." I smiled, finding her waiting at the end of the corridor.

"Quick," she whispered. "This way. Kate's room."

"I thought her room was below?" I whispered, tiptoeing to the tiny bedchamber at the end of the hall.

"Yes, but this one's her retreat room. I remember her saying from here she can see directly down to the study. There's a hole in the floor. See."

The tiny room, decorated in various shades of pinks, overflowed with lace trimmings, dolls, beaded lamps, and pearled cushions. I stopped by one of the paintings gracing the wall, a pretty landscape featuring a rose garden.

"Don't stand there gaping," Angela hissed. "We've work to do."

Her ear was already glued to the floor, and my ear followed suit. The floorboards were cold without the rug's protection, but the hole was large enough for one eye to see at a time. Angela and I agreed to take turns.

"Has nothing been left for his son?" Mrs. Eastley asked. "Nothing at all?"

"No, ma'am."

"But I have his note here."

I imagined her waving it before them, the copy of the will Sir Marcus and I discovered in Max's desk.

"It's witnessed," rumbled Jackson.

"*One* witness," noted the attorney. "*Two* witnesses are required."

"But it's his boy! Anyone can see that."

No one disputed the fact.

"My lord?" prompted the attorney. "Lord Roderick?"

"I'm afraid my brother left no legacy in his formal will for the care of his son. The handwritten note came to my attention upon my brother's death and given the unfortunate state of my brother's estate, and the illegitimacy of the child, I will contest the note should it go to court."

"But!" Jackson spluttered. "It's not a note, it's a will, and *you* said—"

"What I promised, Jackson," a sighing Rod reiterated, "shall stand. Your grandson and Mrs. Eastley will want for nothing and as soon as the estate is in order, I shall settle a sum upon them, or, if Mrs. Eastley prefers, an annuity to be paid over a period of time."

"I prefer an annuity," said Mrs. Eastley, her swiftness in tone suggesting her desire for a quick, painless settlement.

Her father did not agree.

"I want more for me girl! And more for me boy, too, as I'm helpin' raise him. Ye brother were no good, knockin' up me girl like that—"

"Father, please," Mrs. Eastley pleaded. She possessed a quality I found almost alien to her parent. Perhaps she'd gone to a select seminary or private school? This might explain her marriage to the late Mr. Eastley, a man of some standing on the island, by all accounts.

"My Rachael ain't like the others," Jackson insisted. "She's well-bred, married well, and I like to see her widowhood well funded since she's got to raise Trevalyan's brat."

"Father, I *said* I was happy with the annuity."

"Oh, I can't bear this!"

Angela and I exchanged a look of shock.

"I can't endure *any more*!" Kate let out a wretched cry. "I won't hear any more about the child!"

"Surely the particulars can now wait until a more congenial time," Roderick proposed after the outburst. "The hour has grown late."

Sleep deserted me.

I lay awake, listening to the wind whistling against the windowpanes. A fierce howl stirred outside and I wrapped the coverlet tighter around me. Due to the nature of the weather, one could safely assume the Major and the others had been invited to stay overnight at Somner.

Major Browning.

I allowed my thoughts to drift to his windowpane. I glared into the still darkness of the night. When a lady's letter failed to solicit a reply it generally implied utter disregard or worse, complete disinterest. "I trust you received mine," he'd said on our first meeting. Received what? A mere postcard detailing his current post and where I might write him? How thoughtful! Just like his ilk to expect ladies to write to him while he enjoyed the pure pleasure of choosing to whom, how, and when he responded.

The door opened, and Angela crept in. Awake, I monitored her stealthy approach. What had kept her so long below? Or, more importantly, who?

"Oh, you're awake." She jumped, concealing her edginess with a dismissive yawn. "The others are still down, drinking brandy. The men, I mean." She chuckled to herself in the darkness.

The chuckle went on to no further elaboration and I did not ask. A wave of tiredness overcame me and I clutched my pillow, thinking of poor Josh Lissot lying awake in his cold prison cell for a crime he may not have committed.

It wasn't the night's fancies. I believed Josh Lissot was innocent. I felt it instinctively. He may have *thought* he'd murdered Max, but his hand hadn't delivered the fatal blow.

I went down early and slipped out the terrace side door. Again, its eerie creak arrested my attention. No one would emerge for hours, except Arabella, who had retired soon after me the night before, and I intended to make full use of the morning. I headed not in the direction of my usual morning walking circuit, but down the drive.

I thought to hire a conveyance from the nearest farming tenants and luck proved with me. Spotting a farmer slashing his fields, I waved and upon seeing me, he soon stopped what he was doing to speak to me.

He started at the sight of me. "From the big house, are ye?"

At this time of morning, I suppose ladies did not venture outdoors. "Yes I am, and I am keen to get to town. No one else is about so I'm wondering if you have a bicycle I can borrow?"

"No. Not one in good workin' order, miss. Not for a lady like yeself, anyhow."

"I should like to see it regardless, if you don't mind."

He shrugged, rather annoyed I'd stopped him at his work to look at a bicycle not fit for a lady.

To my surprise the bicycle seemed perfectly equipped for the job, though rusted, and I was reminded of my excursions with my friend Lizzy Forsythe, riding down the lane and meeting boys. Lizzy, a pretty, voluptuous creature given to attracting male attention, had me ride her brother's old bicycle while she flaunted herself atop her pink handled and beribboned show pony.

"The bicycle is perfect." I thanked the farmer and, wheeling out the conveyance, took the first left.

Nothing could stop me now. The wind in my hair, I relished the freedom, the independence, and fun work of pushing myself to town. I remembered the way vaguely from our outing, and following the signs and the winding road, I cycled to the place where they held Josh Lissot. Kate had glanced forlornly at the building in the square, and on this cold winter's morning, I appreciated the architectural lines of what might have once been a very fine town hall.

Nobody attended the stark front desk. I hesitated to ring the bell, glancing at the large ticking clock on the wall opposite me. A quarter to nine. I didn't suppose they began work so early on the island.

Disappointed, I turned away to wait. If I'd thought for just a moment, I would have brought money to buy a hot pasty from a bread shop I'd seen on my way in.

After a good twenty minutes, a voice echoed from down the hall.

"Can I help ye, miss? Are ye from Somner House?"

I nodded, slowly. I didn't remember the sergeant's face, but he'd seen me at the house and I smiled my best shy smile. "I've come to see Mr. Lissot. I know I should have waited for Mr. Fernald but I was up early."

The sergeant looked past me to the street. "Ye cycled all that way from Somner House, miss?"

"Why, yes." I blushed. "I know I shouldn't really have come without Mr. Fernald's permission, but could I see Mr. Lissot for just a minute? It'll be your secret and mine. I won't breathe a word of it, I promise."

"I ain't suppose to let anyone see him."

"But Mr. Fernald won't find out. Please. I've ridden all this way and I'll be quick."

Still unsure, he flicked through his stack of keys before leading me down a deserted corridor. I noticed the old paint peeling off the walls and shivered. If Fernald came back early . . .

There were only four cells, each with a door and small alcove bearing bars. Cold, dismal, and spartan, each with a bed and a chair.

Josh was glad, if somewhat bemused, to see me.

"Daphne." A slight smile crept to his bloodless lips as he rose, a shadow of the man I'd met at Somner, now gaunt-faced, unshaven, the artistic light driven from his eyes.

"Do come in; I'd offer you a seat if I could." He directed this comment to the young sergeant who quickly rushed off to retrieve a seat for me.

"Just a few minutes," he warned upon return, closing and locking the door behind him.

"Aren't you afraid to be alone with a murderer?" Laughing, Josh perched himself on the edge of his slat bed.

"Murderer? I don't believe you did it, Mr. Lissot. That's why I'm here."

His sad eyes studied the ceiling and a scowl furrowed his brow. "Did she send you? Did Kate send you?"

"No . . . I am here of my own volition. It may sound preposterous, but I have very good reason to suspect you've been framed for the murder of Max Trevalyan."

A bitter laugh escaped his lips. "But I hit him! Whacked him jolly hard, too, when he put his hand to Kate's throat. He fell, slumped to the ground, blood oozing from his head. Needless to say, it wasn't a pretty sight."

"But did you check his pulse?"

His tone sounded weary when he answered. "Yes. We did that. He was still breathing, shallowly, where we left him but—"

"Alive," I emphasized. "Just suppose for a moment that someone *else* stumbled upon that path, intentionally or otherwise. Just suppose for a moment this someone else delivered the fatal blow." I paused, thinking hard. "You mentioned his head was bleeding, but according to Mr. Fernald, his smashed *face* rendered him almost unrecognizable. Is that how you and Kate left him?"

"Sweet Thomas, no! At least, I don't think so." He stopped to reflect. "It was dark . . . can't say. Did leave an awful mess up at the house. We had to clean the path when we dragged him out."

"Through the terrace door . . . the *creaky* terrace door."

He frowned, puzzled.

"Hugo heard the door open three times," I explained, but he still seemed puzzled.

I asked if he and Kate went out through that door only

once. Slowly comprehending my meaning, Mr. Lissot endeavored his best to recall. "Three times, *three* times," he kept saying to himself. "I remember Kate opened it the first time, dreading the noise, careful though she was as we pulled the body through, and yes! I remember Max's shoe dragging on the surface. No! It got stuck in the door . . . yes, I remember now. It got stuck, fell off actually, and we had a devil of a time shoving his foot back in . . . but that's only *twice* that we had to open the door. We didn't enter back in that way. Not the terrace door. Kate was too scared of the noise arousing suspicion."

"Exactly!" I smiled.

A contemplative silence emerged between us and the faintest hope lingered in the air. "I know Kate has pleaded with you to retract your confession and she is right. You were *protecting* her . . . you had to strike him . . . you thought you'd killed him but you didn't."

"I didn't," he said, and frowned, still disbelieving the possibility of another chance. "But if it wasn't me, then *who* did it?"

I smiled again, coy, radiant with my small success. "When we find the person who opened the door the third time, the person who tried very hard to incriminate you by circumstance, then we'll know."

CHAPTER FOURTEEN

Sir Marcus was quick to extinguish my triumph.

"You'll have a devil of a time convincing our friendly hunchback to own up to the fact. And more of a devil convincing that dolt Fernald to pay any heed to it."

"A dolt?" I queried, half amused. "I see you've enjoyed a leisurely breakfast." I indicated with my hand to where the Major and everyone else dallied outside on the open terrace.

The day was fine and sunny. Still a little cool, but windless and thus perfect for a terrace affair. I spied Jackson raking leaves a few meters away and wondered if he decided to do the task in order to eavesdrop.

Who was I to judge him if that was the case? He had more reason than I, merely a curious guest. His daughter and grandson were heavily involved in the Trevalyan business. *I want more for me girl,* he'd said, clipped and curt. Had that ambition led him to search out Max Trevalyan that night and "do him in," as he would put it?

But Jackson had no reason to do so if he believed in the power of the will Max had signed. It was a useless scrap of paper in the end, and his daughter had preferred the offered annuity from Rod. This showed a shrewdness to her character I found fascinating and sensible. Complex layers existed beneath Rachael Eastley's cool façade, I was certain of it.

Inspired by such reflections, I began to compose a short story in my mind. "The Mysterious Widow." No ... "The Noble Widow." She arrives in a new neighborhood much like Helen in *Wildfell Hall* and she bears the secret of her nobility and an air of mystery all her own. However, both make her a subject of interest and speculation in the little town.

"Well, well, here you two are hiding!"

Slipping through the terrace door, Angela's smirk had a knowing quality to it. "Lover's nook, is it?"

"It's nothing," Sir Marcus sighed. "Daphne and I are kindred spirits. Speaking of which, are we still doing the painting day?"

"Oh, yes. Kate *loves* the idea. And"—she glanced chidingly at us both—"the Major and his comrades are joining us, so I've come to rouse you both from your self-imposed and, I scarcely need add, selfish isolation."

"Has Mr. Fernald left yet?" I heard myself echo.

"Horrible man." Angela shivered. "Yes. He left just now with that Eastley woman."

So Mrs. Eastley had spent the night at Somner. I wondered if she'd stayed up to enjoy a lengthy sojourn with the Major?

I told myself I didn't care.

But I did.

Angela set about preparing a place in the sun where several easels and stools and all the accompanying paraphernalia littered a section of Jackson's newly mowed lawn.

Despite the merriment of the occasion, I did not feel in the mood to paint. I felt like writing my story, yet I carried myself to an easel and worked diligently on my tower, using the tips and pointers given by Kate.

"It's quite impressive," remarked Peter Davis.

"Thank you," I said, leaning across to inspect his work.

"My fledging attempt is atrocious." He shook his head, and I laughingly sympathized with him, studying his madcap sketch of what vaguely resembled some kind of distorted garden.

"It's meant to be the forest where Max and I crashed," he said, smiling. Then his face took on a more serious note. "A tribute . . . to old times."

We were a little apart from the others and I nodded understandingly. "The great war affected so many lives. They were all torn asunder, as the expression goes. I only wish I had been more a part of it. I would've liked to fight alongside the men."

"Why didn't you, Miss du Maurier?"

"My parents. Literally penned me in. Probably a good thing, considering my impetuosity would have led me to do something rash resulting in my demise, or worse."

Mr. Davis appeared to follow my line of thought. "Yes . . . there are things worse than death."

His comment inspired the strokes of my paintbrush. I painted the essence of Roderick's gloomy tower, its beating heart, bleak and forbidding.

"Interesting . . ."

I'd recognize that slow mocking drawl anywhere.

"Major Browning." I dipped my head in a civil form of greeting. "I trust among your *many* talents, you can paint, too."

"No," he admitted with affability, showing his atrocious attempt at a portrait painting.

Mr. Davis and I chuckled.

"We're all not born to be as talented as Lady Trevalyan."

I followed Mr. Davis's admiring gaze to where Kate stood, adorned in her amber satin artist's cape, gorgeous and as radiant as the piece of art she fashioned.

"It's a portrait of your sister," the Major announced, "and look how delighted Angela is."

Angela, to my intense horror, was posing for the portrait, reclining and flaunting herself upon the grass, one shoulder exposed and the remainder of her chest draped in a loose, scarlet shawl.

I flushed with embarrassment. She looked little better than a low-class trollop or a dancing girl, her lips and cheeks dusted a theatrical rouge. I reminded myself that she *was* an actress to avoid an unsightly sisterly remonstration.

Major Browning must have noticed my blanched face. He suggested we take a walk. At any other time, I would have found an excuse, but as Elizabeth Bennet experienced when Mr. Darcy asked her to dance, I simply couldn't think of one.

To walk away seemed the most prudent course of action. Feigning ignorance at the offer of his arm, I knotted my hands behind my back as we strolled toward the pergola. I spoke of the weather and mentioned Sir Marcus's painting and the Major obliged by making the customary replies.

"I feel sometimes you slot me into one of your melodramas," he murmured as we approached the stairs leading up to the pergola.

I marched to a seat, lifting a jagged brow. "To talk by rule is sometimes best."

He paused to reflect. "I've read that quote somewhere before."

"Have you? I'm impressed. It's from Jane Austen's *Pride and Prejudice.*"

He opted to lean against the post rather than take a seat beside me. "Austen's your favorite author then?"

"No. I prefer the darker Brontës. *The Tenant of Wildfell* or *Wuthering Heights.*"

"You're a pessimist," he mused. "A *romantic* pessimist."

"I beg to differ. I am not in the least romantic."

"All writers are romantics."

His keen gaze drifted over my person. I colored under the intensity. The man possessed a magnetism and he knew how to use it.

"Mrs. Eastley is charming, is she not?"

"Charming?" the Major goaded, sitting down, cupping his chin in his hands as he studied me in languid repose. "Yes, she is a charming mother . . . a mother protecting the interests of her child."

My eyes met his candid expression. "Perhaps . . . perhaps she's afraid . . . afraid her son might fall with a sudden accident like his father if she contests the will. I thought her merely noble but it's *sense* directing her . . . sense and fear."

"My sentiments exactly," said the Major as I drew in a quick breath. He grinned. "What else have you deduced, Inspector du Maurier?"

His playful voice failed to lure me out of my silent reflections.

"I see you and Sir Marcus have become very friendly."

"Very," I agreed.

He cleared his voice and did I imagine it, or did momentary distaste flicker in those dark eyes? "You intend to marry him?"

Now I was the one to suffer shock. Marry Sir Marcus!

"The notion hasn't occurred to you? You astonish me."

I replied at length. "I feel as if you're making a running commentary on my love life. I would appreciate if you would desist."

He bowed, his lips tugging in amusement. "Your sister, on the other hand—"

"Oh, please, don't speak of her," I implored, and perhaps the desperate note appealed to his sense of honor. He did not press me on the subject, but instead made move to return.

When we rejoined the party, they were in the process of packing up the equipment. I went back to my easel. Mr. Davis had started to attend to my brushes, washing and drying them and laying them back in the container.

"Forgive me, Miss du Maurier," he said, "but I thought you'd finished."

"Yes, I have. Thank you . . . it was kind of you."

He smiled. "The last thing anybody wants to do is clean up. Painting's such a messy business." He half grinned at the blue streak running down his sleeve. "And what's worse, I'm a dismal failure!"

"Can't be as bad as Bella's," Angela laughed as she and Kate led the others back to the house. She certainly had assumed an aristocratic and haughty confidence.

Mr. Davis offered to carry my easel, and together we crossed the green. "Your sister's an actress? Is she a very good friend of Kate's?"

"Yes, very. They've known each other since the war. When did you first meet Max, Mr. Davis?"

"At school." He chuckled at some distant memory. "We were inseparable, much to our detriment and our parent's distress."

Having learned something of Max Trevalyan's character, I well understood this inference. Two boys, embarking on adventures, often led to trouble. I pictured the school expellings, lectures, times of enforced distance, and unauthorized reconciliations.

"My father and Max's parents both passed away during the war," Mr. Davis went on. "They were vastly relieved we both had an occupation by then."

A shadow crossed his face, transporting him to a faraway place. Perhaps to the good old times, those school summer days, training and relaxing at the club between missions, and now . . . his best friend dead under highly suspicious circumstances.

He did not, I found out over a subsequent pot of tea, attribute any blame to Kate, as he casually referred to Max's less than desirable qualities. And she, in turn, regarded Mr. Davis as something of a savior.

"Dear Peter," I overheard her sighing to the Major, her hand resting over her heart, "he's shielded me from so many bad moments. The three of us had many laughs, too," she added gaily.

But the gaiety rang false. Her feelings seemed to remain with Josh Lissot, no longer in residence at Somner playing the charlatan. Did she feel love or guilt? Guilt because he suffered the crime of protecting her? Or love beyond the playful affair?

Time would prove the decider. For now, she appeared concerned only with helping Josh escape the hangman's noose.

Angela, for one, rejoiced in their separation. "It's just what Kate needs," she told me. "Time and distance from all men."

After tea, the Major and his lieutenants took their leave, and I strolled out to the front of the house to bid them farewell. His fingers lingered over mine in parting and I shook them free. He'd return. All too soon for my liking.

"You won't believe it," Sir Marcus relayed to me later. "The Major's agreed to assist our Katie girl."

I feigned a tepid interest, though I was desperate to learn more.

"He's off to see Fernald now, I wager. Let's see what becomes of it, shall we?"

I went to the library that afternoon.

So lost in my loving exploration of the upper shelves, I failed to note the presence of someone else in the room.

"Are you interested in history books, Daphne?"

Roderick adorned the armchair by the window, his sleeve cuff emerging from the large book he held.

"Forgive me for disturbing you." I swallowed and hastened to the door.

"Why leave?"

Words failed and the question floated above us unanswered, like a swirling summer's leaf.

"Don't go," he urged, this time leaving the security of his chair.

I faltered as hearing those resonant tones from Roderick seemed as out of place as I felt.

"We have many books at Somner . . . I trust one of them tempts you?"

I raised my eyes upward, along his tall, masculine frame. I realized a smile tempered his lips.

"The tower tempts me, in fact . . . I should like to see it again," I blurted, searching for something to say.

After I quickly took my leave, I called myself a complete idiot. I was no blubbering female. What uneased me about him? He was not a dashing, heroic lord, but a mystery I couldn't quite decipher. Could his mystery conceal a murderer?

CHAPTER FIFTEEN

I saw Kate before dinner.

The events of the day had left me bone weary. Time for a cavelike retreat, a warm meal in bed, and a good book. However, I considered it my duty to seek out Kate first. She was seated at the dressing table of her room looking pensive, blankly staring at the mirror, reflecting in some private thought that troubled her. I hadn't properly seen her room, this room on the lower level down the hall from the breakfast parlor where I'd caught her and Josh Lissot. The room, a former sunroom of a curious L-shaped design where rows of arched mullioned windows spanned around the corner, possessed the best light in the house and I could see why she'd chosen it. The windows alone were the finest in Somner, one wrought-iron latch left open on the window facing full west to allow in the light and the fresh, salty sea breeze.

Unlike her retreat room abovestairs, the decorations in her lower quarters followed the African theme of the house. From the giant old-world four-poster bed dominating the end corner with its sweeping white silken drapes and spiraling towers, to the multicolored weave rugs lining the faded carpet, it was a room for artists and lovers. Filled with warmth, vibrancy, paintings, chaos, mess, order, it was a room to indulge every whim.

A faint smile touched Kate's lips. "Oh, it's you, Daphne. I thought it might be Angela."

Putting aside her grim thoughts, she resumed a cavalier attitude, remarking on the day and its endeavors, how nice it was that Angela arranged the painting outdoors, and adding the odd tease or two with reference to Major Browning. She also mentioned Peter, her brows lifting quizzically regarding him. "You've quite a few beaus to choose from at present. Who's the current favorite?"

"I saw Mr. Lissott this morning," I said, avoiding the subject.

Face drawn and eyes downcast, she listened gravely to everything I had to say.

"I feel dreadful," she confessed, rising from her chair. "Josh and I . . ."

"You don't have to explain," I murmured. "If the Major presents this information—"

"Yes!" Her eyes glowed new hope. "That is the answer. He's the *only* one who can talk sense to Fernald." She shivered. "I don't like Fernald . . . there's something about him."

Yes, I felt that way, too.

"Oh, Daphne." She embraced me. "I'm so glad you and Angela came to Somner . . . what do you think of her portrait?"

I stopped to critically appraise the painting by the open window Kate promptly shut. She'd captured Angela's facial expression perfectly, her languid pose a trifle daringly sensual. My parents wouldn't approve, but of course I said no such thing to Kate. I gave a polite response, seasoned with the appropriate praise and admiration, and asked what she intended to do with it.

"Showcase it in a new exhibition," she divulged. "I've been working on a few pieces for a while." The hope suddenly vanished from her eyes. "Josh and I were going to do one together, with Sir Marcus's backing."

"Will you still go ahead?"

"I don't know. How could I when he . . . when he—"

"May swing for the murder of your husband?" I summed up dispassionately. I didn't mean to sound so brutal. Perhaps it was the writer within me, painting the plain facts as they stood. "I'm sure the Major will point Mr. Fernald—"

"Yes, yes," she cut in, her voice becoming a distant echo, "but if *Josh* didn't do it, then who did?"

The same question haunted me into the next day as I ate my breakfast.

It could be anyone, any resident at Somner or nearby on the night of the murder.

One fact remained glaringly clear. Whoever had disfigured Max's face had a propensity for violence. Jackson appeared to be the mostly likely candidate. Perhaps he'd consulted legal advice and learned that *two* witnesses were required on the will and had come to Somner that night with the intention of rectifying the problem? On his pursuit for the master of the house, he'd found him lying on the path leading to the beach. He'd seen him there so vulnerable, and anger coiled inside of him when he thought of his cheated daughter and grandson and then—

"Miss du Maurier, does a visit to the tower suit you now?"

Roderick Trevalyan loomed out of his chair at the head of the breakfast table.

I smiled and replied that visits to towers always suited me, noting on my quick ascent to fetch a shawl that he'd dressed in his overalls. Did he intend to work in the boatshed? Intrigued by this prospect, and keen to get away before Bella heard of our plan and invited herself along, I met him outside.

"You are a very contrary man," I began upon reaching the beach track.

"Contrary?"

I decided to see whether it was possible to tease Roderick Trevalyan. "Why, yes. You are born to be lord of the manor, and still you favor the man of the land archetype. Or are you," I paused to reflect, "Hermit of the Tower?"

He laughed. A pleasant sound, musical, alert, alive.

"Well," I prompted, "which is it?"

"All and none," came the eventual rejoinder.

"No girlfriends or wives to change your ways?"

"None," he laughed again.

"All the better for it, perhaps," I went on. Did he truly feel comfortable with me? "Some are unhappy unions."

He nodded in silent agreement.

Then he said, "If you were thinking of my brother and Kate . . . theirs was a dismal fate. I shall not speak ill of the dead, but my brother was not a good man. He wasn't a kind man. Partly because of the war and partly because he'd always been that way."

I nodded. "Erratic. Unpredictable. Cruel."

His brows drew together at "cruel."

"He couldn't help it. He destroyed everything closest to him. Even his friends turned away from him, except Davis and Kate. She's been a good wife to him and tried to keep up the pretense."

"Of the happily married couple," I finished, noting the sudden pallor of his face. Following his gaze to the cordoned-off section of the track, I led him past it. "I've spoken a little to Mr. Davis," I admitted, putting on my shoes as we reached the end of the strip to climb up the hill. "Friends at school. Friends during the war . . . what happened over there probably preserved the friendship for all time."

Roderick nodded. "Yes. Davis saved him. Has done so on many occasions."

Mercifully, the wind had lessened its assault and I enjoyed the trudge up the hill. "Kate said the same thing." We reached the tower door and I paused to appreciate its Baltic beauty. "I am so envious. I should love to live in a tower like this." Or a lighthouse. Or a castle. I wasn't fussy. My wild ramblings managed to extract another low chuckle from Roderick.

Drawn first to the bookcase in the tower's library, my fingers soon located a book hidden at the back.

"Oh, not that one!"

Roderick Trevalyan seemed most insistent to the point of desperation.

I held the book from him. "I'm no missish prude. Can't I at least read the title?"

Holding the book out of his grasp, I gave him a beguiling smile. "Aha! I see you *are* a romantic soul at heart." Lord Byron's verses. It was an entire book devoted to romantic love, its pitfalls, its euphoric allurement. The subject interested me vastly, and I asked if I might borrow it.

His secret passion for poetry thus detected, my companion retained a decidedly darkened expression.

As he began a monotone tour of his beloved tower, I noted that the tribal decorations alluded to Kate's strong influence in his life.

"She's my sister-in-law!" He became stricken at the suggestion.

"Yet she's a . . . femme fatale," I crossed the line cautiously.

Roderick sat down with a sigh. He hung his head in his hands. "Once, she came here, *once*," he reiterated. "It was over Max again. She came here to escape. She wanted to stay for a time."

"Did you let her?" I asked.

"Yes, but not as you imagine it. I'd not touch my brother's wife. I'm not that sort of man."

I was impressed.

"I do *care* for her," he went on, guarded, yet eager to unload the burden he'd been carrying for far too long. "I *did* care for her"—he paused, perhaps wondering how much to confess—"in a wrong sense, for a time. She was my brother's *wife* and all I wanted to do was to protect her . . . from him."

It appeared many men were in the business of protecting Kate Trevalyan. She had three chivalrous knights: Josh Lissot, Roderick Trevalyan, and now, I daresay, Major Browning.

"She stayed at the tower a few times," he continued, looking around his chamber for the fleeting memory of her. "I slept in the boatshed."

"But most of the time they remained in London?"

"Yes. Max was only interested in weekend parties and the like, never the land."

I caught a glimpse of righteous indignation underlying the thin layers of his guarded tone. The biblical passage suddenly blazed through my mind, *"you have been weighed in the balances and have been found deficient."*

A chill scalded me. If a family's honor and survival depended on the removal of one member, was Roderick Trevalyan the kind of man to murder and disfigure his own brother?

No, I couldn't believe it of him. I'd sooner suspect Arabella of a private vendetta than Roderick.

Yet the fact remained. He had a strong motive for removing his brother, permanently.

Roderick and I deepened our friendship that day. For some unknown reason, this man of intense privacy and few words liked me. Perhaps he'd thought me a dowd when I'd first entered Somner House. Winter forbid extravagant dressing, but under Kate's skillful élan I had emerged, I am daring enough to say, a beauty.

I had enjoyed the attention, especially from the Major.

Sir Marcus remarked upon the attraction. "Have you settled your differences then, Daphne girl?"

He'd taken a liking to calling me Daphne girl, after the fashion of Katie girl, which I despised. I reminded Sir Marcus he lacked the appropriate Irish heritage to behave in this glib fashion, but it amused him.

"The Irish hide nothing." He grinned, marching smartly into Hugo's forbidden domain. "Unlike you and the Major, and all members of this house for that matter," he added, his purpose clear as we descended upon the kitchen.

Hugo scurried away.

"Never thought I'd live to see the day a hunchback turns into a frightened rabbit," mused Sir Marcus, swinging a kitchen hand towel Hugo had left on the cutting table. "I daresay he is troubled, for dinner was not *au fait* last night."

Unequivocally, I accepted his assessment.

"The meat was *half* cooked and those carrots! They tasted like bricks!"

"So you're claiming the apron tonight?" I asked.

He nodded, gaily inspecting the supplies. I shook my head with a gentle laugh, declining to participate and deciding on a walk instead.

Rachael Eastley lived in a ramshackle cottage on the outskirts of the main town. It was a two-story cottage resembling a town house divided by a thick hedge of overgrown shrubbery. Up above a balcony looking out to sea, strands of wisteria and ivy scaled down the dark gray stone brick walls.

Opening the tall, thin, rusty gate, I dodged a jagged ensemble of mismatched cobbles up to the front door, hoping I'd find her at home. I knew she worked at the local pub, but three o'clock in the afternoon seemed a safe time to visit.

A moment's hesitation gripped me before I knocked on the painted red door. I knew nothing of this woman or how she'd take to me showing up in my Sunday best. I don't know why I chose to dress thus, even snatching one of Angela's hats to wear at the last moment. Perhaps I felt the need to present myself in a professional sense, like one of my mother's important social calls.

The door was opened by a grim-faced old woman.

"What ye want?"

"To see Mrs. Eastley. Is she in?"

"Who's askin?"

I paused. "Say . . . a guest from Somner."

Her eyes quickened at this—a visitor from the "Big House." I hadn't seen much of the island, but I suspected Somner House far surpassed all other residences in the area.

The door closed in my face. Only to swing open again a moment later. Bidden inside by the stern-faced serving woman, I encountered the tiniest parlor I'd ever seen, beautifully decorated with a table bearing fine lace cloth and chairs covered with embroidered cushions. A small fireplace, unlit, glimmered to the left, as did a narrow flight of stairs leading to a second level.

The serving woman disappeared to what appeared to be the kitchen as I removed my hat and gloves. I looked for photographs or other clues as to the life of Mrs. Eastley, but there was nothing in the parlor other than a neat, cheerful welcome.

Low voices resounded down the tiny hall and I held my breath in anticipation. The serving woman burst through the door and behind her appeared the serene face of Mrs. Eastley. Carrying a book in her hands, she set it down on a passing hallstand before indicating we sit at the table.

"Tea, Nanny," she spoke in a firm but fluid manner.

"Miss du Maurier, isn't it?"

Suddenly questioning the wisdom of my visit, I nodded. In the falling light, Mrs. Eastley's radiance cast a welcoming glow into the embers of my story. But did I feel guilty, coming here, partly for inspiration, and partly out of curiosity? No. Quite the contrary.

"I hoped you might come," she said, lowering eyes that had no right to possess such thick, curling lashes. "Major Browning speaks highly of you."

I blinked. "I . . . er—"

She smiled softly. "My husband knew him. He served under him for a time."

"Oh," returned I.

"So, it was, in effect, almost a first acquaintance when we met the other day."

Her countenance turned a mild peach color and I blithely continued my perusal of the room, indulging my imagination.

"I hear you're a writer, Miss du Maurier. What do you like to write?"

Nanny swaggered in, noisily bearing the tea and cake tray. Her clumsy attempts seemed out of place, like everything surrounding the mysterious Mrs. Eastley.

"Thank you, that will be all, Nanny." Mrs. Eastley smiled when her erstwhile companion refused to leave.

Mrs. Eastley served the tea. I admired her delicate hands and wrists, hands unscarred by hard labor. I burned to ask questions; however, I replied in answer to hers on my writing, why I'd come to Somner House, and where I lived in London.

"You say your husband served under the Major?" I asked in a blunt manner my mother would have been horrified to hear.

"Yes. Sugar? Cream?"

"Neither, thank you. I confess I've come for a visit as you intrigue me, Mrs. Eastley."

I left my statement open to interpretation and a hint of the peachiness returned to her face.

"Might I ask, is your mother deceased?"

I hated myself for the brutality of my voice, especially on hearing her gracious, unoffending reply.

"Yes. She died many years ago of consumption."

"And you've always lived on the island? Has your father always served at Somner?"

"It's a hereditary job. My family have always served the Trevalyans."

I sipped my tea. "Your mother . . . were her family also islanders?"

"No."

I lifted a penitent brow. "Forgive me for my rudeness, but I'm curious to learn more about Somner House and the island."

The apology failed to appease Mrs. Eastley, but she smiled her acceptance, before seeing me to the door.

CHAPTER SIXTEEN

It would take time to break down Rachael Eastley's defenses. I was reticently pensive that evening after my visit to the mysterious widow as Sir Marcus, Mr. Davis, Kate, Angela, and I lingered around the fire. Since Roderick had retired early, Bella no longer found a reason to stay. I think the rest of us felt acute relief at her withdrawal and a casual easiness ensued to the sound of Mr. Davis and Kate humming wartime tunes. Sir Marcus, Angela, and I did not know the songs so we opted for a game.

"I daresay I'm rather brain weary for cards," Sir Marcus confessed. "Can't it be something a little less . . . strenuous?"

"Charades," Mr. Davis suggested, but nobody was in the mood for charades.

"Secret loves?" Kate flashed a smile. "My life is an open book so why should not all of yours be?"

"Pity Bella and Rod aren't here," Angela put in, refilling the gentlemen's brandy and her own glass of wine.

"I only do secret loves with cigars," Sir Marcus declared, and Kate invited him and Mr. Davis to use the house supply.

"My brother-in-law rarely smokes." She gave a carefree shrug.

"I don't think," I ventured with a smirk, "Roderick and Bella are in possession of secrets."

"Oh, you'd be surprised." Kate's quizzical eye scanned the room, watchful for the gentlemen's return. "Bella's been in love with her cousins for years. Max told me about it once. Cousin Bella"—a sly grimace lurked at the corner of her mouth—"is possessed of many dark, hidden passions. In truth, I wonder why she stays on . . . hoping to at last conquer Rod and marry him?"

Angela snorted. "She's the strangest girl I've ever met. What reason does she have to be so secretive?"

"Hidden, dark passions?" Mr. Davis, resuming his seat, tapped the corner of his lighted cigar. "We all have them . . . and secrets."

"You?" Kate's friendly hand nudged his elbow. "You don't have any secrets. I know you too well. You're the first to divulge over a glass or two."

"*Little* secrets. But *big* secrets are a very different thing altogether."

Now he'd intrigued all of us.

"Big secrets, Mr. Davis?" I teased. "Perhaps you are a great artist only *pretending* to paint ill for our sakes!"

"No," he returned, "I'm not that gracious. If I were a great artist, I'd . . . I'd, oh dash it, I'd paint Kate her dream world—to hang on the wall."

Kate visibly softened at this euphoric statement and Angela stiffened. "Perhaps Mr. Davis has a confession to make?"

"I do." Standing up, he took Kate's hand in his. "I've loved you for as long as I can remember. I admired you before you became Max's, and when you became Max's, I slowly fell in love with you. The secret has plagued my soul daily, hourly, knowing I could never act upon it: my best friend's wife."

Astonished, yet not so wholly surprised at his wine-induced proclamation, Kate set down her glass and closed both her hands over his. She met him squarely, her eyes searching his, wondering, disbelieving, and flattered. "I don't know what to say . . ." The uncertain words echoed through the mausoleum-like silence of the room.

"Say nothing," Mr. Davis urged. "For my love for you is beyond words."

I slept well, dreaming of the beauty of Mr. Davis's declaration. Fit for a novel, yes. Fit for a hero, yes.

But would Kate accept him? Now that she was free to enter another marriage if she so desired? Or would Lord Roderick try to win her hand? Or Josh Lissot, pining away in prison?

She had no want for admirers. They abounded everywhere, some waiting for years for her freedom from her dastardly husband. Lord Rod, for me, would tread cautiously on the subject.

However, since our talk in the tower, I doubted whether he felt any true love for her. Her plight aroused his chivalrous nature; he found her attractive, charming, her personality infectious, but love? No.

Needless to say, when the morning arrived, I had to write. Inspiration burned within, and the skeleton of a novel began to take shape. After jotting down random notes, I sat chewing on the end of my pencil. Rachael Eastley was a fascinating subject, she deserved a story of her own. In the meantime, however, I contented myself with finishing a short story. I weaved a mystery element into an ending in which a long-lost love, long thought dead, returns to stop his lover's wedding.

Proud to have completed what I believed a short fiction worthy of publication, I made a copy and walked into town to mail it off to *Punch* magazine. I did not tell anyone of my submission; I wanted nobody to know, especially not Angela. I couldn't endure her mocking criticism if I failed.

When I returned to the house, Angela greeted me in a panic.

"She's with him right now. They've been locked away in the study for hours!"

My growing uncertainty accelerated. "I assume you mean Lady Kate and Mr. Davis? Why should it concern you so desperately?"

"Oh, what would you know!"

Her face became a quivering mess of emotion. This was not my poised, self-assured Angela. She was no longer able to hide her distress from me.

"Whatever it is, you can rely upon me to keep your secret," I said, urging her to quit pacing the parlor like a lion.

Finally, she wavered, considering, and I saved her from saying the words. "Has, er, Kate ever returned your affections?"

She bit her lip.

I nodded. "Has, er, Kate ever, er, entertained relationships of this kind?"

"Yes."

I couldn't say I was shocked. To close one's eyes to reality served little, and whereas in the Victoria era, when such affairs were regarded worse than a scandalous death, times had changed.

The Great War changed everything as dreamlike, almost blissful innocence seemed to vanish, exposing all the crude rudimentaries of life. I had long suspected Angela of harboring a secret, all the months spent away in the country, never divulging her friends' names.

Her quick glance surveyed me. "Don't speak of this to *anyone*."

I gave her my solemn promise.

I met Major Browning on my return to our room.

Nearly colliding on the front step, he smilingly dodged me one way. I took the opposite side and the unavoidable occurred, a clash of bodies, minds, and temperaments all at once.

"On the case again? I hope your visit to Mrs. Eastley's was . . . fruitful."

How did he know I'd been there? Too proud to ask, I paused in my ascent up the stairs.

"Like your visit to Mr. Lissot," he added, standing tall, smart, and roguishly sophisticated.

My chin lifted to an arrogant angle. "Have you come to see Lady Trevalyan?"

"No, actually, I came to see you."

"*Me?*"

"Yes, you, unless there's another Miss Daphne du Maurier in the house?"

Not comfortable with the sudden rush of elation at this statement, I managed a polite acknowledgment. He looked fine, and though not prone to sighing like some females of my acquaintance, I softened. My breath shortened, too.

"Why don't we take a walk? You like to walk, don't you? It's where you stumble upon things."

"Don't you mean bodies? Please note I did not *find* Max Trevalyan this time, Major Browning, and I am glad of the fact."

He nodded, guiding me gently out of the house. "It is not easy to see a body for the first time. Consider yourself fortunate you missed Max Trevalyan on your morning walk."

"Whoever killed him hated him. I don't think it was a random act of violence."

"Nor do I."

I glanced up ahead. I hadn't ventured this way before; the new copper and green leaves promised an early spring, the earth was damp from the winter reprieve. I imagined how lovely it would look in a few months, in the height of summer brilliance. Suddenly, it seemed very natural for me to be walking the grounds with Major Browning.

"How are you enjoying your stay at Somner?"

The Major's low resonant voice caressed my ears. Heart racing, I sought to bring my foolhardy emotions under control. He inspired too much in me. He was a veritable danger. "Oh . . . it's . . ."

We circled an open, untended path. I thought of Jackson and wondered why he'd neglected to tend this part of the garden. Perhaps the wilderness that encompassed Somner House had waged war against domestication just as I waged war against Major Frederick "Tommy" Browning.

Hearing the light laugh betraying my amusement at his chummy nickname, he lifted a caustic brow.

"Do you then . . . delight in a murder?"

I was horrified at the suggestion. "A preposterous notion, Major Browning. *I* did not orchestrate these happenings in any form, and I am as innocent as I was in the Padthaway affair."

He choked out a cynical cough.

"It's not my fault *things* drift my way," I snapped to his thinly disguised insinuation.

"Or perhaps the Daphne boat willingly drifts into them," he tempered as we completed the path circuit.

I stood still, enjoying the cool afternoon breeze rustling my hair. The house never looked better than it did now, emblazoned by the dull glow of a setting sun, burnt orange intertwined with pale hues of lilac, amber, and muted silver. It appeared almost ancient thus bathed and, standing alongside of me, the Major appreciated the view as well.

"Fernald is releasing Josh Lissot this afternoon . . . that is why I came to the house."

Startled, I stared up at him as I remembered Mr. Davis's declaration of love. Would a duel on the green follow the return of the vanquished lover?

"Daphne." The Major's laugh brought me to reality. "This is not a *novel,* but real life."

"Yes, yes." I nodded. "Danger . . ." Biting my lower lip, I decided to update him regarding Mr. Davis and he listened to everything I had to say with his usual diligence.

"And what are your suspicions in regard to Lady Trevalyan's current affections?"

Due to my all-too-recent conversation with Angela, I said I did not know. Who could know a woman's heart? It could turn in a number of directions.

He refused to let me off so easily.

"The Daphne du Maurier I know is never in want of an opinion."

"And if I do not care to share it?"

He shrugged. "It won't matter except to deny you the glory if your suspicions are proven correct."

I studied the slow upward curl of his mouth. "How did you know I'd been to visit Mrs. Eastley? Did you follow me?"

"Unintentionally," he admitted. "I was in town and I saw you. Did you glean much from the widow?"

"She's hiding something. Fear perhaps?"

He frowned, reflective. "Fear for her son foremost—"

"Followed by fear of her fierce beard of a father."

It was his turn to laugh. I loved hearing the melodious sound; it warmed and humored me.

"I hope"—he hung his head in false humility—"you have forgiven me for my lengthy absence and we are friends again?"

"Comrades," I put in after a lengthy reprieve.

"Well, then," he said, proffering his arm, "shall we inform the lady of the good news?"

Neither of us anticipated her gut-wrenching reaction.

"What? Released?" She sat down in the parlor, her movements slow and mechanical. Within moments, Mr. Davis strolled into the room and her countenance fell. "Josh . . . Mr. Lissot. Fernald's let him go." Her huge eyes encompassed the Major. "Oh, thank you, thank you, thank you . . ."

"It's Daphne you should thank," the Major informed.

"And me." Sir Marcus wandered blithely in. "Why does everybody always forget about me?" He went on to give Kate a hearty embrace. "There you are, Katie girl. He's free. Your conscience can rest."

Bolting out of her seat, Kate sauntered to the far wall. "No, I cannot rest, not until I know the truth." Her knee overturning a small table, she waved off any comforting attempts. "Oh, dear . . . my mind is in turmoil."

"What's wrong?"

Floating down the stairs, Angela went straight to her and persuaded her to a chair. With all attention focused on Kate, I alone caught the quizzical look in Mr. Davis's eyes. He was questioning Angela's attentions to Kate and how it would affect his suit.

I shouldn't have enjoyed the scene with all its crimes of the heart, but I did. It made for a very intriguing drama in the wake of the murder, and considering Josh Lissot's return and Mr. Davis's proposal, one hastened to wonder what would transpire in the next chapter.

CHAPTER SEVENTEEN

Grateful for the Major's influence in obtaining Mr. Lissot's temporary release, Trevalyan invited the Major back to dine at Somner. The dinner meant to serve the double purpose of thanking the Major whilst welcoming a partially exonerated Mr. Lissot. But was he truly welcome now?

Sir Marcus and I debated.

"Davis has put her into a quandary. We'll have to see which horse comes in first. It's not always the strongest or most obvious one, you know."

To protect ourselves from Bella's eavesdropping, we had decided on an evening stroll. It was cold and I shivered as the sea air whirled around us.

"Should have brought a wrap." Clicking his tongue, Sir Marcus elegantly slid out of his coat and placed it on my shoulders. I thanked him and told him he was a gentleman.

" 'A gentleman.' Alas, that appears to be my sad vocation in life. The Gentleman of the Cloak . . . speaking of gentlemen in general, glad to see you and MB have mended the breach. Had my doubts, I did. The fiercely independent proud Daphne—"

"I'm not proud!"

"Stubborn. You are very stubborn where men are concerned. Your sister told me."

Annoyed with Angela for once again exploiting the affairs of a younger sister, I determined to set the record straight. "Just because I weigh their words and actions doesn't mean I am proud or stubborn."

"Aha. Seeing them all as potential characters, eh?"

"Perhaps," I admitted. "What else did Angela say?"

"That you're in love with the gallant Major."

This time, my face turned scarlet. "The little . . . trollop. I have *never* divulged such secrets—"

"So it's true? You're in love with him?"

"No, it's not true," I returned hotly.

"I think it may be."

I sighed. "It's not what you think. We are entirely unsuited to each other. Besides, he's a . . ."

I paused, nudging Sir Marcus. "Is that Bella Woodford?"

Sir Marcus squinted. "Yes, I believe so."

Both of us stood there watching her tear out of the house, a fountain of tears streaking her face.

"Bella . . . wait!" Roderick burst out of the house, his cryptic eye quick to detect us. "My cousin is upset," he explained. "Have you two been outside long?"

He was wondering how long we'd been standing there, and perhaps, how much we'd overheard from our place in the gardens.

"Not long," Sir Marcus replied. "Is there anything we can do?"

"No." Frowning, Lord Roderick took his leave. At the door,

however, he turned to say, "My cousin and I have no attachment, if you are wondering."

"Strange comment," I breathed to Sir Marcus after he'd left. "Perhaps she expressed her true feelings for him now that he's Lord of the Manor and he rejected her?"

"Possibly," Sir Marcus owned, "but I see a different version. *Perhaps* they quarreled over Kate or you, for instance."

"Me? What do I have to do with Bella running off in tears?"

"Because, dopey, his lordship might be *interested* in you. Romantically."

"No. That cannot be."

I turned a deeper shade of scarlet, examining my words and actions. Had I encouraged Roderick? Had I flirted with his affections? "It has to be over Kate."

Sir Marcus whistled and we parted ways at the base of the staircase. I longed to upbraid Angela for talking about me and I found her sitting alone in the darkened breakfast parlor, brooding, her hand clutched under her chin as she stared unseeing out the window.

I began to storm over to her and say "how dare you" when her expression stopped me. It looked almost murderous.

She jumped when she saw me.

"Daphne! You have a very bad habit of sneaking around like that. Are you spying on me? And where's Sir Marcus? Hiding behind those drapes?" A single tear rolled down her cheek. "Don't know what I'm doing here anymore, Daph. I stayed on for Kate's benefit, but now, I think it's time to leave."

"Oh, no, we can't leave. Not yet. That's running away."

Every instinct rebelled against the idea of leaving just when things were starting to get interesting, and I'd finally begun to enjoy myself, but perhaps I spoke too quickly.

"Why do you want to stay?" Her accusing eye scathed me. "It's cold and boring. There are no shops or theaters here to entertain us, and I find the present company most *tepid*."

I suddenly understood the reason for her sullenness. She and Kate had quarreled.

Seizing a nearby cushion, I sat cross-legged before her on the floor. I had never seen Angela so withdrawn and gaunt and I felt a little sorry for her. Everything usually seemed to go her way, but not this time. "Of course, we'll leave if you wish. Do you know if the boats are operating now? I can ask Roderick tomorrow if you like."

"Oh, I don't know," she groaned, shielding her face from me.

She hardly ever cried, nontheatrically, and I felt ill equipped to deal with the situation. What was I to do? Angela wasn't a warm affectionate hugging sort of person; she detested such signs of weakness, so I just sat with her and eventually persuaded her to go to our room. "It's not good to sit alone in the dark," I advised, and she meekly followed my guidance.

"I wonder if . . . I wonder if she'll marry him."

She was speaking of Mr. Davis.

"Is, er, Mr. Davis well set up?" I said, shepherding inside our room and closing the door. "I mean, can he support her?"

"More than Josh Lissot," Angela snarled. "But she's a fool if she makes the same mistake again. I've helped her through the whole Max affair. I won't do it again. She was warned, you know, about Max. But she didn't listen."

"She liked his looks and his estate." I shrugged. "She's not the first to make such a decision." I paused. "What do you know of Mr. Davis?"

Chewing on her lower lip, Angela lifted a dismissive shoulder. "His parents died during the war, leaving him a handsome flat in London and an income." Yawning, she clapped her hand over her mouth. "Other than that, I don't know much about him."

"So, he's a gentleman of no profession," I mused to myself aloud, "who plays the piano and has harbored secret passions for his best friend's wife all these lonely years."

"Oh, he hasn't been lonely," Angela corrected. "There've been countless girlfriends, from what I hear, but none of them obviously matched up to Kate, so I suppose that's why he's now made his move . . . now that she's free."

Her voice echoed with bitterness and the grim acceptance of reality. Kate Trevalyan needed someone financially settled and Mr. Davis fulfilled the requirement, having the London flat and the income to support her current lifestyle. On the other hand, Mr. Lissot, while handsome, young, and virile remained the struggling artist, chased about for back rent and constantly on the run from creditors. "Do you think Roderick's in love with Kate, too?" I asked Angela before we lulled ourselves to a contemplative sleep.

"Not anymore," came the decisive laugh. "I believe *you* have conquered there, little sister."

I refused to believe I could have made such an impression on the dour Roderick Trevalyan. Though, on reflection, we did share a love of poetry, and I had to admit that his estate was a definite virtue.

I waltzed, needless to say, on the way to the breakfast parlor only to encounter Arabella, her vicious glare stalking me as I helped myself to coffee and toast.

Angela was right. Bella had guessed or suspected her cousin's interest in me, and rather than hide her disappointment, chose a course similar to Miss Bingley's in *Pride and Prejudice*. After refusing to pass the jam bowl on my third request, I said, "Miss Woodford, do you not hear me on purpose? I asked you three times to pass the jam."

Casting a glance to Roderick, where he sat perusing the morning paper, she gaped at me. "I, er, did *not* hear you, Miss du Maurier."

She most certainly *had* heard and sensing Roderick's immediate interest in our dispute, I gingerly applied a spoonful of the surrendered jam bowl to my toast. Whatever Sir Marcus's objections concerning the Somner House kitchen, they kept an excellent jam and I complimented Roderick on it. I then offered him coffee as I poured my own, which, no doubt, further incensed the dark-eyed Bella sitting opposite me. Accepting my gracious offer with a warm smile, Roderick proceeded to engage me in conversation, drawing fresh spots of angry color on his cousin's face.

Throwing down her napkin, she sauntered out of the room.

Lord Roderick looked after her, slightly embarrassed. "Forgive her, Daphne. Bella's not a happy person. She never has been."

This admission perked more than one set of ears about the room, and I spied Sir Marcus pretending to be fully immersed in an upside-down copy of *The Times*.

"Yes," Roderick said quietly while I stirred my coffee, "Aunt Fran is something of a tyrant and poor Bella's tied to looking after her . . . the brief reprieves here at Somner are her only escape."

Seeing Kate, Angela, and Mr. Davis adjourn to the sunny terrace, I lowered my voice to the confidential tête-à-tête. "I think, my lord, your cousin is in love with you."

"If she is, she's no reason to be. I've never thought of her that way."

"Did your brother?" I lowered my eyes.

"Yes."

"Oh." I didn't know what else to say.

"She's more in love with Somner," he went on. "She'd love to be mistress of Somner and Max's inheritance appealed to her. As for him, she was a brief amusement."

A brief amusement. I hoped nobody would ever call me a "brief amusement."

"You mustn't blame Bella. She was young and vulnerable at the time."

"And in love with Somner House," I reminded. "Was it a shock to her when he married someone else?"

"Yes. It was a shock as he'd given her an engagement ring."

"They were engaged!"

"One foolish summer. Max, from what I understand, was drunk. He never meant anything serious but Bella took it to heart."

"What happened?"

"He demanded the ring back. She refused so he packed his bags for London and told her she'd never be welcome at Somner again."

"But she was here when . . ."

"Yes. She came every summer, as usual. Max just ignored her."

"And Lady Kate, how does she manage to . . ."

"Tolerate Bella? She feels sorry for her and thinks it would do more harm than good to banish her from Somner. After all, Somner is a second home to her and my parents treated her like a daughter."

She had hoped to marry Max and make her refuge her home, but Max had humiliated her by bringing home a wife.

Had she resorted to murder?

CHAPTER EIGHTEEN

Josh Lissot arrived early the next day.

I was returning to the house from my morning walk when I saw the car. He stepped out without a backward glance at the driver and stood for a moment on the flagstones.

"Hello," I called out.

He flinched.

"Welcome back. We are all glad you are back."

He said nothing but I read the silent question in his eyes. He wondered what kind of reception awaited him, what the future held, and why the police had let him go.

I slipped my arm through his. "Come inside. It's eight o'clock. We can breakfast together."

"Thank you, Daphne. It's kind of you . . . and thank you for coming to see me."

Once in the parlor, he said he'd go and change first and I followed suit, meeting him and the others a little later. Outwardly, everybody greeted him with friendly relief, commiserating over what he'd endured while in the prison house. There was no sign to indicate the transferral of Kate's affections from Mr. Lissot to Mr. Davis. Perhaps she deferred her decision as a kindness to Mr. Lissot, but I believed otherwise. I believed she hadn't yet decided.

Betraying an inner qualm, Angela remarked upon it as we dressed for dinner. "She doesn't have to choose. Oh, I wish she would follow my advice, return to London and set herself up independently! She doesn't need a *man* to support her and Sir Marcus can obtain painting commissions at the snap of a finger."

"That may be so," I replied, finding it difficult to choose between the gray skirt and cream lace blouse or the beaded black dress. "But considering how much she suffered with her first husband, she may want another. A kind, caring one to make her believe in love again."

"Gosh!" Rolling her eyes, Angela snagged the zipper on her skirt. "You make me positively ill! All men are not worth two pennies rubbed together. They're not faithful or true and they invariably go for the pretty and racy ones and they age very badly. Why, consider Heathcliff. He just got worse and worse. He never truly loved Cathy. She was just a possession to him."

The mention of *Wuthering Heights* made me decide upon the black dress. Elegant and simple, I'd enhance it with my mother's pearl set: pearl drop-earrings and a pearl-studded comb. Sweeping up my hair, pins protruding from my mouth as I endeavored to achieve a classic French style, I squinted into the mirror. "No, you're wrong. Heroes exist out there, otherwise why would we fictionalize them? Granted, they're not perfect, but who is?"

"Well," huffed my sister, "I still think she's an idiot if she marries Davis or Josh Lissot."

"Perhaps she'll choose Sir Marcus," I joked, dusting a small amount of rouge over my cheeks. "After all, if it's comfort she desires, he has the best address out of all of them."

"Perhaps, then, *you* should encourage him. You're gallivanting around with him enough as it is, and you cannot pretend that *Lady* Daphne of Clevedon Court doesn't sound good."

"It does sound good." I allowed myself to indulge the brief possibility of becoming the mistress of an estate in which all doors were open, every confidence shared. The same tantalizing picture no doubt had occupied Arabella's dreams.

I confess to a certain degree of nervousness as I descended the stairs. Roderick awaited me at the bottom and the marked attention he bestowed upon me in front of the Major and the others betrayed his singular interest. I couldn't help but wonder if this interest coincided with his desire to lessen Bella's designs.

True to form, Major Browning raised a cynical brow, his dark gaze moving surreptitiously to Roderick. I smiled at him and feigned innocence, glad, in fact, of the additional company. The Major and his men occupied one end of the table, Roderick, Kate, Bella, and Mr. Davis at the other. The rest of us sat in the middle and I noted Josh Lissot's scowl growing heavier by the minute. Was the love affair with Kate over then? Or was she using discretion considering her recent widowhood and Mr. Lissot's near escape from the hangman's noose?

"You play decoy, Amadeus, while I'm on watch."

Nudging my chair, Sir Marcus rose and after allowing a modest time to pass, I followed him.

He was waiting for me out in the corridor.

"Now the plan is . . . when they all go to the parlor, you take the piano stool so that I can see where the lovers sit."

"What! Are you mad? I can't play the piano and there's no piano in the parlor, so I don't know what you are talking about."

"Oh, yes, there's a piano in there," he grimaced. "For Mr. Davis. Our Katie girl wishes him to lull us to sleep with a *love* melody."

I lifted a brow at the evident sarcasm. "Don't believe in love, do you?"

"Infinitely," he assured me. "Especially after good food and wine. It's the between parts which bore me, but I've a hunch Cupid is in the air tonight and will light the way."

"The way to the murderer?"

"Or a murder*ess* . . . shhh! Alas, they emerge."

He bounded away, leaving me to linger in the hall as Roderick and Kate led the party to its adjournment.

Play the piano. My first instinct was to run away.

"Arrest my eyes. Miss du Maurier appears to be lacking an escort."

I began to feel ill. The person I least wanted to see me make a fool of myself stood there in the shadows.

"I left my coat in the dining room," the Major explained, strolling by with a grin. "I thought I had better fetch it before the performance."

I felt considerably ill and hurried to the room before the Major haunted my steps. Sir Marcus had his reason for wanting me to play the piano and obviously had announced my recital to the others. I groaned. There was no escaping now, no running away. I drew in a quick breath, entered the room, and marched straight to the piano facing the back wall.

The party had begun to relax around me. Wineglasses twinkling, pleasant smiles all around, amiable conversation and reluctantly, I slid onto the cool, leather chair.

"Daphne, what are you doing?" Angela cried. "You can't play!"

Trust one's sister to trumpet one's failures. Ignoring her, I stroked the keys, trying to remember a tune I'd learned years ago. The result, I'm afraid, came out very raw and from the corner of my eye, I observed the Major and everybody else's sudden silence.

Sir Marcus alone clapped.

"Daphne." Angela hurried over. "I think you should let Mr. Davis play."

"Yes," I humbly admitted, slowly rising and retreating to a darkened corner of the room as Mr. Davis began Mendelssohn's *Songs Without Words*.

"He plays very well." The Major strolled over to me.

"Unlike myself?"

"Anyone can play," he responded to my slightly loud tone. "But I cannot help but think you are acting as a distraction."

"A distraction? Don't be absurd, Major Browning. I've no reason to engineer a—"

"Or is it"—his smile eluded me—"too much champagne for a little girl to handle?"

Now he'd enraged me. *A little girl.* How dare he imply such a thing.

"Despite your assumptions, my playing had nothing to do with any beverage I may or may not have consumed."

A knowing grin continued to play on his lips. "I daresay you and Sir Marcus are engineering something."

"Mr. Davis," I said, quick to divert his suspicions, "do you think Kate will accept his proposal?"

The Major shrugged. "The man in question is well positioned."

I followed his gaze to where Kate turned the pages for Mr. Davis. "Whereas poor Josh, languishing there in the corner, is not so well positioned." I shook my head. "How sad for him . . ."

"The love affair is not over."

Startled by this admission of superior knowledge, I raised a curt brow. "No? Do you hold the lady's confidence then?"

"Brooding does not look well on you," he replied, a faint smile on his lips. "I note it is a favorite façade of yours—the cynical soul—the writer within philosophizing and drawing from life to insert into books."

"You mistake me, sir—"

"Do I? Can I ask you a question?"

This sudden turn in conversation lured a reflective musing on my part. What did the Major hope to achieve by drilling me? Did he care about my writing? Dare he be showing an *interest* in my writing, and, in turn, me?

"There's certainly plenty of scope for characters here," the Major observed. "We know who the victim is: Max Trevalyan. But who's the hero, heroine, and villain in this tale, Miss du Maurier?"

The use of my formal title attempted to rebuild the wall between us. I swallowed, fiercely wishing he did not know me so well. Nothing escaped the notice of Major Browning. I was sure he filed everything away to use at will.

His question inspired me to try to unlock the inner workings of his mind.

"Dear Frederick . . . your first name is Frederick, is it not? You seem to be the beholder of many secrets. Why don't you tell me who my characters are."

His lazy eye perused me. "You overestimate my talents. I am not a guest of this house, *you* are."

"However, you still have the propensity to influence events. Mr. Lissot's return for one. We have no doubt he owns his temporary release to your interference."

"Not interference," he corrected. "Reasonable persuasion. And he is not out of the fire yet, so to speak."

"So he's still a suspect along with the others," I said under my breath, surveying the room. Mr. Davis continued to play a beautiful concerto, but he'd lost his page turner. Kate and Josh Lissot now occupied a divan near the fire, both engaged in a low, earnest conversation. Unlike the previous day, no tension strained her face. On the contrary, she smiled often, laughed once, and her eyes softened as she placed her hand on Mr. Lissot's knee.

"Lissot's a fool," the Major murmured. "He'd do better to keep away until Mr. Whitt arrives."

"Mr. Whitt?"

"Chief Inspector Whitt. Due in on the next boat, by all accounts."

"See! You *do* know everything. How did you find out?"

"It is no secret. Courtesy of your Lord Roderick."

"He's not *my*—" I stopped short, looking at the man in question. I couldn't deny a certain attraction to him, admiring his stern work and moral ethics, his sense and education.

"He's a better choice than David Hartley," the Major remarked, "though not entirely exempt in this affair."

"Why would he murder his own brother?"

"Look around you. To save the family fortunes."

"Yes, but he's not a violent man, nor the kind to resort to—"

"Not by his own hand, but a hired one?"

"Jackson the gardener. He's the only kind of nefarious character I can see delivering the blow."

"How do you not know Lord R and he did not come to some kind of arrangement?"

It was true.

I didn't.

"It's a mystery," the Major sighed at length, retrieving his coat from a nearby chair, "and time for me to retire. I shall leave you to your . . . deliberations, Miss du Maurier."

He bowed curtly and left.

I watched him go, feeling suddenly a little lost without his company. I didn't know what to do with myself. I didn't feel tired, nor did I feel like talking to anyone in the party, least of all Arabella, who eyed me curiously from where she lounged beside her cousin. Roderick, I noticed, looked stiff and ill-at-ease and as I bid my farewells, he immediately rose and lingered over my hand.

I climbed the stairs, enjoying the small triumph. Beyond a doubt, I'd certainly captured his interest. What should I do? Encourage it? How did I feel about the man? I *liked* him and respected him, but, he was a little too reserved. Did I feel a romantic attraction? I couldn't say, but I imagined passion lurked somewhere beneath his cool façade. Why else would he seek to hide a book of poetry? Was he ashamed of these safely guarded emotions and desires?

Or was he, like me to some degree, afraid of love?

"I've *delicious* news."

Sir Marcus's big face invaded my sun. And right in the

middle of the final chapter of *The Tenant of Wildfell Hall*. Did the man have no comprehension of decency?

Stealing the book away, Sir Marcus faced me with a schoolboy grimace. "Delicious, mouthwatering news, my little Daphie. As it so happens, I witnessed an event last night of momentous magnitude."

I waited for the revelation.

"Like Othello, Mr. Lissot believed his love had rejected him for another."

"Rejected! She *rejected* him?"

"Well, not entirely," Sir Marcus reflected, squeezing a seat beside me though there was clearly not enough room for the two of us on the divan. "This is rather cozy, isn't it?"

"Yes, and?"

"*Brotherly*," he insisted, his face all innocence. "You needn't fear for I have no designs upon you at present, though I suspect you'd make a jolly good wife."

"Thank you." I smiled. One couldn't help but smile at his ridiculousness. "Where did this momentous event take place?"

"In a moonlit garden." Sir Marcus sighed. "It was *so* romantic . . ."

"But of what import?"

"*Hasty* Daphne. One must build the scene, not plunge headlong into the swamp. Swamps are horrid, murky places; don't recommend them at all." He shuddered, pausing for effect. "Here is how it happened: after all you boring people went to bed, I wheeled myself into Lord Rod's study for a cigar. The night air enticed me outside, yet I soon snuffed out an absurdly *good* Cuban, more's the pity, when I spied our lovers behind a tree. Or was it a hedge? I can't remember, and in any case, it doesn't signify. What *does* signify is that I heard all, bones, heart, and soul. It almost made me weep."

He affected a false tear.

"The hero pledged his *undying* love for the lady, then accused her in the same breath of betraying him."

"With Mr. Davis?" I interposed.

"The same," Sir Marcus nodded, "and I wondered if he, too, might be lurking around the place. Snag the premonition! I had to tear my eyes away from this tragic beautiful sight to do a reconnaissance around the garden. I returned to find the two lovers embracing. Oh!" He raised his eyes, a hand over his heart. "And then I made my speedy escape, leaving the two to er, *commence* whatever it is they were going to commence. If you ask me, Lissot's gone against all reason to pursue her while still a subject—"

"Because he loves her."

I scarcely heard my own voice. It echoed like a drifting whisper carried away by a summer's breeze.

Because he loves her echoed back at me.

CHAPTER NINETEEN

Dinner promised to be very awkward that eve.

Having no wish to partake of it, or listen to Angela's out-raged protests regarding Josh Lissot and his inability to care for Kate, I planned to do the only sensible thing: stay in bed and read a book.

"You should come down." Lingering by the door, Angela's lips curled. "I suppose there's no attraction now the Major's not here? What of Lord Rod? If you want my advice, Daphne, there's more than a fair prospect for you. I've a mind to tele-phone Papa about it, for I can see the two of you living in that dreary old tower, leading dull and uneventful lives surrounded by books."

I lowered my book a fraction.

"See!" She smirked. "You're reading a history book!"

"It's a history of the island," I said, and shaking her head, she left me in peace, returning an hour or so later.

"You're *still* there. You should come down. Roderick asked after you."

My face turned red. I could feel it.

"You really ought to save him from Bella," Angela prompted. "That girl won't take *no* for an answer."

Trying to ignore her chatter, I continued flicking the pages until a face caught my attention.

Sitting up, I fanned the pages backward.

"What the devil are you doing?"

"I saw something." And there it was, a photograph of Max Trevalyan and Mr. Davis, brothers in arms, standing before their warplane. Stunned at the inclusion of this all-too-recent image, I checked the printing date inside the front cover. It had been published three years after the Great War.

There was a brief commemorative inscription below the photograph, too. " 'Local landowner Lord Max Trevalyan and friend Mr. Peter Davis . . .' "

The photograph must have been taken before one of their missions. Perhaps it had been the one where the Germans had shot down their plane, leaving them stranded in the forest, alone, unprotected, and wounded. I had to find out. Roused to action, I located my robe and hastened down the hallway, book perched under arm.

"You can't go down looking like that!" Angela protested, hurrying behind. "What did you find in that book anyway?"

"Oh, nothing of any great importance. Just a photograph."

Approaching the drawing room, I suddenly reconsidered my state of dress. My mother would be horrified by such a spectacle, and as my mother was not at Somner, Angela played the role.

"Think of Roderick," she hissed. "He will disapprove."

"If he does," I retorted, "then he is not worth winning. I won't allow convention to rule me."

Angela lifted her eyebrows in warning. She did not want Roderick to think any less of me. Just as I was poised to heed her warning, Sir Marcus hooted, "Aha! The deserter deigns to join us!"

I quickly scanned the room, relieved to find Roderick and Josh Lissot absent. Kate looked particularly flushed, entertaining the company with some kind of scandalous reading, judging by their faces.

"Continue reading, Katie girl." Lazily perched upon one of the divans, Sir Marcus battled with a score of disobedient cushions. "I am curious as to Daphne's opinion."

To humor the party, I listened, my ears growing redder by the minute.

"The Marquis de Sade is too obscene for my little sister," Angela smirked. "She prefers the old romantics . . . and fairy tales."

"So do I," Mr. Davis defended, and I thanked him with a smile.

He offered to take me into dinner.

"I'm not really dressed for dinner." I laughed by way of apology.

"It doesn't matter . . . in these circumstances." Mr. Davis waved away my protests and escorted me into the dining room, seeing me comfortably seated. It was a gentlemanly consideration, I thought, often lacking in most young men of my acquaintance.

Roderick and Josh Lissot were already there, heavily engaged in a private discussion. No one seemed to take offense to my robe, and I suppose if I had thought to put a feather in my hair, nobody would have looked twice.

As the others entered the room, Josh looked tense, managing a warm smile when Kate trailed her hand across his shoulder.

I felt my companion's keen gaze upon her. Poor Mr. Davis. After loving Kate for years, he languished in the wake of his dramatic confession. Certain he regretted the public avowal to some extent, I strove to make light conversation and brought up the photograph in the book. "This is why I came down, really. Did you know they used the photograph?"

He took the book from me, surprised to see himself there. "Max must have done it. He liked fame, in any form. Those were wild days, but we survived. We were the lucky ones."

"Max was injured more than you were, was he not?"

Mr. Davis nodded. "Thankfully, for we'd both not be here today if I had. One of us had to drag the other out of the plane and across the field . . . away from the Germans."

I tried to imagine the scene. Blasts hurtling through the sky, the eerie sound of the German bombers approaching before the earth-rattling tanks made their invasion into the village. It was just as Kate had captured so vividly in her paintings.

"Max won the medal of bravery," I said, scanning Mr. Davis's quiet concentration on his dinner. "How did that happen when *you* saved him?"

"I offered it. Max needed it more than me. His wounds plagued him terribly and it was quite some time before he recovered."

I thought of the drugs, which evidently turned to severe dependency as Max attempted to lessen the pain. Or maybe they were not to blame for his many vices.

"Not many would give up their reward like you did," I murmured. "I trust the gesture was appreciated."

"It was," Mr. Davis insisted, declining a glass refill from Sir Marcus. "As I watched him hobble to the award ceremony, I knew I'd done the right thing. Like they say, there's more pleasure in giving than receiving."

I wondered why he continued supporting a libertine like Max Trevalyan. As I'd learned, he had a very active social life in London, many friends and connections, so why bother with Max?

"I can see you're confused. Sometimes I'm confused, too, why I kept trying with Max all those years. I suppose, like Kate, we worked on 'reforming the rake.'" A chuckle escaped his lips. "You'd understand that, being a devotee of romantic fiction and a novelist."

"Oh, I'm not a novelist, Mr. Davis. At least, not yet."

"Call me Peter," he smiled. "And I trust you will be one day."

So did I, most passionately. Publication of a novel was something every writer dreamed of and yet few achieved.

Which reminded me of the short story I'd sent off in the post. I told myself firmly I'd not give into depression if I heard nothing, for news came very slowly to the island.

"I'm afraid I have to leave tomorrow," Mr. Davis said. "I have to see my uncle. He lives on one of the islands."

"Oh? Shall you return?"

"Absolutely," he returned with a smile. "It's just an island hop for two days. You must understand, Miss du Maurier, I cannot leave Somner until this business is settled. Someone murdered my best friend, and I won't rest until the murderer"— he glanced caustically at Josh Lissot—"is punished."

CHAPTER TWENTY

"Did someone say 'island hop'?"

Inspired by Mr. Davis's excursion, Sir Marcus seized on an idea. "I daresay that's a splendid idea. I shall make all the arrangements. I'm very good at outings, you know. What do say you, Lord Rod? We could all do with some cheering up."

Everyone focused on the man who had recently lost his brother. "I suppose it would be something to do."

"Exactly so. Tomorrow too soon? How does the weather fare?"

And so a day trip and picnic dawned and I, for one, could not contain my excitement. I longed to explore all of the islands and was delighted to hear the party had settled on Tresco.

Transported in a convoy of motor cars to the ferry, we parted with Mr. Davis, who caught a different boat to see his uncle on St. Mawes.

"I do hope you'll be able to join us later," I overheard Kate say to Mr. Davis as we parted ways.

"I don't think so. Uncle William has a penchant for keeping me once I arrive. Another time, perhaps."

He left and I caught a fleeting glance of sadness drift over Kate's fine features. Was she thinking she should desert the penniless Mr. Lissot to marry the man who'd loved her so devotedly all these years?

I asked Sir Marcus.

"It's devilish odd: this Katie/Josh business. Are they together or are they not?"

As we were about to board the small schooner ferry, Sir Marcus and I lingered back from the others. "I don't think she's made a decision yet. She may feel guilty for deserting Josh."

"Guilt is no reason to stay." Sir Marcus's logical utterance accompanied us down the sunny ramp.

The day promised fine weather blessedly free of wind and rain. Such days were rare during winter and the sunshine inevitably brightened everyone's mood.

I sat next to Arabella on the boat. She looked quite attractive, abandoning her spectacles and donning a plain white summer's dress, her lank brown hair tied back with a red ribbon. Kate and Angela dressed similarly whereas I had opted for a skirt and blouse as was my custom, and we all took the precaution of bringing coats and umbrellas.

The men carried baskets from the kitchen and Roderick stood with the captain up in front. They chatted the entire time and I realized he felt more at ease with the working class than with people of his own. I began to understand the spartan tower, the overalls, and the boatbuilding business. Yes, it all suited the quiet, unobtrusive man. He'd make somebody a very good husband one day.

"Are you," Bella dared to ask me during the voyage, "and my cousin . . . ?"

Words failed her. Her desperation drew a profound sense of pity from me. *Unrequited love.* It mustn't be kind.

"You were very close to both your cousins, weren't you?" I replied, keeping my voice low and sympathetic. "I daresay within the family they hoped you'd marry one? I felt a similar attachment to my cousin at one time."

"It was my mother's fondest wish," she confided.

"And you love living here on the island, don't you?"

"Yes, I do."

"In answer to your question," I whispered, "I can say there is no attachment at present between your cousin and I—"

"And will you promise there never will be?"

She reminded me of Lady Catherine in *Pride and Prejudice.* I was Elizabeth Bennett being asked to steer clear of the quarry.

"I wondered," she went on, "if you and the Major—"

"Oh, no. We're just . . . friends," I decided at length.

"Sir Marcus mentioned Padthaway. Is that where you met the Major?"

I had no desire to embark upon a dissection of that period of my life. Fortunately, we arrived at our destination and the jolt sent me upright. Steadying myself, I maneuvered away from Bella so she and I could not continue our conversation.

Sir Marcus, of course, had noted the exchange. In fact, he noted a great deal too much.

"I think you're hiding something from everyone," I teased. "Are you a private investigator or a closet chronicler?"

" 'A closet chronicler.' I rather like the sound of that. . . . Watch your step, Daphne girl. We trudge a very fine path here."

Tresco. I especially looked forward to visiting the abbey

and the old shiphead museum, with varying figureheads dating back to the early nineteenth century.

Roderick willingly assumed the role of tour guide, betraying his passion for seafaring. I opted for the seat beside him on the hackney carriage that met us down at the dock.

"It became more than a hobby these last two years," he uttered with pride. "My little boatbuilding enterprise . . . the warehouse you visited up at the tower."

"Oh, yes. The tower," I echoed.

A tiny smile played at the corners of his lips. "You are an unusual woman, Daphne. Not many women envisage it as you do. They all seem to exclaim 'how can you live there!' "

I shook my head. "It makes me indignant. A tower is a wonderful place to live, though I suppose it gets very cold in the winter?"

"I've improved the heating capacity to a large extent. Surprisingly, parts of Somner are colder than the tower in winter, if you believe me."

"Why shouldn't I believe you?" I took a sideways glance at him. "Don't you ever fancy living on the mainland? London?"

"No," came the firm reply. "These islands are my life. I feel just as Augustus Smith must have felt in 1834 when he came to Tresco and built his house and gardens. He dedicated his future to creating a life on the island."

"Do you know the family at the abbey?"

"A little," he admitted. "You, I think, will fall in love with the place once you see it. It is like something out of a dream . . ."

"But your Somner House is very fine," I reminded him, "and your cousin is just as dedicated."

Roderick missed my humor, but understood my meaning. "I have told her again and again—"

"It's all right," I whispered. "But she does love you and the island."

"I know she does," he said, raising his eyes as if the fact were a thorn in his side, "and I've made the offer to her and Aunt Fran to live at Somner, but Aunt Fran despises the sea air. It is the isolation of her gentle country village she prefers where she's lived her entire life, so it's understandable. Bella, on the other hand, cannot leave her entirely and, to some degree, is trapped. I often say she should marry a good man. I tried to introduce her to a few but the society down in Devon spawns a disastrous lack of prospects and Bella refuses to spend time in London 'hunting a husband,' as she would say. She finds the exercise abhorrent."

Pride, I thought to myself. For if she really wanted a husband, wouldn't she make the effort? No. For years she'd planned to marry Max or Roderick and live on the island. Perhaps she hoped, in time, Rod would agree to enter into a marriage of convenience for companionship. In a prudential light, it would be a good match, as Roderick would need an heir.

The lack of an heir brought Mrs. Eastley and her son promptly to my mind. "I called upon Mrs. Eastley," I admitted to Roderick. "It surprises me she has no designs on Somner. Have you had much trouble with her father?"

If he was surprised by my interference, he didn't show it. "I'm afraid Max promised Jackson more than what is reasonable. Of course, my brother wasn't in a proper frame of mind at the time."

A slight frown passed his face, perhaps recalling how Sir Marcus and I had broken into the drawer and read Max's will.

"It seems he never was, now that I look back upon it. Even from childhood."

"Mentally ill," I whispered, "worsened by circumstance?"

"Yes," Rod confirmed a moment later, lightly touching the outward frame of my hand. "You've summed it up perfectly, Miss du Maurier."

Our first stop, the Abbey Gardens, proved a sweeping terrace of over twenty thousand rare, wonderful, and exotic plants from South America to the Mediterranean to South Africa and even New Zealand. The first walk captivated us from the start. It felt like we had entered another world, like the lost Lyonesse of King Arthur, perhaps. I'd read a little about the Isles of Scilly, but visiting this place sent a shiver of appreciation through my bones.

Exotic balmy palms, the essence of spiced plants, the unusually shaped flowers; every square inch had been carefully thought out and planned to achieve the look of a wild, random beauty, all surrounding the magnificent ruins of the twelfth-century church of St. Nicholas Priory.

Unstintingly loyal to any colossal mass flaunting splendid gray walls and ruined arches, I sighed in wonder at the towering proportions standing proud by the river, closing my ears to the running commentary on flora and fauna. The Abbey House and its cascading landscape interested me far more than the tour. I stopped to wonder who had lived here in the past and who enjoyed the house and its surroundings now.

"I will inquire whether the family is at home," Lord Roderick said to me, strolling off in the direction of the house.

I took another path, a path of scented hedges and fragile stone steps creeping to endless exotic niches. The garden's beauty arrested me, as did the house, and upon locating a garden bench from which to view the house, I sat down and daydreamed. I daydreamed I was the mistress of the Abbey House, and this was my garden.

"If I were a policeman, I would think you drunk with beauty."

The voice was teasing and all too familiar.

Keeping my eyes closed, I crossed my arms. "And if I were a police inspector, I would think you illegally on a case not your own. What are you doing here?"

Dressed in casual brown trousers and an olive green sweater, Major Browning strolled into my sunshine. Blinking open my eyes, I enjoyed the way the light danced across the fallen tendrils of his slightly unkempt hair.

Humor danced in his eyes. "I am merely here to enjoy the scenery . . . as are you."

"The devil you are. How did you get here? Did you follow us? Did you know we were coming?"

"Nice view, isn't it?" Without invitation, he sat himself beside me, stretching out his legs and resting his arms on the back of the bench. "I do so love to visit Tresco when I have the chance of it . . . and it so happened an opportunity arose and—"

"Do you know the family?"

"Yes. I am on intimate terms with Major Dorrien-Smith. Perhaps you've heard of him?"

I shook my head.

"He collects plants. You'd like him. Charismatic old fellow who's not, surprisingly, at home."

"You know that already?"

"Of course I do. I caught an earlier boat than you."

"Oh."

"Is there any news, Miss Sleuth?"

"I can't say, but, speaking of sleuths, Major Browning, when is the police chief to arrive? I suspect you are in possession of that information."

He shrugged. "Next day or so. Business is booming these days, particularly with random acts of violence on the islands. If Max Trevalyan had not been who he was—"

"Then nobody would have bothered to come," I finished for him.

Sighing, he moved closer to me.

I turned to him. "Do you mean to infer Max Trevalyan's case may now be resigned to the forgotten confines of a file?"

" 'The forgotten confines of a file,' " he repeated. "Lovely, Daphne. Quite lovely."

I beamed.

"But too wordy. 'Resigned to a forgotten file' reads much better. It's much more . . . *succinct*."

"And what authority do you have on the matter, sir? Are you a publisher, editor, or even a reader?"

"I am a *great* reader," he avowed.

"Is that so?" I lifted a contemptuous brow. "And what do you read? The latest yachting magazine? *London Life* weekly?"

"You do me severe discredit." He frowned. "I read upon a variety of subjects. From Shakespeare to Socrates, Dickens to du Maurier." He paused, an elusive grin twigging at the corners of his mouth. "Oh yes, I read your uncle's book."

"Did you really?" I was most impressed. "There aren't many copies available."

"I know," he groaned, "but having met his niece last summer, I decided to find out how the family wields the pen. How is your penmanship coming along, by the way?"

"Intolerably slow!" I said, but added that I'd managed to finish a short story.

"What kind of story?"

"Fiction. Just a silly little short work of fiction."

"You could have written a novel about Padthaway."

"I know . . . maybe one day I will. I'll have to change the names and the plot, of course."

"Of course," he agreed. "And have you sent off your story for publication yet?"

I didn't want to answer. I didn't want my fear of rejection shared among my peers, for I expected the parcel to be returned to me, red marks lining my typewritten pages, topped with a printed rejection letter. *Dear Miss du Maurier, I'm afraid your story does not suit our magazine at this time. . . .*

"I think it's a remarkable vocation, writing. You have the power to create anything."

For once, he sounded sincere and full of admiration. "Tell me something. Why did you follow me here?"

"I did not follow. Remember, I have some business with Dorrien-Smith. He asked me to bring him a certain plant."

"I thought you said the Major was not at home?"

"He isn't. He asked me over a year ago, but I thought it a good time to fulfill his request—since I am in the area and Lord Roderick told me of your plans to visit Tresco. Pure coincidence," he assured me, stretching out his long legs to further enjoy the sunshine and the view. "Yet can you imagine my delight to find you on the island. Now you tell me how you are enjoying this dubious little house party."

"Dubious?"

"Well, you can see for yourself how guilty they all appear."

"You are mistaken. We both know Josh is no murderer, and as for Sir Marcus, he is my friend."

"A risqué friend."

"No more than you," I retorted.

"Oh," he smiled, "I am delighted to hear I am your friend again. Gallivanting around the world's greatest estates and mixing with high society must produce a forgiving nature in you. But, by and by, did you know your friend Sir Marcus is 'Mysterious M'?"

"No!"

"But yes. Wonder what he shall write about this affair, hmmm?"

I gaped at him in utter disbelief, followed by shock and denial. I began to shake my head. It couldn't be true. However, thinking over the past weeks, from the very first day I'd met Sir Marcus, the possibility unfurled like the sails of a ship. It made perfect sense. Sir Marcus was the famous gossip columnist Mysterious M who reported on society's scandals and mysteries. Nobody knew his identity, but now that I thought about it, Sir Marcus was in the right position with the right contacts and he had the likable and trusting personality to do the job. "The phantom of society revealed," I murmured, unable to curb my astonishment. "Yes, that explains his experience with listening devices and so forth."

"What listening devices?" the Major asked.

"Oh." I saw I'd betrayed myself, so I relayed the conversation Sir Marcus and I had overheard between Kate and Josh Lissot. This led to other confessions; I couldn't help myself, for the Major's attentive, handsome face, keen to hear and to talk, encouraged me. I hadn't experienced such a rush of excitement for a long time and I think, I hoped, he felt it, too. Perhaps I allowed the fine day to carry me away in a romantic fancy, but something sparked between us that day, and I was eager to hold on to it.

"I love this place." His wistful appreciation brought fresh color to my cheeks as we strolled around the gardens later in the day. "I came here as a boy . . . and I never forgot it."

"It isn't a place you can forget. Serene and . . ."

Angela's raucous laughter spoiled the moment.

"Your sister sounds like she's having a merry time," the Major remarked, stepping to the side as the others descended upon us.

I tried not to scowl as Kate struck up an instant flirtation with the Major, bringing quick pallor to Mr. Lissot's cleanly shaven face.

"We are going to the museum," Angela announced gaily, usurping the role of tour guide. To the Major, she held out her hand. "How delightful to see you! Shall you join us for the picnic? We've *plenty*. You simply must join us, mustn't he, Roderick?"

"Yes, please do." Roderick, returning from the house, shook hands with the Major. "I am glad you have joined our party. Are your men here with you?"

"Sadly, no."

"Then we are very happy to have you." Angela nudged my arm. "Aren't we, Daphne?"

"Y-yes." A strangled sound emerged from my voice. "Very."

We headed for the museum, Roderick and the Major sharing a private chat while the rest of us lagged behind. So, I was wrong. The Major had been invited; he had not intercepted our plans and decided to follow. I felt a pang of disappointment.

"Daphne." Sir Marcus took my arm. "It was my idea to invite the Major. Does he join us for you?"

I glanced up at him with a secretive smile. Mysterious M, are you? Yes, it fit.

"What say you, Daphne girl? The Major is a shady fellow. He claims bad weather brought him to the island but I think he has come for another reason."

"Oh? What reason?"

"I think he's come for a woman."

I tried hard to swallow the lump rising in my throat. "You mean Kate."

"Yes, but not in the way you think. Although she has not admitted it, I believe she invited him, you know, at the same time we all received our invitations. I think this whole little holiday of ours is a diversion."

"A diversion for murder?"

Sir Marcus lifted his shoulders. "Perhaps, my girl. Perhaps."

Walking into the museum, I concentrated on the Valhalla collection. As I strolled past each relic born from the sea, from various shipwrecks over the ages, I envisaged each tragedy. Pausing by a painting of a beautiful woman dressed in a flowing royal blue gown, I stared up at her face and whispered, "Hello, Katherine Trevalyan. Did you murder your husband?"

"No, I didn't," came Kate's response from where she stood just behind me.

CHAPTER TWENTY-ONE

"Want to go outside? I fancy a smoke."

"I don't know what to say," I blurted. "Please forgive me."

"There's nothing to forgive." Snapping out her silver cigarette case, Kate smiled. She lit her black ebony pipe and stared out over the green as we moved onto the hall's veranda. "I know everyone thinks I did it, but I'm innocent. If I'd wanted Max dead, I would have paid someone to do it."

"And you didn't pay someone—"

"I know it looks that way. That horrible man Fernald twisted all of my words . . . and Josh's. He won't give up until he pins this murder on us both and"—she laughed—"I mean, who else could have done it but the wife and the lover?"

"Jackson?"

"Jackson," she said, her eyes narrowed, "and his daughter."

"They could have hoped to gain an inheritance," I went on, remembering that she did not know Angela and I had eavesdropped on the reading of the will.

"Fools. Roderick will be kind, but he won't give up Somner now that he has it."

"As has Arabella."

She looked at me and laughed. "Daphne, Daphne, you have a mind for a murder case. I prefer to think Max died of a random killing. If only we weren't so isolated, it may well have been the case. But he had a knack for making enemies faster than friends."

Seeing Angela and the Major a short distance away, I said: "I'm sorry for my silly ramblings, Kate."

She gazed at me then, her huge blue eyes turning sea green with tears. "You do believe me, don't you, Daphne?"

"Yes, I do," I replied, but I didn't. I didn't trust the way her eyes shifted when she spoke, or the way her brow furrowed. It was as though she was contemplating and choosing her words very carefully. She was too careful for innocence.

Hackney carriages carried us on a short tour of the island before we reached our picnic destination near the Trevalyan cottage. Despite my misgivings, I endeavored to be a pleasant companion and dismissed all thoughts of murder from my mind. I wanted to enjoy the fine day, the fine food promised us by Sir Marcus, and the scenery.

I thought of my poor parents in cold London, and Jeanne in wintry Paris. No, I wanted to be no place else but on that island, breathing in the fresh sea air.

The cottage, rented by the Trevalyan family over the years, resembled an old rectory one might find in the heart of Hertfordshire, gracing the far side of a sloping hill strewn with tiny blue and white flowers. Long grass bowed to the hum of a mild breeze and a maze of pale pink primroses grew up each side of the cottage.

Upon walking down the modest clipped path leading to the ancient stone house, I wished Angela and I could have rented the lovely place for ourselves. The caretakers, Mr. Trent and his wife, a contented plump couple of middle years, warmly greeted us.

From the moment we arrived, the couple bustled about, directing us down to the lake, where we planned to conduct our picnic, and I noted the particular regard bestowed upon Roderick. A gentle smile and nudge of approval here and there indicated their support of his inheritance. I pictured Max here, bringing his latest mistress, and I wondered if Mrs. Eastley had spent time at the cottage. When she found herself with child, had Max brought her to the cottage to bide the time until the birth?

Mrs. Dorcas Trent interested me. A robust Cornish woman with shrewd eyes, she missed little and I saw her place a sympathetic hand upon Kate's shoulder as we walked down the path.

"Daphne, do help me with this thing."

I hurried ahead to where Sir Marcus labored with a cumbersome gramophone.

"So you are Mysterious M?" I teased, pinching his arm and grabbing one side of his load.

Snagging his finger on the gramophone, Sir Marcus scowled. "I most certainly am Mysterious M, and if you breathe a word of it, I'll—"

"You don't have to worry." I smiled. "Your secret is in very safe hands. I won't breathe a word of it, I promise. Are you writing a piece on Kate and the scandals of Somner House, perchance?"

He colored. "It was my intention, but after Max . . . I don't know. Now, here's a good place to set it up."

"Music by the lake," I mused. "A charming idea."

Mrs. Trent instructed her husband to set up chairs by the lake and our men assisted Mr. Trent while she spread the blanket over the grass. In no time, a picnic laden with bread, fruit, ham, and cheese emerged to the lulling sounds of a beautiful composition.

"It's called 'Jazz in New York,' " Sir Marcus informed, trying to inspire us to dance.

I shook my head, preferring to keep my legs outstretched on the grass and to watch the black swans swirling in the lake.

Lord Roderick took a place beside me. "You're not going to dance with the others?"

From the corner of my eye I surveyed Kate and the Major engaged in a fox-trot, Josh and Angela laughing beside them. "No. You?"

"Certainly not." He grinned and reclined there in companionable silence.

After a time, I turned to him. "This is like a dream."

"Yes, it is, but I'm afraid to believe it . . . to believe what I hope is possible."

This dire admission drained some of my sleepiness away. "Why don't you believe good times are possible? They are yours for the taking. You don't need to bury yourself away in your tower, you know. It takes courage, but surely such happiness is worth the gamble."

"You're speaking of love," he laughed, his voice so soft it echoed with the afternoon breeze.

"Love is not alien to you." I reminded him of the book of poetry I'd seen at his tower. "If it were, you would never keep such a book on your shelves. I find the fact that you do most . . ."

My voice drained off. I couldn't find the word. I didn't want to encourage him unnecessarily, yet I felt the urgent need to promote the belief that love prevailed over all else. No struggle surpassed the truest love. I believed it with every fiber of my being, yet I, sadly, had not experienced it.

"Oh, Daphne," he murmured, not daring to face me, "I love how you live each day with such optimism. I sincerely hope your time at Somner hasn't been too catastrophic?"

I assured him it had not. His brother's death, though I dared not admit it, had interested me far more than it should. Was it a callous disregard for the victim, or a growing obsession with my study of life, the study of people and their motivations? I wondered.

"I wish I knew who murdered my brother, but he had so many enemies, who can tell?" Roderick asked.

"Jackson the gardener seems your most likely suspect," I said. "He has the greatest motivation. A daughter and grandchild to think of."

"No," came the gentle response.

I languidly turned my head to see Bella sprawled out as I was upon a blanket beside Sir Marcus and Angela. In amongst this happy crowd lay a resplendent Kate and the dashing Major. "Your sister-in-law says that she's innocent as well."

"I am sure she is. A man had to have done it, judging by his face."

I lowered my eyes.

"It's curious, you know, I thought Max was invincible. He survived the war and many scrapes in it only to die . . . like that."

"Whatever he did, he didn't deserve such a death."

My words echoed in the ensuing silence and Roderick suggested we join the others at cards. I stayed a little while apart, sensing the Major's amusement at my antisocial behavior. At social events, he had the upper hand, whereas I paled into the shadows.

When Mrs. Trent came to take away the basket and dirty plates, I offered to help and followed her inside the cottage.

"Bless ye, dearie, ye didn't 'ave to help me. I can do it on me own."

"Oh, I know you can. How long have you been here, Mrs. Trent?"

"Oh, a few years now, ever since I got married. It's a bit quiet and I miss Penzance, that's where I grew up, but it's a good livin' workin for the Trevalyans."

"It must have come as a great shock, Lord Max's death. Did he ever come here with . . . friends?"

I'd caught her unawares and her guilty expression answered me.

"I suspect she had the child here," I went on. "Is it true, Mrs. Trent? Did Lady Kate know of it?"

Mrs. Trent looked outside. "She knows everythin'. Lord Max had many vices, but at least he didn't keep secrets."

"She wanted a baby . . . Lady Kate. It must have been heart-wrenching when her husband's mistress bore the son she can never have."

Mrs. Trent arched her brows. "Well, that's the way of it. I know nothin' more of the matter."

I turned to leave her, knowing she thought I spoke out of bounds. But I had one last question. "What did you think of Rachael Eastley?"

"A lady. Not born one, mind."

Yes, but was she a lady with secrets?

CHAPTER TWENTY-TWO

"Daphne, what on earth are you doing out here?"

"Oh, hello Josh. I'm interested in this particular flower. Do you know what it's called?"

"I don't blame you." He grinned, kneeling down beside me in the garden. "I'm not very good with cards either. That's why I went for a walk, hoping . . ." He glanced down the hill to where Kate stood clapping her hands. "Women! I can't make them out."

"I am a woman, sir."

His keen eyes studied me. "So you are. But you're different somehow. You see people and you glean the beyond. I've watched you, you know. One has to keep aware of the quiet observers."

I laughed. "I am not entirely a hermit."

He smiled, his haunted gaze intent on the merry card group.

"I suppose it's too early to ask if you and she—"

"Plan to marry?" Scowling, he took the unusual blue flower from my hands. "Kate is like this flower. She's like a wild thing who has to be protected. How I wish I had better means to do so!"

"Both of you never imagined there would come an opportunity where marriage would become possible."

"No," he agreed. "We did not."

"And now it's awkward?"

"Devilishly awkward! I don't even know how to treat her. Friend? Lover?"

"Will she marry you?"

"I don't know," he murmured. "When this business is over, I guess we'll see."

"They cannot arrest you again, surely."

"They can and they will. For who else do they have but me?"

I followed his retreat down the steps to the others. Greeting him with fervor, Kate suggested we take a walk before we were due to catch the boat home.

Josh's lips tightened. My heart went out to him. He didn't know whether to go or to stay as he was forced to accept crumbs from his changeable lover.

"A walk," Sir Marcus protested. "After all this food and wine? I daresay that's a criminal offense."

So the party, save Sir Marcus, started out for a late-afternoon walk. The shoreline lay not far from the cottage. We strolled along the beach and into the hinterland beyond, exploring, absorbing the delightful sea air under the watchful eye of squawking seagulls.

What I enjoyed most was just listening, to the sound of the surf rolling into the solid backs of the rocks; to the crunch of the soft, sandy beaches beneath our feet; and the gentle breeze blowing across the hills.

"Hullo there!"

I stopped and shut my eyes. I could no longer hear the sea air. "Major Browning, you are not helping my cause at all. Shhh. Listen."

Grinning, he watched my effort to stand perfectly still and unruffled by his presence. "I think it only *proper* to advise that the wind is lifting your skirt, Miss du Maurier."

"I know it is but I don't care. Hear the storm coming? It is growing and shall strike soon."

And it did, with dire precision. A sudden lightning streak across the darkening sky and I jumped into the Major's arms.

"You should predict more often." His laughing breath caressed my forehead. "It's not every day you jump into my arms."

"I did not jump *willingly*," I pointed out.

"*Willfully*, you did. *Willfully*, you want to kiss me."

He was right. I did. There was something comforting about a storm brewing on the horizon and being wrapped in his arms. Throwning my pride to the wind, I gave myself to him completely, moving so close that I could feel his breath on my neck. I had taken him by surprise for once.

"Daphne!"

"Browning!"

"Now there's a name." Waving to our friends on the opposite headland, the Major reluctantly let me out of his arms. "Mrs. Daphne Browning. *My* Mrs. Browning."

"You are wrong. I shall never marry you," I avowed, nearly slipping on the rocks before he steadied me.

"I am never wrong," the Major returned, climbing down and holding out his hand for me to follow. "The fact is you need a husband to look after you. Otherwise, lightning will strike your head one day."

"I'm not an imbecile," I retorted. "I can take care of myself."

We'd reached a sharp stretch of jagged rocks. I faltered at the wide gap and he gallantly proffered his hand once more.

"I know you can take care of yourself, Miss Independent. Jump across now before the rain comes."

Grinding my teeth, I accepted his helping hand. We had nearly caught up to the others and must have looked a sight, running back along the beach to the cottage, the rain and thunder pelting down upon us. We all sat with blankets around ourselves within the fire-blazing parlor of the cottage.

"We'll have to stay. We can't go back now," Roderick declared.

A party of guests, stranded at her humble, wayside cottage by the sea, all demanding food and lodging for the night was quite the unforeseen occurence, but Mrs. Trent handled the situation with aplomb. Disappearing and reappearing, she pronounced the rooms ready and waiting, and to my eternal distress, it appeared that I would have to share with Arabella. Angela and Kate were in one room, Roderick and Sir Marcus in another, and Josh Lissot and the Major were designated the study enclosure.

Fresh towels and basins of steaming water awaited us in the bathrooms. I realized this was the primitive offering of a bath in such circumstances, and I offered Bella the opportunity to go first. She accepted without reservation, and I waited on the hastily made bed, quivering from the cold.

Eventually, she emerged and apologized for taking so long, to which I lamely smiled. Once inside the bathroom, I rolled my eyes. Could I survive a night with Bella? I knew she considered me a threat. When I emerged in my towel and began combing my newly washed hair, she eyed me with a tinge of hostility.

I sat down on the edge of my bed to dry my hair and put it in some kind of order. "Oh, did you ever think we'd be stranded here overnight!"

To my amazement, Bella, curled up in her swamp of warm blankets, sent me an uncharacteristic smile of quiet, self-assurance mixed with curiosity.

"Is there or is there not something between you and my cousin?" Her whisper shot out in the semidarkness.

"I . . . I cannot tell you," I stammered truthfully.

"Or is it the Major? I've watched you two together, too, and I won't allow you to hurt my cousin. He's doesn't like to be played."

I was about to answer "I am not the kind to do so" when my pride got the better of me. Knowing it would annoy her, I answered her question with a question. "I might ask something of you. Are you in love with Rod or with Somner House?"

She laughed the nervous schoolgirl laugh one makes when discussing boys and secrets. Discarding her blanket, she began to undress, stripping almost bare before me and parading her lithe figure about the room.

I turned an abhorrent eye. She did it for the purpose of an exhibition, to shock, to prove she was a desirable woman.

Determined not to give her any recognition, I feigned complete nonchalance. Outside, the wind howled as lightning flashed, and from down the hall, the gramophone started playing a French song I hadn't heard since the war.

Eager to get away from Bella and sacrificing my vanity by leaving my hair unset, I strolled out of the room and into a dream.

Lounging by the window, Major Browning lay reading a book, his profile partially softened by the lamplight, a gentle smile upon his lips as he listened to the lilting caress of Edith Piaf's "*Non, je ne regretted rien.*" The rest of the room, a collage of floral-covered chairs, faded carpet, burgundy-and-cream-striped wallpaper cluttered with small pictures of various animals and children's faces, and lamps, a dozen lamps adorning every nook and cranny, blurred into the background.

Since I approached quietly, the Major didn't see me at first. Choosing the opportunity to linger awhile in the shadowy hallway, I studied the man of many faces. Scotland Yard trusted him. My father respected him. *I* should rely on him. He had an interesting face more than a handsome one, I decided, his nose not quite aquiline but distinctive, his cheekbones and jawline well-defined, all leading down to the sensual curve of his mouth.

A peaceful radiant warmth accompanied me as I walked into the room. As his long fingers caressed the pages of the book, I choked away a sigh of longing for what could not be mine. A man like the Major was too well-liked by women to be anything more than a friend, and suddenly, seeing him in this repose, I wished it wasn't so. His hot gaze now fell upon me, slowly dissecting every inch of my unkempt appearance. A slow smile played at the corner of his mouth. He rose out of his chair and ever so subtly caught me, his hands cupping my face and his lips engaging mine in an ethereal, intoxicating kiss. Forces out of my control gripped us both and I suddenly understood the danger of passion.

"Well, well, here's a to-do."

Gaping dramatically from the door, Sir Marcus whistled.

"No, no, go ahead, my friends. I'm not one for interrupting romantic interludes."

Scarlet-faced, I detached myself from the Major. Fleeing to the safety of the vacant parlor, I proceeded to engross myself in the business of finding another record to play as, blessedly, Mrs. Trent announced the time for dinner and asked if we would like a predinner drink.

I said yes, hastily. Sensing my distress, Sir Marcus slid to my side the moment the others entered the room, all convivial and noisy as usual. Had I really wantonly kissed the Major? Had I really given him a glimpse of my inner soul, the secrets I guarded so passionately?

"There, there." He proudly patted my hand. "All fixed and all's well, as Shakespeare says." He next whispered, "I'm so relieved you're not a prude, m'girl. Though I *am* distressed you didn't pick *me* as your kissing partner."

I sipped my champagne and allowed it to drift straight to my head. I didn't care. I had to forget my momentary lowering of the guard. To no one had I shown what I'd shown Major Browning, a man who chatted amiably with Kate Trevalyan and Arabella Woodford as if nothing had occurred between us.

Thunder rumbled outside.

"How glorious," Angela laughed, clapping her hands. "We're stranded!"

"With only the clothes on our back," echoed Roderick, his curious, questioning eye darting from the Major to me.

I blushed. Did he know? Had he seen us? Oh dear. If he *had* seen me with the Major, what must he now think of me? Did he think me a wanton gadabout?

Roderick's good opinion mattered to me. He had displayed

a romantic interest in me by opening his mind and his heart and I did not wish to repay the compliment by flirting shamelessly with another man.

Apologizing for the lack of time to prepare a proper meal, Mrs. Trent shepherded us into the cramped dining parlor adjacent to the kitchen. It proved a tight squeeze accommodating all eight of us around her walnut country table. Her best linen and dinnerware had been brought out of the cabinet on the far wall for the occasion.

"Smells delightful," Sir Marcus said as he sniffed the air. "Roast beef and potatoes and Cornish pasty pies. Heaven!"

Bottles of wine lay open on the table and the Major swiftly rose to his feet to see to the ladies first, and then the gentlemen. Draped windows kept the terror of the storm outside, its odd clap of lightning and thunder heightening the drama of the occasion.

"Where on *earth* is Josh?" Kate muttered, poking around. "His dinner will grow cold or lies in deep peril of Sir Marcus devouring it." Smiling as Mrs. Trent brought out yet another tasty dish, she covered Josh's plate with a napkin. "It smells absolutely delicious, Mrs. Trent. You're a marvel . . . doing all this at the last minute."

Mrs. Trent beamed. Eager to impress, she left us to help ourselves to the roast beef and vegetables and potato pie wrapped in pastry.

"If Josh doesn't show up soon," Sir Marcus warned, heaping his plate to a pinnacle of splendor, "I'm afraid there won't be any left! And it's no good trying to hide that plate from me, Katie girl. I know exactly where it is."

"I ought to fetch him," Kate said, but the Major, as he was Josh Lissot's designated roommate, offered to do the duty.

He returned almost immediately, his face whiter than I'd ever seen before.

"Whatever is the matter?" Kato, half laughing at a quip of Sir Marcus's, looked up with an innocent, childish gaze.

"Mr. Lissot . . ."

There was a long pause.

"Mr. Lissot," the Major attempted again with a deep swallow, "is dead."

CHAPTER TWENTY-THREE

"Dead!" Angela shrieked. "Are you jesting, Major? Is this some kind of a midnight ruse?"

"No, it is not."

Dropping her knife, Kate sprang to her feet. "Whatever do you mean? It has to be a ruse! It must be! He can't be *dead* . . ."

She raced off toward his room. The Major tried to hold her back, indeed, he tried to hold all of us back, but like a herd of elephants, we hurried down the hallway and into the bathroom.

Poor Josh Lissot, murdered in his bath. A knife stuck out of his heart and I turned away, sickened at the sight of blood. It was tragic, but in death, he never looked more beautiful. His luxuriant black hair had curled around his face where a surprised expression remained fixed. I felt ill, so did the others, and Kate wept. Sliding to her knees, she hugged the corpse, her anguished cries cursing whoever had done it, whoever had committed the foul deed.

———

I don't think any of us slept that night. There was little to do; no authorities could be contacted in the middle of the night, in the midst of a wild, raging storm. We were stranded upon yet another island as mere visitors. Alone, we bore the tragic horror of Mr. Lissott's death, and I felt it most keenly after our conversation on the hillside. He had been so charming and kind and artistic; it seemed a dreadful waste of life.

"Why would anyone want to murder Josh?" Arabella whispered to me from the darkness of our bedroom.

"I don't know . . ." my voice trailed off, trying to think of a reason.

I couldn't find one. All I knew was that there were seven of us left and therefore seven suspects, nine including Mrs. Trent and her husband, but what reason could anyone have for stabbing Josh Lissot in his bath?

"It's very odd," Bella murmured despondently. "Poor Mr. Lissott. I don't know why Kate is so fickle. She's had many lovers and she was never a faithful wife."

"Was her husband faithful to her, though?"

"Max?" Bella laughed, a strange bitter laugh. "Goodness, no. And I suppose I can't blame her, really, for seeking love elsewhere. But I'll never forgive her for toying with Rod. You made him see other women are worthy of his affection. Not just her. That there *are* other women out there, ones just as interesting and desirable as she."

I registered the pain in her voice. Mentally assessing each possible suspect, I succumbed to the ugliness of it all. Death was never pleasant, but these crimes were particularly brutal.

I cursed the murderer, whoever he or she proved to be, for Josh Lissot was a good man and he deserved a better end.

I imagined Kate awake, crying, unable to believe that her

lover lay a stiff corpse a few feet from her bed. I grieved with her, secure in the knowledge that Angela would comfort her.

The morning confirmed her deep reliance on all of her friends. She needed them to help her through the dark tunnel of her life. She confessed her love for him to all of us, tearful, unable to eat her breakfast or even sip a cup of tea. She inconsolably grieved for the man she loved, who had suffered acutely on her behalf. He had been arrested and incarcerated, then liberated, only to meet with such a death.

The morning also brought with it the burning clarity that a murderer resided amongst us. *A serpent within the garden of discontent,* I scribbled down on a sheet of paper whilst sipping my coffee. There was little else to do. Numbed by the horror, we waited. We consoled Kate. We listened to the men discuss the business of the body.

It was quickly decided that it must accompany us back to St. Mary's and taken to Mr. Fernald.

"It's a good thing his boss has arrived," Sir Marcus said. "I doubt that man would ever catch a killer. He's too . . ."

"Priggish?" the Major suggested.

"That's not quite the right phrase, but it'll suffice. He failed to come up with a plausible end to poor old Maxie and now Josh at his bath. Disgraceful! Who'd kill a man at his tub? Most inconsiderate. Very ill-mannered and unmanly a thing to do."

"Don't trivialize the matter," Angela snapped from a far corner, holding Kate in her arms. "Can't you see it's distressing her?"

"Well, it's a distressing matter," Sir Marcus defended himself. "And if I appear heartless—"

"Yes, heartless," Angela insisted.

Seizing an armchair opposite me in the lounge room, Major Browning lifted a brow. "You are mesmerizing, Daphne." Bending his head low, so that only I could hear, he said it again.

"Mesmerizing," my soft echo transcended the silent chasm between us. "How does one know one is mesmerizing?"

"When one hears it from an ardent admirer."

I turned a deeper shade of scarlet. With him so close, so alluringly close, I completely lost my resolve.

"There shall be an inquiry, I suppose, into this death?" I brought the subject up purely out of fear to continue the other.

"More than an inquiry. And everybody has a motive. Even you."

"Me?"

"Inspiration," he teased. "Make a murder. Write a story about it. I can see you selling your story to the paper."

"I'll never be a journalist," I retorted. "I prefer fiction. And speaking of motivations, what are Sir Marcus's and Bella's then? They can have no reason for wishing Mr. Lissot dead."

He clicked his tongue. "The only one who is exempt in this affair is Mr. Davis . . . for he wasn't present at either."

"Or Rachael Eastley or her father, for neither are here now." I pointed out.

We both sat in silence. Sir Marcus soon wandered in, Lord Roderick not far behind him.

Offering my chair to Sir Marcus, I offered silent comfort to the long-suffering Lord Roderick as he patiently listened to Mrs. Trent's prattle.

"We'll have to rip out the bathtub," she told her husband, "and shut off the room." She shivered. "Ungodly thing to happen."

"We'll do no such thing," her husband challenged.

"Oh, yes, we will. It's awful and I'd be too frightened to stay . . ."

I drew Roderick away to the window to avoid the confrontation.

"A storm passes and another begins," he spoke, staring at the pale sun on the tranquil garden outside.

CHAPTER TWENTY-FOUR

We were all relieved to return to St. Mary's Island.

It was the grisly duty of the Major and Lord Roderick to bear the makeshift hessian bag containing the body. They were careful to shield Kate's eyes from it as much as possible, Angela's help being enlisted again, and Bella and I were called upon to oversee everything else.

"The murder weapon was one of Mrs. Trent's kitchen knives," Bella nudged me. "It's frightening to think one of us did it, isn't it?"

Her sharp eyes searched mine.

"Somebody must have had a reason to hate Josh," I surmised.

"You naïvely believe *logic* must always provide a reason for murder? Who defines logic, Miss du Maurier? You? I?"

Her reasoning haunted me because of its rationality.

Little conversation ensued for the rest of the drive. Arriving at the house, we all dispersed and I began to mix a little laudanum for Kate.

"No, *opium*," Kate pleaded, sprawled upon the bed in her

retreat room, for she professed she'd never again set foot in the downstairs bedroom, which had featured so extensively in her life with her dead lover.

Shoving her purse to me, Angela gave the instructions and I was dispatched to mix drugs. I'd never done so before and I felt decidedly uncomfortable. Angela said Kate needed something stronger than laudanum and asked who were we to say no under the circumstance. However, I would have preferred the recommendation of a doctor.

My task became harder when I saw Hugo hovering over the kitchen bench. Tired and irritable, I was in no mood to wait for him to finish cutting up vegetables. "I am in need of a spoon, Hugo. Quick, if you please."

Slowly putting down his knife, he gave me a passing sideways glance. I looked at the knife and shivered.

Fetching what I required, he returned to his vegetables and I returned to the darkened room. Drapes drawn, Kate moaned appreciatively when I put the tonic I'd mixed into her hands. "Oh, thank you, Daphne, thank you."

I watched as she faded into sleep, a smile on her face.

"It's the essence of supreme calm," Angela said. "I'll watch over her . . . you can go, if you like."

I nodded, watching Kate Trevalyan sleep, wondering how she'd ever recover losing a husband and a lover.

When I emerged from my room some hours later, I hesitated on where to go. Who did I want to see and whom did I wish to avoid?

Creeping downstairs and out the front door, I decided to go and see Mrs. Eastley. She'd find the news alarming, and in the delivery of it, I hoped she'd betray a confidence. I believed she was somehow involved in Max's death, and that her serene face was merely a veil to hide the truth.

Having put in the effort to come all this way into town when what I really needed was a good, long sleep, I pushed my hand on the door when advised she was not at home.

"It's quite important I speak with her, Nanny." I added the title as an afterthought, exactly as Mrs. Eastley did.

"She's workin'. If ye must see her, ye'll have to go there."

"Thank you." I smiled, and asked for directions.

I still had difficulty equating my well-bred Mrs. Eastley with the local pub and its auspicious name, the Fiddler's Pipe. In my estimation, Rachael Eastley did not belong to this world; I fancied her as a Victorian lady or a governess, soft-spoken and modestly dressed in widow's weeds.

Upon entering the bar, considering my intrusion, I came straight to the point.

Shock spiraled in her large eyes.

"We're all vexed over it," I went on, "*two* murders in such a short period of time."

A frown marring her delicate forehead, Mrs. Eastley silently removed her working apron. Leading me to a private room, she thanked me for taking the trouble to inform her in advance of these terrible tidings.

"The murder occurred at the cottage of Mr. and Mrs. Trent."

The news startled her as we leaned against an obliging wall in the cleaner's room.

"Mrs. Trent helped deliver your baby, didn't she?"

The answer was long in coming. "Yes. How is Mrs. Trent? You left her well, I trust?"

"Troubled, to say the least."

"In the early days," she said, a light laugh escaping her lips, "long ago now, Max and I used to meet in this room. Dear Max . . . he had a gentleness to him back then. The drugs killed it, more surely than any war."

"Are you afraid for your son's life?" I whispered after a moment's silence.

"Not from Roderick Trevalyan. I'm sure he'd never do anything to harm the boy."

"But from someone else?"

"Yes," she breathed, sighing. "I don't trust Arabella Woodford. I never have. I fear *she'd* hurt my boy if he were ever to venture into Somner House."

In appreciation for Mrs. Eastley's confidence, I shared my own misgivings about Bella.

"I believe *she* finished Max off after my father witnessed Josh Lissot and Kate Trevalyn drag him out of the house."

"Could your father have killed Max to protect you?"

"Oh, he'd *threatened* to do so often enough, but I know my dad. To kill Max when he had agreed to his demands doesn't make any sense. Dad wants Somner for my son, who is the true heir. You know these old families in Cornwall often include illegitimate contenders to title?"

"Which is why you're still afraid. For your son."

She nodded in the darkness, retying her apron. "Daphne, *do* be careful up there. Please, let it not be *you* next."

I left Hugh Town decidedly uneasy. Rachael Eastley's words haunted my every step as I crossed the fields of heather and made my return to Somner House.

"Somner House," I whispered, "a subtle peril grows within you and all those around you. What is your secret?"

My uneasiness increased the moment I hung my coat by the front door. An eerie silence pervaded the empty parlor, the grotesque paintings of war too true to life.

The door creaked behind me and I jumped.

"Forgive me." Mr. Davis blundered in, shrugging off his greatcoat. "I should be more soft-footed. My mother always said so. Oh dear, is something the matter? Where are the others?"

By his countenance, I could see he hadn't heard the news yet. I lingered in the corridor, wondering if he'd betray his relief at his rival's death. "How is your uncle? I trust you found him well?"

His brow furrowed before he smiled. "Oh, he's not really my uncle. A friend of the family, but we've always called him uncle. He likes to fish— Dear me, are you all right, Daphne?"

I told him of the murder.

"Josh Lissot! Dead! But how? When? *Who?* Blast! I wish I was there. I wish I was on hand to . . ." He glanced upstairs. "I have to go to her. I have to see—"

"I don't think that's wise right now." I stopped him. "She's sleeping."

I neglected to mention the opium but I guessed, having known the couple so intimately all these years, that he was aware of Kate's occasional indulgence.

"Oh, I see . . . yes, you're right. Sleep is the best thing. She's had too many shocks, and if you're going up there, can you check on her for me? Give her a message?"

"Yes, I can, if my sister allows it. She's guarding her."

"Kate is very lucky to have your sister. My message is just an embrace. Will you do that?"

"I will," I promised.

When I went to look in, the room was very dark, and the lamps were turned down low. I heard the peaceful breathing of a deep, dreamless slumber and there the two of them lay, like frightened children, wrapped in each other's arms.

On the little bedside table, I glimpsed a discarded note. Tiptoeing closer, careful of the treacherous floorboards beneath my feet, I reached over to retrieve it. So slow and methodical in my movements, I knew I'd not wake them, not in the midst of a drug-induced lethargy. I began to read the tear-blotted scrap of paper.

> *Kate,*
> *I'll kill myself if I can't have you.*
>   *Not after all we've been through.*
>   *Please answer me. You know I didn't kill*
> *Max and I long to take care of you as my wife,*
> *even if I am of little means.*
>   *Kate, Kate,*
>
>   *I love you,*
>   *Josh.*

My heart swam with pity. Could he have taken his own life? How loathsome and how tragic and I wished—I wished—I could have talked him out of it. I wished I'd paid more attention to him that day on the hillside. The fragile flowers we had so admired were represenative of him—not his erstwhile lover. She must have given him her answer that day.

I felt ill. I wish I'd been there for Josh instead of wandering off and enjoying the Major's company. Why hadn't I been more thoughtful? Why hadn't I even bothered to look for him? One look at his face and I should have known . . .

Once in my room, I went over the day in my mind. I had been too immersed in my walk and Major Browning's kiss to perceive anyone else's pain. Josh had walked with Bella and Roderick most of the day, if I remembered correctly, while Kate, Angela, the Major, and Sir Marcus had sauntered on ahead.

Suddenly, all thought deserted me and I drifted to sleep. I dreamt of a dark sky and ferocious birds circling the tower, restless with their beaks and barbed teeth, resembling rats. I stood their victim, partially concealed inside the tower, praying the shadows kept me safe. The sky turned red and Rachael Eastley's face appeared out of a mist, perfect and serene as she looked over Max's body and began to laugh, her black hair blowing in the wind.

I woke with a fright. Hunting for my clock, I saw it was five thirty. I tried to sleep a little more but the nightmare prevented me from it. Frustrated, I switched on the light to write. Scribbling down a wild collage of random names, thoughts, suspects, desires, secrets, motivations, actions, personality traits, and background information. I eventually circled four names. Content, I awaited the new day.

"I have to know who did it!" I announced, barging into Sir Marcus's bedroom.

Darkness enshrouded his body as he plied a pillow over his head. "Oh, go away! Whoever it is, I've only just gone to bed."

Navigating my way through his discarded clothing, I yanked back the drapes. My startling action caused him to turn seedily on his side, propping up his head, one eye open and his brow testy.

"I know who did it," I blazed on, triumphant. "At least, one of these four." I shoved the piece of paper before his blood-shot eyes.

"Blimey, girl. Can you write any smaller? I can scarcely see a thing!"

"It's the whiskey, not my writing," I informed, sitting down beside him. "So this is how you keep a room. . . . I'm afraid us being married won't do at all, for you are decidedly too messy."

A lazy shrug rolled over his shoulders as he sighed, collapsing back onto his pillow to read the names on my list aloud. "Bella, Jackson, Kate, and . . . *Kate?* Have you gone mad? Have you taken leave of your senses?"

"Yes, and no. If you think about it, everything revolves around one person: Kate."

"And the saintly Mrs. Eastley? She doesn't fit into the equation?"

"She is merely a mother protecting her son. She has no motivation to kill his father."

"It's . . . possible that you are correct."

"Thank you for your confidence in me."

"I suppose you and Major Magnificent have worked all this out."

I gave him a woebegone look. "Why ought we when Mysterious M is on the case?"

He blinked, and a curl of pleasure wound its way through his quivering lips. "I must say, I am flattered. You know another word for flattery is 'to gloze.' Scribe that down, novelist, in your doodles."

"Doodles? I certainly do not doodle."

Sitting up, he failed to make any effort to correct his mis-shapen, spiky hair or the fallen order of his singlet. He did, however, snatch a blanket to conceal his bed-shorts with some modicum of dignity. "You do realize, Miss Daphne, you have compromised yourself by coming here in all this lather to see me."

"Oh, please. We're in the *twentieth* century now—"

He coughed. "I beg to differ. Your parents, I am sure, would severely disapprove of you entering the apartments of a bachelor, unchaperoned."

"But Angela—"

"Angela," he declared, sounding very much the schoolmaster, "lacks your refinement."

I assumed he was teasing me and called him the "Chief of Gloze" in return. A deep-throated laugh rumbled out of his mouth.

"Shhh! We'll wake them."

"Wake whom, Miss Daphne? The drugged or Miss Wooden Woodford? If it's the latter, I'd dispense with the pretenses. She already knows you're in this room by now. She keeps tabs on all of us."

My face turned scarlet.

"And will probably publicize the fact at breakfast . . . to ruin your honor in the eyes of your copious suitors."

"I do not have copious suitors."

"You have two. Major Magnificent and Lord Roderick Trevalyan. Perhaps Davis, too . . . he seemed rather taken with you. Ah," he said, tapping his lips thoughtfully, "perhaps our Katie will now accept his proposal? It's either him or Rod. She is the marrying kind of girl. Needing money . . . and security . . ."

"That's no reason to marry," I snapped.

"I've offered her an alternative," Sir Marcus admitted, referring to his role as a rich benefactor. "A living, as my secretary. And I can set her up in her own studios if she wishes and support her until she gleans out enough patrons of her own."

"That was very kind of you," I replied, slightly envious.

"But, of course, she refused."

"She refused! Why?"

"I don't know. You're a woman. You work it out."

To do so was to paint a picture first of a woman who needed to be cared for, nurtured and cherished, protected and loved at all times. And I saw that her best choice was Mr. Davis. Friendship and intimacy and a happy marriage would free her to pursue a career as an artist. Mr. Davis would only be too happy to oblige, knowing better than any how much she had endured with Max. Max and Kate, the answer lay somewhere in their tragedy.

"Don't sit there gaping like a mummy," Sir Marcus scoffed. "You might start drooling and I won't wipe up the dribble, I warn you."

"I'm sorry. I must go."

I fled from the room before he could stop me.

I couldn't be stopped until I knew the identity of the murderer for certain.

It was a risk that I alone must take.

CHAPTER TWENTY-FIVE

I thought of the great detectives G. K. Chesterton and Sherlock Holmes. I was no great detective, nor did I aspire to the title. It was people who interested me, their desires, their secrets, their regrets, their loves, hates, and revenges.

That's why I placed a letter under suspect number four's door before rejoining Angela in our room.

"Isn't it a glorious day, Daphne?" Yawning, Angela twisted herself away from the window.

I joined her at the window. Somner House in the morning. Nothing could compare to the exotic pattern of trees winding to the beach, the strange call of the island birds hiding in the branches, the sea air rustling those wintry leaves.

"Aren't you glad you decided to come along? I told you it would be interesting."

"Yes, interesting," I murmured. "Two deaths and one sister who seems strangely happy about the fact."

"Oh, pooh! If you knew half the things Max did to Kate, you'd be glad, too."

"I was speaking of Mr. Lissot."

Her mouth hardened and I watched her return to her side of the room to sort through her clothes.

"And how is our Kate? And how are you?" I whispered.

"Fine," she snapped, maintaining an air of indifference I knew she didn't feel. "It's Kate's life. And if she chooses him, Davis will provide handsomely for her. She won't want for anything." A grim smile appeared on her lips. "Men! Who needs them? They're a blight, a weakness, a plague among women. But I cannot dissuade her. She insists Davis is a good man who will cherish and protect her. Cherish and protect! Ha! It sickens me to hear it."

After a moment's reflection, I spoke my fears. "You do see we're in danger here, don't you, Ange?"

She eyed me sharply. "Danger?"

"There's a murderer on the rampage. None of us are safe."

"Max was murdered, but Lissot took his own life, Daphne."

"Yes, I know. I read the note."

The force of my confession struck her. "Did you *spy* on me last night?"

"By accident," I protested.

I shivered, though the room burned with the sun's morning light. I envisioned Angela reading Josh Lissot's note, tiptoeing to where he lay in his bath, plunging the knife into his heart, shoving her hand over his mouth so he couldn't cry out. I studied her from the corner of my eye, sickened to see an ugly purple bruise emerging on her left arm. "How did you get that?"

"Get what?"

"That bruise on your arm."

She averted her eyes. "Oh, I ran into the door of the cottage."

Since the Major's ongoing residence in the house, I took more trouble with my appearance, though I was loath to admit it.

"Angela, can I borrow your pink lipstick?"

"Sure." Gliding to the window, Angela hurled her makeup case to me.

Opening the silver case containing a cache of theatrical wonders, I rummaged through to the desired item. It was when I zipped the case back up that I noticed the blood. Blood? I dropped the case as though a snake had bitten me. The pouch was large enough to have concealed a kitchen knife. Shaking, I painted my lips pink to the sound of Angela singing, nausea squirming in my stomach.

Perhaps she'd forged Josh's note? Perhaps he'd intended to kill himself and at the last minute needed help and Angela obliged?

I shook my head free of such nonsense. It was a preposterous notion . . . Angela, no, no, not even an intoxicated Angela, could have committed such a heinous crime.

"Hurry up, Daphne, we'll miss breakfast."

Pinning my hair up halfway as I walked down the stairs, I prayed my face did not betray my fears. Nervousness had a penchant for reflecting on my face and I must not allow my suspect to guess my identity.

As the clock in the dining room struck nine thirty, I shivered. Who was I to stir up a hornet's nest? I doubted even the best detectives lowered themselves to use a baited note to flush out a suspect.

"Sir Marcus said you woke him." Adjusting her spectacles,

Arabella eyed me with the contented smile of a well-fed cat. "I wondered what all that noise was in his room."

I felt the heat rush to my face. Roderick, I noted, quickly discarded his paper and the Major's brow flickered upward as Kate stirred her coffee, cooped up in the far corner with Mr. Davis and Angela.

"Splendid news," Sir Marcus grinned, hitting his coffee cup with a spoon. "Daphne is to become Lady Oxley. Cannot compromise a girl rousing a bachelor from his bed, now can I?"

"He's joking," I laughed, careful to avoid the Major's inquisitive gaze.

Sir Marcus gave me a severe frown. "You wound me terribly, Daphne girl. I do quite fancy you as a wife, you know, waking me up early in the morning with a hot cup of tea."

Mr. Fernald's superior, the chief inspector assigned to our case, called an hour later, as we'd all repaired to the outdoor terrace to enjoy fresh tea and sunshine. Hugo let him through the door and I saw Kate shudder.

"Good morning, ladies and gentlemen."

Inspector Zoland, a bald man, short and well-dressed and with gray hooded eyes, waved his cane at us. "After reviewing the facts, I am of the opinion that Mr. Lissot did not take his own life, but was, in fact, murdered. And as for Lord Trevalyan's untimely demise, I am not satisfied as to the cause. My lord, I shall prevail upon you to allow me to interview your guests."

"You are welcome to conduct your interviews in the library, Inspector," Lord Roderick offered.

"We'll interview each of ye in turn . . . startin' now," Mr. Fernald declared.

My distaste for the man increased as I witnessed how much he enjoyed wielding his power to inspire fear in others. Did he abuse this power, I wondered? Was he susceptible to bribery?

"Miss Daphne." Fernald's voice sent my heart pounding. "If you will come this way, if ye please."

Stumbling to my feet, conscious of all eyes intent upon me, I obediently followed the policemen.

I began to tremble. Why had they chosen me first? Surely they did not suspect *me*? What reason could I have for murdering Josh Lissot or Max Trevalyan?

Enclosed in the library where books no longer radiated comfort, I wrung my hands together. I missed my father. I missed his strength and authority in the face of a creature such as Fernald. It was clear he meant to conduct the interview with the chief inspector looking on, making notes in his little pad.

Fernald opened his leaf pad. "I want to know your precise movements on the day Mr. Lissot was murdered. There was a storm. What time did you arrive back at the cottage, Miss du Mure?"

"It's du Maurier." I glared at him. "And I never carry a watch but it must have been around five o'clock. Yes." I nodded, remembering the sky.

"You shared a room with Miss Woodford that night. Give me an exact account of what you did upon your return."

I stammered through the events of the evening.

"So, ye say you went to the lounge room early? Can anyone vouch for this claim? Mrs. Trent, perhaps?"

"Major Browning," I whispered, heat rising to my face. "He was there also."

A slow curl emerged on Fernald's too-thick lips. "You and the Major . . . are intimate?"

I shot to my feet. "Certainly not! And I *resent* the insinuation."

"But ye've a habit, Miss du Maurier, of poking into places, don't you? Sir Marcus's bedroom, for one?"

My face turned redder. I don't know how the man had come upon this information. Had he been eavesdropping outside the breakfast parlor while waiting for his superior?

"Sit down, Missy."

I sat down, wishing I had the fortitude to throw a book at him. He was the most odious man I'd ever met and I vowed to make him into a villain in one of my novels. A horrible creature who preys upon the innocent . . . a tyrant . . . a tyrannical innkeeper, I decided.

"I cannot conceive Miss du Maurier's motivation to stab Josh Lissot at his bath," Inspector Zoland observed from his seat. "But the sister is another matter."

"Angela?" I feigned surprise. "*Kill* Josh Lissot? Are you mad?"

My mind raced ahead. Was Angela to be interviewed next?

"I think this one's hidin' something," Fernald said. "She's trying to protect somebody and that somebody would be a sister, eh?"

Eh? I bit back a retort.

"I am hiding nothing," I maintained, folding my arms across my chest.

"When did you last speak to Mr. Lissot, Miss du Maurier?" Mr. Zoland asked.

"Before the storm."

"Did he seem upset? Out of sorts to you?"

"Yes, he was worried about how everything would turn out."

"His innocence proven so he could marry Lady Trevalyan?"

"Yes, I suppose so."

"One more question, Miss du Maurier. In your opinion, was Josh Lissot a man capable of suicide?"

I delayed my answer in hope of protecting Angela, but Josh Lissot deserved my honesty. "I don't know."

Once dismissed, I let out a sigh of exasperation just as Bella advanced upon the library door.

Smiling, she moved toward the door handle and I moved out of her way. If anybody had something to hide, it was she, I grumbled to myself.

Eager to forget the whole affair, I escaped to the gardens, to a little corner I'd found where a stone wall covered with climbing roses, clematis, and wisteria looked out to sea. Numerous pots with struggling pelargoniums, verbenas, and heliotropes stood as lovely guardians to a luxuriant border hedge shaped into a circular oval design. There was no garden chair in the middle so I sat cross-legged on the green lawn and caressed the soft grass. The promise of spring blossomed all around me, and I longed for it.

" 'For throughout every new mystery and journey / Is an expanse of new stimulus for all eternity.' "

Blinking twice, I looked to my side to see Roderick Trevalyan.

"May I join you?" he asked.

"Y-Yes, of course. It is your home, my lord."

He sat down and I smiled. "You will get your suit soiled."

"I care not," he shrugged, looking back at the house. "I never did care for the privileged life. I am far happier building boats."

"And reading poetry. Who was the poet you quoted just now, by the way?"

"Me."

"True? Why didn't you say so before?"

He raised a modest hand. "I've done it since a boy. It's a private passion of mine, one my father hated. So did Max. But my mother encouraged me and one day, without my knowing, she'd shipped off my compilation to London and they accepted it."

I was astounded. "They accepted it? Just like that?"

"Yes, I have a published copy in the tower, if you're interested."

"Here I dream of being a writer and you are already one! It's very selfish of you to keep this talent to yourself, you know."

A light laugh drifted from his lips, bringing out the blue of his eyes. A deep Mediterranean blue, I thought.

"Daphne . . ." His eyes deepened with new meaning. "I know we have only known each other a short time, but nothing would give me the greatest pleasure if you would agree to be my wife."

I was lost for words, but flattered beyond belief. I didn't know what to say.

"You needn't answer straight away. No doubt you'll need time to consider the proposal and I've no wish to press you. Take as long as you like. Take a year, if need be. I will still be waiting for you."

That meant a great deal to me. He considered my needs before his own, further proof of his very good character. A good man. He almost fulfilled all of my criteria. Except he lacked one critical element. Like all young women I imagined how it ought to be, the romance preceding marriage, that flush of instantaneous joy, that wild abandon symbolizing absolute clarity . . .

A clarity I felt with only one man.

Major Frederick Arthur Montague Browning II.

I did not tell Angela about Roderick Trevalyan's proposal.

I had no wish to hear her laugh.

CHAPTER TWENTY-SIX

"Horrid senile creatures!"

Cursing, Angela strode into our room after her interview. "How dare they infer *I* did the deed to win Kate. Ha!" She scoffed. "I showed him the letter. It proves Josh took his own life because he feared Kate would not marry him. It wouldn't have worked. There would be no money. She's struggled enough with Max to start a new struggle."

"But shouldn't love defeat all?"

"Remember Marianne and Willoughby from *Sense and Sensibility*? Marianne thought so, too, but later she realized that if they'd taken that course, one party or the other might begin to resent life and regret the choice."

"So Kate's chosen Davis and money?"

"She's not said yes to Davis *yet*," she fired back.

I let a minute or two pass between us. "Ange, please say you didn't forge Josh's suicide note."

She stopped sorting out her laundry, turned to me, and I read the answer in her eyes.

"But *why*? Why did you do it? You could get into trouble if they find out."

She began to cry. "I had to protect myself, Daphne."

"How did you copy his handwriting?"

"I've seen his letters to Kate. He likes to leave little love notes around for her. They're everywhere."

"You invaded her privacy?"

A whimsical smile touched her lips. "You've done the same, little sister, so don't judge me."

Sickened, I faced her squarely. "Did you push the knife into Josh?"

She glanced away, to reflect, to choose what to confess, and what to keep secret. "It's funny." She shook her head, resuming a seat on her bed, like a caught-out child preparing for the parental lecture and punishment. "I've seen a few threaten to do it before but I didn't think he had it in him . . . or that I should be there to witness it."

I joined her on the bed, squeezing her hand. "What happened? How far and to what extent did you assist him? Angela! How could you?"

She shrugged off my hand. "I didn't do it. When I found him, I tried to stop the bleeding, but it was too late. I'd just run back to fetch my bag. Silly me, I'd forgotten it, otherwise I'd have never been there to hear his cry." Tears spilled down her cheeks. "Oh dear, Daph, I'm in real trouble. That odious Bella saw me exit. She told them, no doubt, and when they match the timing, they'll charge me. *Charge* me with murder!"

I held her close, patting her back as she sobbed all over my blouse. "So you found him in the bathroom with the knife at his chest."

"Yes, yes. But by the time I reached him, he was dead," she said through her sobs. "It was awful . . ."

I pictured the scene, thinking hard, desperate to find a way to help clear her name.

She shut her eyes. "The blood . . . I'll never forget the blood."

"Surely, Mr. Zoland will believe you if you tell the truth."

"No, he won't." Hot, salty tears blinded her eyes. Inconsolable with fear of losing her future, of facing the unavoidable scandal and a prison sentence, or even death, she began to shake. "I'm so scared, Daphne, I'm so scared. . . ."

"So am I." I hugged her tight. "So am I."

Later, I learned that Angela had played her usual nonchalant self to Mr. Zoland. She'd been vague on details, and said she'd seen no one.

The lie would go against her and I anxiously glanced at the tiny clock ticking away in our room. Zoland and Fernald were in conference, comparing their notes, deciding my sister's fate.

"Have you confessed all this to Kate?" I brought Angela a cup of tea as she lay inert on her bed, her eyes staring at nothing.

The staring eyes closed. "No. She'd never forgive me for not saving him. She wouldn't understand."

"She deserves the truth. I will help you, if you like."

New hope blazed in her eyes. "Would you? But I mightn't be able to see her before they take me away this afternoon."

"If they do, you'll just have to be strong," I said, assuming the elder sister role.

"I'll kill myself!"

Expecting her dramatics, I waved my finger at her. "No,

you won't kill yourself. You've too much to live for and I'll find a way . . . I'll find a way, I promise."

The vow rolled off my tongue as a curt knock sounded at the door.

Angela froze. "They're here. They've come for me already!"

"Shhh!" I ordered, getting up to answer it. "Try and be calm."

I've never felt so relieved in all my life to see Sir Marcus's shining face at the door. "Oh, thank heavens it's just you."

"Who did you think it was? Is that Angela crying?" His head poked curiously into the room. "Bad time?"

I nodded, closing the door so we could talk in the corridor.

"Er, is Angela all right? Anything I can do?"

"You may as well tell him," Angela sighed from behind me as she opened the door. "They'll all know soon enough and I don't want you two whispering in the corridor. It's obscene."

Granted entry into our bedchamber, Sir Marcus tiptoed in. "Now it is *you* ladies who are compromising my honor." He swooped down beside Angela. "So, what's the catastrophe, my girl?"

"She lied about witnessing Josh's suicide," I said.

"Aha."

After listening to Angela's story, Sir Marcus paced the room to deliberate. "*Josh Lissot, the lover of Lady Kate, murders her violent husband out of defense. Josh Lissot, the abandoned lover of Lady Kate, takes his own life out of an unwillingness to face the future. An eternal gloomy future, he feared doomed commissions, an inability to pay his rent, and endlessly dodging creepy creditors.* There, how does the column sound?"

"Worthy of the Mysterious M," I said. "Are you sure you did not murder Max to write it?"

"What? *Moi?* Murder to compile a column? I think not.

But, my dear Daphne, I fear we must distract the inspector from investigating Angela's hand in the crime by fishing out the real murderer here—the real murderer everybody's missing."

Suddenly, I remembered the trap I'd laid for my chief suspect and now dreaded the result.

It was not difficult to find the Major, who was draped languidly across a divan humoring Kate, whose legs dangled over the armchair to his right.

I hesitated before entering the room.

She laughed as he endeavored to divert her from all the unhappiness and terror of the past few weeks. She lapped up every morsel.

Resenting my errand, I made an awkward entry, apologizing for the intrusion.

"Oh, it's no intrusion," Kate assured me. "Do come and join us, Daphne. Is Angela with you?"

"Er, no. She's resting."

She nodded while emitting a feminine yawn. How did she manage to retain her magnetism in such circumstances? And then it occurred to me. She and the Major possessed the same quality of composure. They'd been born with it. Rachael Eastley had it, too, and I thought it an interesting character study for a future novel.

Chewing on my lower lip, I petitioned the Major. "May I have a private word with you if you can spare a moment?"

"Go ahead." Kate winked. "I am not one to stand in the way of an engagement."

Amusement was apparent on her face, so I kept my remarks

to myself until we were well out of earshot. "She's free now, you know."

"Who is?"

He stood beside me, his hands in his pocket.

"Lady Kate. She's lovely. She'll make any man a good wife."

"A good wife?"

"Yes, Mrs. *Katherine* Browning . . . it has a ring to it, wouldn't you agree?"

His dark eyes arrested mine. "Since we are on the subject, what is between you and Roderick Trevalyan?"

A telltale color rushed to my face. Oh, no, had he seen me out in the garden with Lord Roderick? Did he think we were together? After he and I had shared that kiss in the cottage?

"If you must know, Roderick proposed and I—"

He laughed. "You are an amazing girl—two proposals from two lords in one year. I salute you."

"It is *not* like that and you know it."

"Not like what? Many would assume it a grand achievement. So, what if one fell through? Roderick Trevalyan may not be as dashing as Lord David Hartley but he's still a *lord* with a *castle* and that's what you want, isn't it?"

His taunt caught me off guard. In my heart of hearts, I had to admit it. I dreamed of marrying a lord with a castle. But what Major Browning did not understand was that lords with castles came in many forms and not always in a literal sense.

"If you do choose this lord and castle, you have my sincerest felicitations."

"You think I'd marry a man just because he owns a castle?"

"It is one of your prerequisites, is it not?" Cynicism and jealousy stained his face.

"No, it is *not* one of my prerequisites. I'd be a dreadfully shallow person if it were. I didn't come out here to talk about this anyhow. It's—" I broke off.

"You are pale." He squeezed my hand. "What's the matter?"

He didn't let my hand go. I glanced at the ground, shifting my feet from side to side.

"What is it?" He pressed my hand again, gentle, yet firm.

"It's Angela . . . Oh, Frederick, I fear she's done something dreadful. She happened upon him as he took his own life. She was at the scene of the crime."

I gazed up at him, watching him slowly digest my words.

"Does anyone else know of this but you and me?"

"Sir Marcus—"

"Sir Marcus! You went to him before me?" Snatching his hand away, he glared ahead of him. "You give that man too much credit. He uses information and scandals to profit from it."

"He doesn't need the money."

"No, but he needs the fame. He thrives on it."

"If he thrives on it, why does he remain anonymous?"

He couldn't deny my reasoning.

"What will happen to my sister? I don't know what to do. Should I telephone my parents? Angela is beside herself. She's convinced they will arrest her."

"She's probably right."

"I'm afraid she'll do something to herself and we've had enough death around here." I despised myself for starting to cry.

"There, there." He drew me within the circle of his arm. "Don't fret, dear girl."

"It was mercy that made her run to him," I breathed into his warm chest, wanting to shut my eyes and remain in his arms forever. I didn't want to face the day. I didn't want to face my sister's future.

CHAPTER TWENTY-SEVEN

They took Angela away, as the Major had predicted.

I stood alone to watch her go, her pale face drawn at the window of the car as she gave me one last backward glance. I'd never seen Angela so afraid, so uncertain.

"I must see Kate," I murmured, mulling over how best to break the news.

I found her resting outside on the terrace, large dark glasses covering her eyes. Even in repose, she looked cool and calm, like an English lady relaxing on the deck of a ship. As I made my approach, she stretched out a casual hand to raise her sunglasses, inviting me to sit beside her in the next recliner.

"It's odd, you know," she said, "I've been mistress of this place for so long, I don't know what to do with myself now that I must leave it."

Adjusting the lever on my chair, I pitied her sad smile.

"I think I will go to town for a while and not make any hasty decisions," she said, and shrugged. "Sir Marcus promises I won't be penniless and Roderick's a generous soul. He's given me an annuity, just like was done for Rachael Eastley."

Her mouth hardened at the name, but no bitterness emitted from her. I liked her the better for it. She was a great deal stronger than she believed herself to be and I said as much, admiring her for what she'd endured with a husband like Max Trevalyan.

"It's strange, Daphne. I always thought I was weak for staying . . . weak for putting up with it, but now I realize it takes a special kind of resilience to survive so long in a warlike marriage in which there is no peace, no security, just terror and uncertainty every day."

"And you did not just face one challenge," I reminded her.

"No," she agreed. "I used to think: if only he were a happy drunkard, or if only he wouldn't keep abusing everything from women to drugs to servants. A mutilator of self and others is what he became. And he enjoyed controlling others because he could not control himself or his mind. He almost drove me to suicide once. I lay there, curled up in the corner like a frightened animal, too scared to move or to breathe. There can be no worse sentence than a marriage such as that, one that strips the soul to its last burning ember."

"You ought to read *The Tenant of Wildfell Hall,*" I said, and smiled. "It echoes your life, but there is a happy ending and I prescribe a happy ending for you, too."

"Oh, do you?" Her lips twitched. "And what is the ending of the book?"

"I have it here. You can read it. After the terror, Helen recovers and marries again. There is a line that says, 'What is it a Doctor prescribes? A second marriage. Yes, a second good marriage is the triumph of love over experience.' "

"I like that," Kate whispered, wiping away the lonely tear running down her face. "Poor Josh, I blame myself. I had to tell him that day that there was no future for us, that I couldn't marry him. I couldn't go and live in his rat-infested flat, I just couldn't. It wouldn't be fair, on him or on me, and neither of us could hope with the added pressure of trying to make a living. You must think me a heartless woman, but Daphne, I am a realist. My head rules over my heart."

I studied her as the sunset filtered through the terrace, the golden light adding warmth to her beauty. I was loath to disturb her peace, but I could wait no longer to tell her of Angela's seeming demise. If she was shocked by the news, she did not show it. Perhaps she had become desensitized to catastrophe.

"When she told me, I felt so sick, sick that my own sister could have witnessed such a thing and could be blamed for it. But she tried to help him. She's sorry she was unable to save him, Kate. She cares for you deeply."

"Yes, but," she said, blushing, "Angela—I don't know how to say this—but she wants more than friendship."

I raised my hand to indicate that I knew. That I knew and understood.

A heavy frown disturbed Kate's fine brow. "You may tell her that she has my friendship."

Little conversation flowed at the dinner table that evening as we each sat alone with our thoughts, covertly eyeing one another, passing stilted, polite smiles across the table.

"Does Mr. Lissot have any family?" I overheard Sir Marcus ask Kate later in the drawing room.

"None that I know of. He did mention a brother once, but I don't think they had anything to do with each other. It sounded as if he lived far away, maybe in Australia?"

"Some attempt should be made to locate him and apprise him of the news," Sir Marcus said, offering to go to Josh's room and see what information he could find.

Kate agreed, disengaging a key from her set and handing it to him.

"Poor fellow," Sir Marcus mumbled. "I'll sort out his affairs. I daresay anything of value will have to go to pay his creditors."

"Yes." The empty reply hastened out of Kate as though she wished a permanent end to the subject.

"You're very artful at eavesdropping." Drifting near, the Major placed a glass of sherry into my hands. "Here, drink it. It will help you sleep."

I wanted to tell him what I'd done. A foolish, dangerous thing if my suspicions proved true. Yet I could not. Having placed the note under my suspect's door, I willingly put myself in danger and I alone must bear the consequences.

Shepherding me to a seat nearest the piano where Mr. Davis played Bach, I asked the Major if he had any musical aspirations.

"None at all," came the quick reply. "I am entirely *de trop* in that area."

"But I thought you were good at everything?"

"Your faith in me does you credit."

"It wasn't a compliment."

Leaning back, he arched his arm casually across the top of the settee. I swallowed.

The action didn't go unnoticed by the rest of the room, either. Bella smiled from her quiet game of backgammon with Lord Roderick, and Sir Marcus winked at me.

Feeling the effects of the sherry tinting my cheeks to a

bright red, I said, "Josh probably had many friends who need to be informed."

"A notice will go in the weekend paper."

Rearranging the cushion behind my back so I could move a little away from the Major without being obvious, I lifted a brow. "It was kind of Sir Marcus to offer to settle the man's affairs. There is Josh's artwork, too. His sculptures might be worth something. What happens to them if he's left no will?"

"There's the brother to be found. He'll make the decision."

"And if he can't be found?"

"I suppose then his closest friends will decide what to do. He was a social man, but like so many before him, the artist perishes. Was it Byron or someone else who wrote of an artist's penchant for hard living, addiction, and voluntary death?"

"Or sickness," I put in. "Tuberculosis claimed so many greats."

"You're a library of information."

His teasing drawl delighted my ears far more than Mr. Davis's piano recital. Sipping my sherry, I allowed myself to enjoy the moment and sensed Roderick's particular gaze upon me, still hopeful I might agree to marry him. I had shared a private word with him prior to dinner and he had pressed my hand warmly, offering his assistance in regard to Angela.

"They cannot condemn her without further proof," he had said, and I appreciated that his interest in me had not wavered.

It was late when I retired to my room. Angela's belongings strewn about the room depressed me and I fought the urge to telephone my father. Angela had begged me not to, not yet. She hoped the whole matter could remain a secret between us, that none of our family need know if they released her.

I had stepped inside, sighing, picking up a few of her discarded items when I noticed the envelope slid under the door. My heart raced as I opened it.

> *Miss du Maurier,*
> *I accept your offer.*
>   *If you wish to know the reason why Max was killed, meet me at the dock labeled "Milton Heath" at eight o'clock tomorrow morning. Come alone. Follow these directions exactly.*

Not for the first time in my life, I was about to do something immensely foolish. Needless to say, I slept very little, my heart thudding as the minute hand on the clock clicked closer to the hour. Turning on the light at six thirty, I hunted for and located my walking skirt, an old blouse, and a cardigan. Not knowing what else to take, I grabbed an umbrella and slipped a letter opener into the pocket of my skirt.

Tiptoeing downstairs, I prayed Hugo was in the kitchen.

"Milton Heath." He stared at me. "Why'd ye want to go there?"

"I can't say, but can you do me a favor, Hugo? Can you please give this to the Major at breakfast?" I handed him a note. "It's important. Please don't forget."

I hurried from the house and down to the beach, following the coastline around to the dock of Milton Heath. The cool air assailed my cheeks and nausea coiled in my stomach. I'd embarked upon the most dangerous enterprise of my life thus far and my inquisitiveness could cost me my life.

I thought of a proper detective. I thought of the Major. Both, I imagined, would never chance that I was about to meet a killer on their terms.

"Don't turn around."

Standing at the precipice of the old rotting ramp, fear seized me.

"And drop your umbrella."

I obeyed, my heart thumping loudly as a blindfold landed over my eyes. I tensed as darkness enshrouded my vision, a lone seagull my only connection to the outside world. My hands were then thrust together and tied with rope.

"This way. Stairs ahead."

Led by the rope, I tested out each wooden plank, thinking of Lady Jane Grey and how she must have felt walking up to the axman blindfolded. A terrible fear suddenly consumed me. If I died now, I'd never see my book published. True, I had to *write* a book first, but had I chosen an artist's fate?

"Sit."

Pushed down onto something hard, I felt the small boat rock. Waves snarled at its sides and I prayed Hugo delivered my message. What if he didn't? I was not naïve. Having arranged this deal with the devil, I had gambled with my life. And for what? A burning desire to know *why* Max had been murdered.

I reasoned that if the killer had been suspected by the police, they would have nothing to charge him with, no evidence whatsoever. I alone had to take the risk.

It was not a long ride but the minutes dragged on into eternity and I was thankful I'd brought along my cardigan. Twenty minutes . . . *twenty* minutes drummed through my mind and I wished I'd studied the map of the islands. I really ought to pay more heed to geographical study as my father said. What island could be so close? Bryer? Could it be Bryer? Or Tresco?

And why were we going to an island? Was it necessary for a confession? Or necessary to murder me, the one person who'd guessed the murderer's identity through a careful deduction of character, motivation, and a little niggling slip of the tongue.

The motoring ceased its rumble and we glided into the opposing docking bay. The boat clanked against the side and I thought of throwing myself at the sea's mercy. However, sense prevailed for I'd not get far with hands and eyes bound, would I?

A chill wind whipped around my neck and I shivered. I couldn't even pull my cardigan up around me since my hands were tied. Thrust to my feet, I was lifted onto wooden decking, the rope binding me to my captor. There was no chance of escape as we walked on, across the beach, and upward to a sandy, grassy track. I faltered once or twice and my captor steadied me, ensuring I did not fall, and at last, we appeared to have reached our destination.

I heard birds above, and the sound of the sea in the near distance. We were close to the beach.

"Stop."

Brought to a halt, I inhaled the pungent, pleasant odor of coffee.

A door opened and I was pushed inside what I imagined was some kind of boathouse. I suddenly sensed the presence of someone else.

"Timas. We've another inmate," announced my captor.

A grunt emanated from across the room. From the grunt, I pictured Timas an old seaman and criminal with no saving virtues. Who was the first inmate, I wondered.

The blindfold ripped from my eyes, I blinked a few times to adjust to the light. We were in a boathouse, yes, a cramped boathouse full of clutter, old ship wheels, sunken objects extracted from the ocean, a tiny kitchen, cupboards bearing rusty food tins and empty whiskey bottles, three or so rooms and two broken windows boarded up with pieces of driftwood. The place had an eerie personality about it and I swallowed, not wanting to know what lay beneath the floorboards at my feet.

Timas proved broader and fatter than I imagined him, with wiry white hair, a great beard, and bulging red-rimmed pale eyes that gleamed at my arrival. His chafed lips smacked together in appreciation and I turned to face my captor, finally.

"You're not to touch the girl," Davis ordered. "Would you like a coffee, Daphne?"

Assuming a completely at-home air, as though we'd come here for a picnic, Mr. Davis loosened the bonds on my hands. He frowned whilst I rubbed the reddened, broken skin.

"I'm sorry for that. Alas, it was a necessary precaution, but I trust you didn't find the journey too uncomfortable?"

"Why?" The question choked out of me. "Why?"

"Ah, yes, *why*. It's the great question, is it not? You rather caught me off my guard with your little note, you know. You don't make a very good blackmailer."

"I have no intention of blackmailing you," I assured him. "I merely want to know the truth."

"Truth," he echoed. "The truth has many faces. Now, how about that coffee? It's a chilly morning."

I shook my head.

"Ah well." He lifted his shoulders to Timas. "It's as the lady commands. We'll go up to the lighthouse now. Give me the key, Timas."

Shuffling through his trouser pockets, Timas produced a large iron key.

Davis turned to me. "I'm trusting you not to run away."

"As agreed: I give you my word."

I was surprised at how calm I sounded. I certainly did not feel calm. I thought of running down to the boat and rowing myself off this island, far away from danger and Peter Davis.

But my curious nature prevented me from running, just as Mr. Davis's arrogance prevented him from rejecting my proposal. He thought himself so immensely clever, so above suspicion that he *had* to know how I'd uncovered his guilt. He couldn't rest until he learned what mistake he'd made, what little inconsistency had exposed him. It was the only trump card I had to play, and I prayed the Major reached me before I found myself in real danger.

"You're a remarkable girl, Daphne," Davis said to me, leading me up a rugged island path strewn with sand-blown long grass and purple and white flowers. "And I'm sorry for the rope. But at least," he smiled, "I did not make you wear the blindfold."

"You are all kindness."

"Ah! A hint of sarcasm . . . now, watch your step," he advised, too chivalrous for my liking, "the island has many dangers. It's a deserted part up here," he went on, tugging me up the path as though he'd made the journey a hundred times over.

"Does it belong to you? This place, the lighthouse?"

"Yes." His emphatic nod confirmed it. "It's my own little bit of paradise."

"It's lovely," I remarked, for I didn't know what else to say. Acting normal encouraged him to feel secure with me. Without it, he'd mistrust everything I said and did, which guaranteed my incarceration. What I hoped for was to convince him to give himself up and win back some level of decency.

My good intentions, however, deserted me upon reaching the defunct old lighthouse, a lonely ruin of a place.

"It's ancient," Davis said. "Once the island's only lighthouse and abandoned in the seventeenth century. When I purchased this allotment of land, the old ruin came with it, but I don't view it as an impediment, do you, Daphne?"

"No," I said as a crow screeched above, gliding to perch on the highest, jagged stone.

"Don't be afraid," Davis grinned. "The locals call it the Place of Crows. It's not really as unfriendly as it looks."

Despite the warmth of the sun on my back, I shivered. Escape was as far off as the sun, I realized, surveying the lithe frame of Mr. Davis. I could run fast, but not fast enough. My only hope lay in the letter knife in my pocket.

Davis stood at the door with the sun on his face, smiling. "Do you care to hazard a guess at the identity of the inmate who resides within?"

His affability disturbed me. Feigning a nonchalance I did not feel, I opted for the surprise and, thrusting the key in the door, Davis opened it, waiting for me to go in first.

I squinted, unsure of entering. What awaited me? A monster?

I stepped inside a circular room, half open to the elements and half protected from them. I turned toward the door in disgust, the smell churning my stomach. The threadbare room bore little furniture, one damp single bed and one bedside table, a huge candelabra, its base littered with new and burnt-out candles, a bear rug, faded, yet of good quality . . . and hauntingly familiar. I'd seen such a rug in Lord Roderick's tower.

Sensing the intrusion, the tenant of this prison rumbled out of the shadows.

I gasped.

For there, carting a stack of books under his arm, was Max Trevalyan.

CHAPTER TWENTY-EIGHT

"Angela! How nice of you to visit me."

I stared at him. "Max? Max, is that you?"

"Yes." He embraced me, squeezing me so tight I lost my breath. "Why have you taken so long to come?" Shaking his head, he clicked his tongue. "Naughty girl, but no matter. Would you care for a spot of tea? I don't know whether they have tea in this establishment." His displeased brow arrested Davis. "Tea? Do we have tea here?"

"Miss Daphne has already said no to refreshments." Davis's smooth reply cut the air of equanimity.

"Daphne?" Max leaned over to peer at me and I recoiled at his stench. "No, I am sure it is the elder, Angela."

"No, it's Daphne," I broke in, astonished. *Max Trevalyan alive.*

I shuddered. If Max Trevalyan was here, alive and well, then whose body lay in the family crypt?

"Hallo, Daphne." A cheerful Max embraced me again. "Good of you to stop by. What do you think of my island? It's all mine, you know. Every inch, every grain of sand."

His sheepish grin did little for my nerves. He'd grown a thousand times more mad up here, alone and forgotten by the outside world.

"I'm afraid the lodging isn't the best, but it has all I need. Don't travel much these days," he yawned. "Too darn tiring. You don't mind if I go and lie down now, do you?"

Without waiting for my reply, he sank down into his little slat bed, stretched out, pulled the blanket up over his body, and closed his eyes.

Davis instructed me to sit.

Guided to an alcove by the door where two wooden chairs lurked, I said, "You've drugged him, haven't you?"

"Bravo!" Clapping his hands, Davis exuded his amusement. "In point of fact, I've only *increased* his dosage. I never drugged Max, nor introduced him to the vile stuff. He drugged himself, after the war."

"Because of the pain?"

"At first. Cigars were getting too expensive, you see, and there was a man we knew near the base. He used to be a doctor, a good respectable doctor until two German pilots murdered his wife and daughter and the authorities were too busy with the war to do anything about it. It turned him bitter, so he turned his hand to a different kind of enterprise."

"Selling narcotics to pilots," I finished grimly.

"And others," Davis confirmed, running a cool finger down my cheek. "You'd be surprised at how many *good girls* fell into the doctor's trap and what they were prepared to do in order to get their . . . shall we say, *fix*?"

"They were victims." My gaze strayed to the sad figure of Max Trevalyan. "I suppose he developed a quick dependency?"

"Yes, you are right. Poor Max. He was always searching for the 'eternal escape.' Now, I've given it to him."

"But how?"

"No. My questions first. What led you to me?"

I knotted my hands together. I didn't know what he intended to do to me, and fear rippled up my spine. I had only a little time to play. Very little. I had to keep him talking while I planned my escape. "There were quite a few things," I began, trying to stretch it out as long as possible.

Arrogance glinted in his eyes. "Very vague. When did I feature on your list of suspects?"

I opened my mouth.

"Yes, I know all about you and Sir Marcus and your little games. I also know he is the most rapacious columnist this side of Europe. That is why he was asked to Somner House."

"But he is Kate's friend. He wouldn't write anything to hurt her."

"No, but I know something you don't know. Kate is not as innocent as she looks. She was planning to kill her poor dear husband. She and her lover. That's why she invited Sir Marcus down. She needed someone of Sir Marcus's ilk and stature to proclaim her innocence to the world. She's very clever, our Katie."

"No, it cannot be true." I thought of the poignant conversation we'd had outside the museum, how her blue eyes expressed her innocence. *You do believe me, don't you, Daphne,* she'd said.

Cupping his chin, Davis tapped his piano fingers across his face. "Proceed. What led you to me? You said a few things. What things? I am very curious to know."

"The painting day."

"The painting day?"

"Yes," I rattled on, wondering if I could make a quick retrieval of my letter knife if necessary. "When we were painting that day, you mentioned the phrase 'there are things worse than death.' I thought at the time you spoke in general, but later I came to realize there was something more significant implied in your words."

"Oh?"

I paused. I'd captured his undivided attention and every moment brought the Major closer to me. " 'Things worse than death' can only mean one of two things. You resent life or life resents you. Something bitter festers inside, something you cannot control."

"You are vastly entertaining," he said. "Go on."

"This festering sore burns and emits desire and when desire meets opportunity, a plan is born. A plan that was part of the desire and the desire is simply to win. Win over Max Trevalyan, this man you claimed was your best friend."

I could see I'd rattled him for his lips tightened.

"You resented Max," I went on. "You always have. He excelled over you in school. He excelled over you in friends. Women chose him over you. During the war, you saved him, yet gave him your medal because in some bizarre way you were also obsessed with him, *pleasing* him, keeping him humored and beside you. He became for you a beacon in life; you fed off his mad behavior and placed yourself in the comfortable role of Kate's protector, this woman who chose Max over you."

Breaking off to catch my breath and survey the sleeping Max, poised so peacefully, like a child at his bed, sedated beyond any decency and totally unaware of it. He was trapped, a willing bird to his cage, having forgotten his former life, his wife, his brother, and even his house.

"Drugs deaden the mind. You knew Max's addiction. You introduced him to stronger drugs and his dependency increased. You thought he'd eventually die of an overdose and Kate would be free to marry you. Or perhaps you thought she'd consign him to a mental asylum? Either way, she'd have her freedom. But there was Josh Lissot, wasn't there?"

Davis's eyes narrowed. "Lissot. A veritable thorn in my flesh. I tried to warn Katie that the affair couldn't last but she refused to listen."

"So you made things difficult for Mr. Lissot by walling up his commissions and rendering him financially defunct . . . destroying a man's pride and an artist's soul. You guessed correctly that he'd take his own life rather than face life without his art and his lover. He had nothing to offer her, nothing left to live for, nothing to aspire to other than a theatrical death."

"Marvelous!" Davis clapped his hands. "You intrigue me, Daphne. Pray, continue."

"Long before Josh Lissot, however, the real duplicity began. When Max failed to die of an overdose, you thought to remove him. You couldn't kill him yourself. You thought of hiring somebody to do it, but your conscience troubled you. Despite all his faults, Max was still your friend, so you decided to grant him his life. I would so much love to know when and how the thought occurred to you." I trusted my plea softened his mood.

"Walking through a London cemetery, if you must know. I saw a tombstone. It said UNKNOWN. FACE UNRECOGNIZABLE."

"I see. And the idea emerged in your mind to find a body, render its face unrecognizable, dress the body in Max's clothes and ring, and voila! Max Trevalyan, a man nobody liked, who had been brutally attacked by his wife's lover, was found murdered. Kate is all alone and she and her friend's would never suspect Max's best friend, who seemed to arrive *after* the incident of the crime."

"How," he shook his head, chuckling, "did you come by a devious mind like my own? Are you full of hidden vice, Daphne du Maurier?"

He said it as a compliment but I rejected it. To be thought brilliant was one thing, to be thought psychotic and to be associated with such minds as his was *not* complimentary. I suddenly recalled the Major saying: "The only one who is exempt from this affair is Mr. Davis, for he wasn't present at either."

"You had the perfect alibi," I continued. "But I am wary of perfection and my suspicions were confirmed when I asked you about your uncle. The briefest flicker in your eyes alerted me to a falsehood."

"I am astounded . . ." Davis said slowly. "What else?"

"The terrace door. Hugo heard it open three times. Upon our return from the island, you blundered in and made the statement that you 'ought to be more soft-footed.' I thought nothing of it then, but later, the inconsistency plagued me. You are a quiet man. Your piano playing is perfect. Accurate. Steady. Yes, steady. That word, that very word, led me to you. You were entirely too steady. Too circumspect."

Listening with full intent, he nodded, as though scribing a mental note to be more cautious. "I still fail to see the significance."

"So did Josh Lissot . . . at first. But on carefully examining his movements that night, he realized he'd only opened the door *twice* at most. Another person opened it a third time to alert Hugo and incriminate Josh Lissot, and then left through the kitchen door. You were there watching, weren't you? You were there watching Josh and Kate in the shadows . . . just waiting for the moment to strike. You wanted to make it appear as if the lovers were guilty. It was a technicality Fernald didn't act on for obvious reasons, but one that clearly exposed a third party—the *real* murderer—you."

Crossing his arms, Davis smiled.

"But really you had the perfect alibi. You never expected anybody would suspect you." Catching my breath, I whispered, my voice sounding very small, "What do you intend to do with him?"

"To do with who? Max? Oh, he's supremely happy here, so I shan't disturb him. Would be cruel to do so and you can ask him later if you like. He has no wish to leave the island."

"But if he were nursed back to sound mind—"

Davis snorted. "He's beyond the point of turning away from the drugs. If released into society, he *will* harm others."

"If restrained, though, are there not clinics who can take him? Even under a false name?"

"Clinics are costly and I am sure if Kate knew, she'd prefer him to be here. He loves it here. Here, he is king of the island."

"But how can you think she would accept this fate for her husband if she knew he was alive?"

Davis affected another nonplussed shrug. "Kate's not as innocent as you think."

"She will not accept you."

"She *will* accept me. Even if it takes a little time. She needs me, you see. As I need her."

He needed to win her, I thought. He needed to triumph over Max. His pride demanded she become his wife, through whatever means necessary.

A horrible dread stuck in my throat. Mr. Davis intended to consign me to the island, too, just as he'd done with Max. Even if I agreed to keep his secret, he'd never release me. He had planned this life for himself for far too long to allow me, a mere nobody, to disrupt his future. I was terrified he'd succeed.

I was given something to drink.

Coffee, delivered in a greenish mug.

"Drink it," Davis commanded, as I sat there, now a true prisoner. I thought of Edmond in the *Count of Monte Cristo* when he entered the Chateau d'If.

Oh, why had I been so foolish? I prayed. I prayed fervently and earnestly. I prayed the Major got my note, in which I told him of meeting Peter Davis at Milton Heath. I prayed he came for me.

"Drink it."

I still delayed over the coffee. "What's in it?" I asked, hoping the calmness of my voice would elicit an answer.

"Nothing like Max's mixture." Chuckling, Davis motioned toward the soundless sleeping Max. "Don't worry. It's merely a sleeping tonic, and you understand, don't you, Daphne, that I have to put you to sleep. I can't have you trying to escape, now can I?"

"What do you intend to do with me?"

"I don't know yet," he replied, honest. "Despite all of this, I am not a monster, nor have I committed a murder."

"Josh—"

"Josh chose poorly. I trust you do not."

I sniffed the coffee under his watchful eye. A sleeping tonic, he said. Closing my eyes, I prayed and drank.

"There's a mat over there you can lie upon, and books for you to read. Consider this a . . . summerhouse. Max shan't disturb you. I predict he'll sleep well into the afternoon."

Davis left, locking the great door behind him.

I began to feel the effects within moments. Dizzy and lightheaded, I wandered around the chamber, searching for any means of escape.

There was none.

None but through that door and the one lone window, which Davis had barred. I saw a baby crow flap outside and fly high into the sky. I wished to be that bird, soaring to freedom. Rubbing my eyes, I sank down, defeated, onto the mattress. My head swam, and all my limbs felt like heavy stones. I lay flat and drifted off to some unknown place, hoping and praying for a miracle.

"Hallo there. Daphne! Daphne, wake up!"

Startled, I opened my eyes to see Max's hazy face peering above me.

He poked me. "Are you alive? Why are you here in this room with me? Are you staying?"

"I'm staying . . . a little while," I managed, attempting to rise. My head still pounded, and I put my hand to my throbbing temple.

"Come on, sleepy head!" Pulling me to my feet, Max's frenzied hand patted my back.

I endeavored to adjust to my surroundings. What I assumed was late afternoon light filtered into the sad little chamber and I groaned. "They gave me something vile to drink."

Max stared at me. "They do that. Want to play pirates?"

"Pirates?"

"Yes, pirates." He scowled. "Pete knows the game. Do you?"

I digested this information. "Mr. Davis plays pirates with you?"

"Sometimes he does, when he's here." Max bit his lower lip. "But I haven't seen him for a while. He said he's been busy. Busy," he scoffed, "always busy, busy, busy."

I nodded through the daze.

"Don't be scared." Max pinched my arm. "Nobody can hurt us. We're safe. Safe and free!"

He rolled across the floor and invited me to do the same.

I declined.

"You're droll, Daphne. Are you a grisly old maid? Want to play cards? Bridge? Backgammon? They're all around here somewhere."

I helped him as he ransacked a box. There was little else to occupy me and I didn't wish to remain alone with my thoughts. I was trapped with a madman. "Is there any way out of here, Max? I want to go for a walk around the island."

Pausing in his frantic shaking of a box and chewing a knotted cord with his teeth, Max thought hard. "Timas. You've got to ask him. He's the one who brings the food. He might let you go swimming. I always ask to go swimming but I'm not allowed." His lower lip formed a sulk.

"Max, do you remember Kate?"

Piercing blue eyes scorched me. "Kate? Oh, her. She's dead."

"Dead!" Is that the lie Davis spun him? "How did she die?"

"She went out to sea in the boat and she never came back."

"She drowned?"

He nodded, his eyes sad and wistful. I applauded Davis's

genius. He had brainwashed Max Trevalyan to believe his stories with childish simplicity.

"Max, don't you miss your home?"

"Home," he muttered, his brow narrowing. "Home's here. I don't have any other home. They took it."

"Who took it?"

"The bank men."

"But what about Roderick, your brother? What happened to him?"

"Rod's gone to London to work. He's busy, too. That's why he hasn't been to visit me. But he'll come one day. And nobody plays pirates better than Rod."

"You used to play pirates with him near the cove at Somner House, didn't you?"

Max looked amazed.

"Do you want to play the game?"

To humor him, I sat alongside him on the floor. Jeanne and I had played something similar as children, on our endless beachside holidays.

Max chose Blackbeard the pirate. I chose Raoul the pirate.

"There's no pirate called Raoul," Max said testily.

"There is. Or, in my story, there is. He's a great pirate. Adventurous and dashing . . ."

"Tell me more about Raoul the Pirate then," a dubious Max demanded. "Where'd he come from? How did he become a pirate? What treasures does he have? What's his ship called? Has he sailed to the Americas? Around Cape Horn? Who's his first mate?"

"Raoul the pirate was an orphan," I began. "He was born of . . . a poor Spanish maid and a Romany gypsy. She had to give birth to him in the forest."

Max shook his head at the poor maid's plight.

"The labor was hardgoing and she lost a lot of blood. In a daze, she saw the towers to a great castle through the trees and thought that if only she could get her babe there, he'd have a better life than on the run from the murderous Russian hordes."

Max's eyes rounded. "What happened to the baby?"

"The lady of the castle found him. She was very sad, as she'd lost her only son and her heart had never recovered. So, when her servants brought her the baby, she took the child and raised him as her own. Her husband accepted the child and they told everyone Raoul was their nephew. They gave him the best education, sent him off to learn all manner of things from books to warfare—"

"Yes, yes, but how did he become a pirate?"

"Raoul was not happy. He longed for the sea. He'd never seen the ocean, only read about it. His aunt and uncle, knowing how much he longed for a sea journey, arranged one for him, and so he set off on his great adventure upon his own ship called the *Liberty*."

Max disapproved of the name. "Why *Liberty*? It doesn't sound like a pirate ship."

"*Liberty* isn't a pirate ship," I reminded him. "When they sailed into the Indian Ocean they came under attack by Turkish pirates. The *Liberty* was captured and her treasures plundered. The captain took Raoul and his men and gave him a choice. They could serve him or die. All but one chose to live."

Max rubbed his eyes. "Raoul chose to die?"

"No, but his first mate did, the man sent by his aunt and uncle to look after him. This man knew that death awaited him should he ever return to the kingdom without Raoul."

Max accepted this with total equanimity. "And then?"

"And then," I hastened, enjoying the spontaneous devising of his tale, "they sailed to Malta."

"Malta! Why Malta?"

"Because the Turkish sultan's envoy had business there. But little did he suspect that in Malta, Raoul would hijack another ship, take half his men, and transform himself into a pirate. The only means of escape was via the coast of Egypt, so he raised up his pirate flag and inspired fear in the heart of the populace for four years."

"Did he never want to go home?"

"No. The pirate life appealed to Raoul as he had gypsy blood. He also feared no future existed for him at home, for his cousin, who was jealous of Raoul's good fortune, was due to inherit the castle. So Raoul became a pirate and plundered the sea of its treasures, especially those fat Spanish galleons."

Smiling, Max said he liked Raoul the Pirate very much but grew frustrated trying to light candles. "It's too dark. I don't like it." Snapping his fingers, he cursed in his patrol of the chamber. "Timas is late and I'm hungry. Are you hungry, Daphne? He should have brought dinner by now and we need fresh candles, too."

Night descended and my heart sunk with the last ray of fading light. "Perhaps nobody is coming?"

"Oh, no," returned my companion. "They never forget."

I failed to share his confidence. Throughout my story, I'd endeavored to keep my spirits up by examining the room and its contents, looking for anything useful that might break down the door. That door was the only way out.

"Don't look so glum," Max grinned. "They'll come. You'll see."

"Have you ever tried to get out when they bring the food?"

Max stared at me. "Get out? Why should I want to?"

"If Raoul the pirate came for you, would you go?"

A slow smile formed on his lips. I took the answer as yes as I stationed myself by the door. "I think someone's coming," I whispered, poised and tense, clutching the letter knife in my right hand. My heart raced ahead. Could a girl of my strength attack a man like Timas? Shaking, I knew I'd have to *try* to attack.

What sounded like keys jingling scathed my ears.

I swallowed hard. I could hear Timas's heavy breathing through the door. Any moment, he'd insert the key . . .

Max leapt to the door just as it opened, barring my way. Sliding to his knees, he beamed up at me as a tray slid at our feet and the door promptly closed.

I shut my eyes, crushed. There would be no opportunity of escaping tonight. Joining Max on the floor, I wondered if Davis had drugged the food. Unlikely, considering he thought me safely locked up for the night with Max.

In the cool of night, after we'd consumed the morsels of flat bread, cheese, and some kind of preserved meat ration, Max said, his voice barely above a whisper: "Daphne, do you think Raoul the pirate will visit us?"

"I hope so, Max," I replied, not allowing myself to believe it. "I hope so."

CHAPTER TWENTY-NINE

Crows pecking at the window awoke me.

Shivering with the morning chill, I wrapped the old blanket tighter around me and drew to the light. Dawn bristled forth, and Max slept fitfully. Observing the spasmodic jerks, I guessed his body craved his next drug installment and I prepared for Davis's return.

I had no idea of how early he came in the mornings, but I imagined routine played a part in maintaining order. Keeping Max prisoner and in good humor suited Davis. It would have been much kinder to have killed him, I thought. What motivated Davis to keep him alive? Did he taunt Max? Or did Max's utter dependency fulfill him in some demented way?

"It's a friendship you cannot understand," Davis said, having brought Timas along to secure his entry into the tower. "Max is nothing without me. I have made him who he is."

"A drug-dependent crazy man?"

Davis sent me a wearied look. "He would have died years

ago if I hadn't saved him. His life has always belonged to me."
Smiling, Davis administered Max's medicine through a needle.
"It's empowering to have complete control over a life. I planned
Max's demise as meticulously as I planned his success. He
won the medal because of me. He *won* Kate because of me.
But he abused his success and so must pay the price."

"It's a game to you, isn't it? And Kate is the prize." His expression changed and I raised a brow.

"Some of the value of a prize loses its shine over time."

His words chilled me.

"We'll breakfast up at the boathouse to discuss your future. There . . . better, Maxie boy?"

A serene glow emanated from my fellow prisoner and my
spirits sank.

"Sorry, m'dear." Davis seized my hands. "Precautions are
necessary."

"The rope burns my hands," I complained weakly.

Hauled to my feet, Davis shrugged. "It cannot be helped."

Lured by the promise of a good breakfast, Max thrust out
his hands for Davis while grinning at me. My spirits sank further as Max's hands were bound by the same rope as my own.
Downcast, I complied when Davis tugged the rope. Sunshine
beckoned and I closed my eyes when its warmth touched
my face.

"Steady now," Davis ordered.

I gazed down at my feet. Hope deserted me. The Major
mustn't have received my note otherwise he'd be here. He
would have rescued us by now.

Flinching at a jab at my side, I glared at Max. He had a
dumbfounded expression on his face as though trying to comprehend why I wasn't happy. I gazed wistfully out to sea.

"Raoul the pirate?" Max whispered.

"No time for pirates now, Max," Davis snapped.

Disappointed, Max whistled his way up to the boathouse. I shivered. The boathouse appeared eerie in the pale light as Timas went to prepare breakfast.

I must have looked terrified, for Max stepped in front of me to squeeze my hand.

"We must escape," I murmured urgently as Davis barked orders to Timas. "Raoul is coming for us."

"Now?" Max asked, all wide-eyed innocence.

"Yes, now."

Hauled into the boathouse, I waited for the information to sink into his drug-induced head.

"Sit down, you two. Breakfast is on its way."

"So is Raoul," I expressed, spurring Max to action.

Davis whipped around as Max's fist thumped him to the ground. The hit was hard but Davis was an agile man. He shot to his feet, only to receive the second of Max's punches.

"Quick," I said. "We must run."

I didn't want to think about Timas. I prayed he hadn't heard us from the back of the shed, but it was only a matter of time before Davis's moans alerted him.

Running out the door, Max managed to rip the rope from his hands as we stumbled down to the beach, spiraling down the narrow, steep path, not caring whether we slid as long as we reached the bottom.

"No sign of the *Liberty*." Max surveyed the scene. "But wait, I think there's a boat!"

I squinted into the light. I couldn't see a thing, but Max dragged me into the freezing cold water. His strength surprised me. I faltered, gasping for breath.

"We'll have to swim," he yelled, pulling me to him. "Hold on to to me. I'll take us."

My feet left the bottom and I kicked hard. I wanted to help but I wasn't a great swimmer and my hands were still tied. My urge to get away from Davis, however, provided enough motivation, especially when we heard the call from the island.

It was Davis. Up on the headland.

"He's coming," I said to Max.

I darted a look whilst wading through the waters. Max hadn't lied. There was a boat. Swallowing a mouthful of water, I dared not glance back but I heard Davis plunge in after us after firing a shot.

"See, it *is* Raoul the pirate! Your stories do come true." Laughing for joy, ignorant of Davis and his gun gaining on us, Max propelled us to the boat.

Another shot fired and Max slumped, his grip slackening. Ducking underwater as another shot fired, I saw the blood swirling all around us, Max's arms growing limp beside his body as he floated away.

He pulled me with him and my terror began. I had to free my hands of my rope or I would sink to the bottom of the ocean. Kicking relentlessly, I thrust the rope knot binding my hands to the pocket of my skirt where I located the knife, praying I didn't stab myself. I took a few turns and desperation clouded my judgment. My weight kept dragging me down and my legs grew tired. Where was the boat? Maybe they wouldn't get to me in time? I tried again, this time not caring if the knife jabbed my hands. Salt water stung my eyes. I couldn't see but I think I felt the rope finally giving way.

My lungs sent me upward. Spitting the seawater out of my mouth, I searched for Davis. And there he was, his deathly grip around Max's throat as the two silent corpses floated life-less, once childhood friends, now companions in death.

I bobbed there in the water, hearing the boat powering to me. The Major rode at the helm with Sir Marcus behind him. I could have wept for joy, and in my weak relief I floundered, the seawater filling my lungs.

I remember no more.

Waking up amongst fluffy pillows, snug, warm, safe, and dry, I gulped down the warm liquid spooned to my lips.

Kate mopped my brow while the Major administered the medicine. It tasted sweet and strong . . . like brandy.

"Is she awake?"

His head poking at the door, Sir Marcus trudged in.

I didn't recognize the room. I could still taste the salt in my mouth. I must have half drowned, I concluded, still bleary-eyed and hazy from the experience. I refused any more spoonfuls. My head swam and pounded and felt heavier than a boulder.

Breezing over to me, Sir Marcus clapped a solid hand to my shoulders. "You're a brave lass, a little foolhardy, it must be said, but a heroine nonetheless."

A heroine. I managed a wan smile. "You took your time. I might have drowned."

"Not the heroine I know." Taking my small hand in his, the Major caressed it with his thumb.

I wavered at the tender look in his eyes. "Is Davis . . . ?"

"Dead, yes." Sir Marcus perched himself on the opposite side of my bed.

The Major answered my next question for me. "They both

drowned. We managed to drag Max safely onto the boat but Davis sank to the bottom of the sea."

"A fitting end for a villain," I heard myself murmur before I recalled Kate's presence in the room.

"It's all right," her soft voice assured me. "It is best it ended this way. Max has his peace now and so does Davis. Poor Peter . . . I never knew. . . ."

"Angela? Does she know?"

"Rod has gone to obtain her release and bring her to you." She shuddered. "I still can't believe that Peter— I can't believe all that he did. It's so wicked, so *unlike* him."

"Desperation breeds dangerous men," the Major advised.

"Thunder 'n turf, you have it all wrong!" Sir Marcus waved a hand. "The man's a complete madman. Where'd he get that body, that's what I'd like to know."

"He purchased it," I said, relaying what Davis had told me. "It seems you can buy anything you want in those dark London alleys. Poor unfortunate wretch, whoever he is."

"Not *poor*," Sir Marcus corrected. "The fellow's got a nice spot in the Trevalyan family crypt, I'll have you know."

He flushed upon seeing Lord Roderick enter the room, my sister hard on his heels.

"Oh, Daphne." Her arms flung around me. "Oh, my little sister, don't *ever* do something like that again. You might have been killed."

"A suitable sibling chastisement," Sir Marcus observed. "But I am one with Daphne. I would have done exactly as she and rowed out to meet a faceless villain."

"No, you would not," the Major replied. "Not without reinforcements. I know you too well, Mysterious M."

While Sir Marcus pondered the truth of this statement,

Lord Roderick waited, ever the patient man, the man who said he loved me and desired to marry me. I suddenly succumbed to weariness and fell to sleep, Max's last words springing to the forefront of my mind. "See, it's Raoul the pirate! Daphne! Your stories *do* come true."

CHAPTER THIRTY

Very late that night, Angela and I sat huddled in bed with a hot cup of chocolate.

"It was good Hugo remembered to deliver your message," Angela began as we analyzed this bizarre and almost lethal holiday. "And good," a slow seductive tease elbowed itself into the cranny beneath my arm, "you had not *one* but *two* valiant heroes to come to your rescue. I shudder to think what might have occurred if they had delayed a moment longer."

I echoed the same acute relief and delight in being rescued by my friend Sir Marcus and the handsome and charismatic Major Browning.

Our ebullience vanished as Angela confessed her terror-filled hours in jail, confined and without hope. "I know exactly how Josh must have felt. When one is pushed to extremes, death seems the only answer."

"I'm thankful you were returned to us before you journeyed down that terrible path." I shuddered.

"What would Davis have done with you?" Angela mused aloud. "Poisoned you, I suppose? Unless he fancied you alive?"

I shuddered again.

"He cleverly ruined Josh's life," Angela continued. "Oh, and I have a good piece of news." Her smile turned to a self-satisfied smirk. "Mr. Zoland has suspended Fernald. It so happens Zoland found Fernald out due to several discrepancies he'd noticed in his method, manner, and the recent stroke of good fortune that Fernald said he received from a wealthy aunt. Zoland's fastidious with details and Fernald has no aunt. It appears Mr. Davis paid him handsomely to have Josh Lissot arrested."

"He sentenced the man to death." My voice sounded shrill in the semidarkness.

"It's a shame," Angela reflected, "that the sea deprived him of a trial, for people like that deserve to be punished for what they've done." She lowered her eyes. "You must promise never to tell our parents what I did, Daphne. You do promise, don't you, Daphne?"

Huddling together, I gave her my promise. "You try and get some sleep now. I might read for a while."

"I took the liberty of booking our passages," she said at the door. "I hope Thursday isn't too soon for you?"

She meant that she hoped it wasn't too soon for Lord Roderick, but my heart went out to another. No, two days wasn't too soon, for I'd learned that the Major planned to leave the next day on the same boat as Sir Marcus.

But dear Roderick. When he'd come to my room I had to give him my answer.

"I'm sorry. I cannot marry you," I said. "I am too fond of you and have too great a respect for you to mislead you. You deserve a girl who loves you thoroughly and I'm afraid I am not that girl."

My confession disappointed him greatly, but I prayed he would find love. In so doing, I earned the immense gratitude of Miss Bella Woodford.

She brought me breakfast in bed the next morning. With her glasses removed, she looked quite pretty and I told her so.

"Thanks." She blushed.

She did not thank me for refusing Roderick, but she didn't need to do so for her face betrayed her joy. The prospect of finally becoming Mistress of Somner House gave her the greatest pleasure.

They exhumed the substitute body and Max took his rightful place in the family crypt. There was no second funeral, though a wreath of flowers appeared on his grave every morning from that day on.

"It's my token," Lady Kate, dressed in black, murmured as I went to pay my last respects.

"What will you do now?"

"Though it would give me unrivaled pleasure to steal Rod away from Bella, I will return to town. I still have friends and a small annuity from the estate. I daresay," she paused, gazing out to the horizon, "I daresay I shall do quite well."

I found it very difficult to see off Sir Marcus and the Major.

"You must write this tale," Sir Marcus gave solemn instructions, "with *me* as the hero. A pirate of the far seas or a dashing swordsman. Indeed, I take no offense to either. Alternatively, you can always look me up and marry me, you know. Mysterious M is in need of a good wife."

"I can recommend one . . . Kate."

"Oh no." He looked horrified. "She is not my type! So, what say you, dearest Daph? Don't tell me you're saving yourself for the dashing Major?"

I cast my gaze to where the Major and Kate stood arm-in-arm.

"Don't wait forever for him. There is always *me,* and comrades should not be long parted. Do visit me at my grand estate and I shall convince you."

"I will," I promised, watching him organize his copious luggage in the motorcar.

"I've never seen a man travel with so much," the Major remarked, and Kate, Angela, and I laughed.

Another car arrived to collect the Major. His men had come to fetch him. Duty beckoned and it was a call any man of credence must heed.

However, my heart floundered. I floundered. I wanted to beg him to stay. I couldn't make any sense of my emotions. Since my rescue, we'd had no moments alone. I had not mistaken the tender look in his eyes, had I? He did care for me, didn't he? We were more than friends, weren't we? I longed for a moment of reassurance, for a moment alone, but it seemed impossible.

"You won't be so foolish the next time, making deals with the devil." He grinned, sweeping my hand up and slowly raising it to his lips.

Since his farewells to the others had been formal and circumspect, I drew a little confidence from his manner.

"And I am happy to see," he dropped his voice to an ardent whisper, "that you are not going to marry a house. Houses are pleasing but they cannot keep you warm."

His lips still lingered over my hand.

"How could you even think it?" I whispered back, my eyes full of what I felt for him. "You know me. You know how I feel."

All joviality deserted him. "I have a mind to kiss you senseless, but that, unfortunately, shall have to wait."

I bit my lip. "Does it have to?"

"Unless," he smiled, "you care to have Arabella Woodford as spectator?"

"Oh, no. I'll wait. I don't want to ruin it."

His hand lightly caressed my face. "Adieu, my girl. Try and stay out of trouble, at least until you get home. I shall call upon you within two weeks."

As we waved them off, pride, oh, hateful pride, prevented me from running after the car. Putting on a nonchalant demeanor, I smiled when Kate shepherded us out to the terrace for tea.

It was immeasurably unfair, I thought, to be the last ones to leave.

CHAPTER THIRTY-ONE

The next day, I praised the stars we had remained on the island, for it began with my hasty sprint to the darkest corner of the parlor where Hugo placed the Somner House correspondence.

A letter, from a publisher, awaited me.

Care of Somner House, St. Mary's Island, Isles of Scilly, Cornwall.

> *December 5th*
> *Dear Miss du Maurier,*
> *We have read with pleasure your short fictional*
> *story and would like to offer you the sum of £25.*
>
> *We wish to publish "The Widow's Secret" in*
> *our spring edition. Please advise the publishers*
> *whether this offer is acceptable to you.*
> *Yours sincerely,*
> *Mr. Hubert Pruce*
> *Punch Magazine*

I blinked twice. Had I read it correctly? Dare it be an acceptance?

"Yes!" Flinging myself into the corner of the room, I hugged the letter to my chest. Yes, it was true. My dream had come true.

And the Major and Sir Marcus weren't even here to witness my success.

"*Punch Magazine!*" Leaping to her feet, Angela seized the letter from me. " 'The Widow's Secret.' " Her eyes sparkled as she tapped the letter on her chin. "I wonder who provided inspiration for that story, hmmm?"

Fortunately, her question went unheeded in the excitement. Kate, busily making plans for her move to London, effusively clapped her congratulations while Arabella mumbled congratulatory remarks.

Since the one whose praise meant the most to me was far away, Lord Roderick filled the void.

"I shall be the first man to subscribe to *Punch Magazine*." He smiled the unadulterated pride of a fellow scribe. "And I shall collect it myself from the post office saying, 'I know the author!' "

Before I left Somner House, I visited the library one last time.

Inhaling the scent of old books, pausing sadly at the desk once belonging to Max Trevalyan, treasuring those elusive moments with the Major, Sir Marcus, and Roderick Trevalyan, I drew a sense of peace, a sense of finality that must lay at the end of any story, and this story had reached its end.

The house whispered its silent thanks. No wastrel master remained to torment it, nor the fearful cries of its former mistress.

Lastly, I felt I must say good-bye to my widow. Tearing out the sheet of paper from my journal, I sat down to compose a letter to Rachael Eastley. I did not mention the story, for it was but a foregleam for the novel I wanted to write one day about the widow she had inspired. I bid my farewells and condolences about Max.

Packed and about to climb into the front seat of the motorcar, Arabella stopped me. "Nice meeting you, Daphne and Angela."

She stood there, rigid, precise, very much the next Lady Trevalyan.

I did not embrace her, but waved a sincere good-bye.

The journey home seemed interminable.

Rather than spend a night or two in Cornwall and Devon as we'd originally planned, Angela and I opted for the short way back to London. After hours on a train, we both needed to be home.

Mother and Jeanne expressed their joy at our arrival.

"Finally." Jeanne rolled her eyes, sliding down the banister of our London house. "I've been bored witless."

Mother failed to chasten her unladylike behavior. Emerging from the sitting room, paper in hand, she raised her eyes to the ticking clock. Shock registered at the unseemly hour before we found ourselves embraced by her warm, loving arms.

"Your father's away," she informed after ordering some fresh tea and bowls of soup leftover from dinner. "But I've received a letter from him. It seems he ran into Teddy Grimshaw, that wealthy America, at the club and we've all been invited to a wedding."

"A wedding?" I gasped, recognizing the name. "Who is the bride?"

My mother smiled, *relishing* her news. "It may come as a shock to you, Daphne, but it's your friend Ellen, Ellen Hami Hon . . ."

Mother sighed. "It is all very inconvenient but he's received three letters from the Baron now and has run out of excuses. It appears, my girls, we shall have to spend the spring in Italy . . . the Villa d'Ablo awaits."